Also by Doris Rochlin

Frobisch's Angel

In the Spanish Ballroom

In the Spanish Ballroom

Doris Rochlin

Doubleday

NEW YORK   LONDON   TORONTO   SYDNEY   AUCKLAND

PUBLISHED BY DOUBLEDAY
a division of Bantam Doubleday Dell Publishing Group, Inc.
666 Fifth Avenue, New York, New York 10103

DOUBLEDAY and the portrayal of an anchor
with a dolphin are trademarks of Doubleday,
a division of Bantam Doubleday Dell
Publishing Group, Inc.

"Miami Beach Rhumba" Lyric by Albert Gamse, Spanish Lyric by
Johnnie Camacho, Music by Irving Fields. Copyright © 1946 by
EDWARD B. MARKS MUSIC COMPANY. Copyright renewed.
Used by permission. All rights reserved.

Library of Congress Cataloging-in-Publication Data
Rochlin, Doris.
    In the Spanish ballroom / Doris Rochlin. — 1st ed.
        p.   cm.
    I. Title.
    PS3568.O3245I6   1991
813'.54—dc20   90-33419
                                                         CIP

ISBN 0-385-26564-6

DESIGNED BY ANNE LING

January 1991
FIRST EDITION
BVG

For Shirley Yarnall and Timothy Schaffner

The author would like to express her gratitude to the National Endowment for the Arts for their generous support.

In the Spanish Ballroom

One

"You don't remember polio, do you?" Juanita wants to know. "You don't remember empty streets, no kids playing, the whole city a ghost town? Do you? Do you?" When it's clear no one will answer, she nails us with her "serpent gaze," the look my father used to say could sear your skin or curdle cream from twenty paces, so potent was its poison. Paulie, who is not quite six, sighs and leans against me, knowing as certainly as I do that Juanita's "look" is mere preamble.

It is a humid summer Sunday in Juanita's house in Maryland, a turquoise-awninged rambler on a cul-de-sac near Friendship Heights, a stone's throw from the District line. Too hot outside to breathe. No stir of birds or cats. No riffle of a breeze in the tall pin oaks. Indoors, in the basement (the area Juanita calls the rumpus room), Paulie and I are freezing because the air-conditioning is set at sixty-five, a waste of energy, I know, but Juanita hollers if I fiddle with the thermostat, and never mind if my fingers are losing feeling and Paulie's trembling with cold. (I've draped an afghan over his bare shoulders, but his lips are blue.) Juanita's in that time of life—hot flashes are killing her. Sometimes her knees go weak, or worse, her heart beats at a crazy pace —*ka chung, ka chung*—like an engine that is idling too fast.

"You don't remember, little babies died."

"Ma," I beg her, "please."

Juanita, warming to her subject, glares, delirious with the fever of remembrance. "Nobody in the playgrounds. Nobody in the pools. They wouldn't dare!" This last she flings at Paulie who is dressed for swimming in his Speedo racing trunks and rubber fins. A diver's mask, the snorkel tube bent out of shape, rests on his chest, rising and falling as he breathes. He is studying his grandmother with a look of naked terror.

"Ma," I warn her, "give it up."

"Maaa," she mimics me. "Sounds like a sheep. Call me Juanita. You're old enough."

"You're scaring him, Juanita." In the two weeks we've been here, Paulie's had bad dreams every night. I've had my fears, too, waking fantasies in which I curse the fates and pace, plotting how we'll get free of her.

"Forewarned is forearmed," Juanita says, eyeing Paulie with a look that strikes me as devoid of love, or any of the tender thoughts a grandmother should bear for her lone grandchild.

"Listen, he's had his shots."

"You don't remember those first shots. Some batches were bad. People got crippled, died."

"That was before Franklin and I were born. Why dredge it up?"

"And before the shots, that serum stuff they used. They doled

2

it out on sugar cubes. We had to line up at the high school to get our share. Like that scene in *On the Beach.*"

"Don't listen to her, Paulie."

"Okay to do your laundry, but not to talk." She's ironing on a board she's placed as close as caution will allow to the TV. The board is covered in gray cotton, torn in spots; trails of raveled padding dangle from the gashes in the fabric like the insides of a ruined, stuffed animal. The TV is flashing rapid-fire commercials —a flying dog, a gaggle of frenzied dancers paying obeisance to a truck. She has the volume turned to Low.

"Talk all you want, but just don't scare him."

Pressing the wrinkles from my favorite blouse, Juanita raises little puffs of steam. The fabric takes on life, stretches and gleams. There are ruffles at the collar and the sleeves that open like pale flowers under the iron's probe. "I had a girlfriend, Janet Polsky. Prettiest little thing. Dark eyes, dark hair, naturally curly. Well-developed for her age, know what I mean? She started with a headache, then a bad stiff neck. Before you could say boo, she couldn't breathe. The virus settled in her lungs. Bulbar, the absolutely worst kind you can get."

"That's it!" I'm on my feet, tugging on Paulie.

"Two weeks in isolation, in an iron lung; then she was gone. My, she was cute. Just twelve years old." Something has caught her eye on the TV. The Sunday matinee, a William Holden retrospective. "Good-o," my mother says. And then, "Poor man. Too young to die. Too absolutely gorgeous." She waggles the remote to get the volume louder.

"We're outta here, Juanita. Time for Paulie's swimming lesson."

"Do you suppose they'll start with *Picnic?* If they show *Picnic,* I'm incommunicado for the next two hours."

There are thuds sounding in the ceiling, my brother Franklin pounding overhead with an old fraternity paddle or my father's walking stick with the carved dog's head for a handle. The house is full of stuff like that, junk picked up at fairs, boardwalk souvenirs from Ocean City, whoopee cushions, teddy bears, and chipped Kennedy plates bearing the likeness of our murdered President looking rueful as though he, too, remembered Janet Polsky.

"See what Franklin wants before you go, would you?" my mother asks.

"No way. Let him come see me."

"Well, you know he won't, so why make it an issue? Why be mean?"

"We'll be back at five. I'm going to have dinner with Reece. If you don't mind looking after Paulie."

"Dinner with Mr. Goodbar, is it?" She looks miffed.

Franklin is thudding overhead. Three heavy thumps and silence. Three heavy thumps again. "If he's that anxious for something, he could come out and ask."

"Oh, well, it isn't *Picnic*. I think I saw this one. A Western."

"I suppose old Bill gets killed?"

"I think Bill makes it, but he's all shot up at the end. What kind of name is Reece?"

"A family name. I've told you."

"Sounds like peanut butter candy."

"You say that every time. It isn't one bit funny."

"Sounds obscene. Reece's pieces, Franklin says. Get it?" Gesturing with a motion of her head toward Paulie, "Why is that child so solemn?"

"He doesn't understand. Besides, you scare him."

"Smile for your grandma, Paulie," my mother commands. "You have a nice swim lesson. But tell Monte no high dive."

"If Monte thinks he's ready . . ."

"You ever hear of broken necks? Snapped spines?"

"Run and get your towel, Paulie."

"Kids paralyzed for life?"

"There's a hot dog in the fridge for him. For dinner. Applesauce."

"They check the chlorine in that pool?"

"Of course they do."

"No matter. He'll pass out from indigestion."

"Why do you say that?"

"The stuff you let him eat. A hot dog," Juanita sniffs. "You ever read *The Jungle?*"

"Sure I did. You saw to it."

"It wouldn't hurt the kid to taste a vegetable."

"I never did."

"Look at the mess you're in," my mother says. Sun streaming through the clouded windows casts gold-green shadows on her face. The basement walls are painted turquoise, her favorite color. The floor is black-and-white linoleum, wide blocks like a Brobdingnagian checkerboard.

Before my mother changed the basement to a rumpus room, it was her workplace where ladies came for electrolysis. There was a section of the basement curtained off, her "treatment room" furnished with a hinged examining table, a cabinet bearing her tools and salves, a rolltop desk, and a swiveling stool on which she perched to work her transformations. She wore a white uniform and thick white stockings, floppy-tongued white shoes that squeaked as she crossed the checkered floor to greet her clients. Franklin and I used to hunker in the shadows watching as they came, trim women with perfect hair, gold bangles on their arms, bright diamonds on their fingers. They'd sidle through the cellar door looking furtive, ashamed, as though some dreadful fate had branded them unclean. "Mama's Dark Ladies of the Sorrows," Franklin had named them. Juanita greeted them with courteous detachment. If she spotted us kids peeking from a corner, she'd growl, "Get lost," before pulling shut the turquoise curtain. If we could manage it, we stayed, eavesdropping. Sometimes the ladies cried aloud or whimpered, pathetic mews like the meek pleas of kittens who were helpless, blind, dependent on some strong maternal force to get them launched in life. "Courage," Juanita used to tell them. "There's no beauty without pain." Franklin and I would cling to one another, disgusted and intrigued, straining to hear the zap of the electric needle. "You know," Franklin whispered one day, "it's not only the face." And we reeled with choked-up laughter, imagining what secret flesh our mother probed and kneaded in her makeshift chamber. When the women exited they looked ashen, defiant—faint lines of pink over their lips, under their chins, and heaven knew where else. They smelled of rosewater and Juanita's secret creams.

There were neighbors who began complaining about cars blocking their drives and the tearfully unthinking women who tottered in high heels over new lawns. For a time my mother shrugged off these complaints (the serpent's look cast at those who were the most overtly critical); then one day she simply said she was going to give it up. She'd been brooding about lawsuits. "One infected follicle . . ." her voice trailed into ominous silence. My father, who was then a printer for the *Star,* good steady work (or so we thought until the paper folded), encouraged her to quit. We moved the TV to the cellar, now christened the rumpus room. We stored suitcases and lawn chairs behind the turquoise curtain. Franklin and I began campaigning for a Ping-Pong table.

"Go see why Franklin's knocking. Can you do me that one favor, seeing as how I'm baby-sitting tonight?"

She does demand her pound of flesh. I grouse that it seems pointless to encourage him, but she waves me off. She's engrossed in the TV. Bill Holden is galloping across a desert plain. From the shadow of tall cliffs, dark figures mark his progress. "Watch it," Juanita cautions. And then to me, "Will you be out late with Mr. Goodbar?"

"Why do you call him that? It's not like he was a rapist. It's not like I met him in some bar."

"Almost as bad, the way you choose to make new friends."

Paulie, wisely, has run off, bent under the crocheted afghan of pink and yellow tulips on an emerald field like a fragile gnome blanketed by flowers.

"You know damn well I met Reece at his place of business."

Juanita drapes my blouse over a hanger. The sleeves extend in rigid wings, a butterfly impaled. "Should I be glad?"

"You should be glad I have some kind of social life. Jeez, Ma, I'm only twenty-five. Would you prefer I live like Franklin?"

"I would prefer you didn't hang out at that fellow's house. You have a home for entertaining."

Oh, sure! Old movies and doomsday tales, with Franklin impatiently pounding upstairs. "Where I go on dates is my private business."

"Is it?" Juanita asks. "Is it?"

We are venturing into quicksand. As if on cue, the music on the TV movie rumbles a fate motif—Bill galloping toward peril. I'm heading for the stairs. "I won't be late."

"But you're going to his place?"

"I don't know where we're going."

"I didn't raise my kid to be a tramp."

"Thanks, Juanita. Nice vote of confidence."

There's a low rumble of drums from the TV, clatter of horses' hooves, the *zing* of arrows. "You ever hear of herpes, AIDS, chlamydia?"

I stumble up the stairs, palms clapped to my ears to dull the sounds.

In Franklin's room another TV set is flickering softly. This one, set upon his dresser, is angled so he can watch the screen from bed if he chooses to. The shades are drawn. The air feels stale and heavy like the rank air of an elevator. He is up now pacing, pounding on the floor with Pop's dog-headed stick. When I tell him, "She's gotten awful. Worse than she ever was," he moves to hug me—as much for his comfort as mine.

"She's a pistol since Pop died. It hasn't been so easy living with her." His smile is secretive and pained, as though he knows some awful stuff that I was spared because I got married and moved away. That tees me off.

"It's no picnic for anyone." I duck from his embrace and move to the Boston rocker near the window. Just to make it clear that I'm annoyed, I start rocking hell-for-leather, glad the noise will carry to Juanita on the floor below. Franklin stands, listless and lost, knowing I'm angry and pretending that he's powerless to make amends. He's wearing Pop's old brown wool bathrobe, tied with a tasseled cord that looks like a drapery sash. His hair is cropped close in an uneven bristle, Juanita's handiwork. I know she's purchased implements and a book on home haircutting, something I disapprove of strongly. Why make it all so easy for him?

"Come on, Linda-love. Don't be mad." He tosses the walking stick on his bed. He offers his most winning smile.

"Don't call me Linda-love. Sounds like a porn star."

"If the shoe fits," he grins.

"And don't try to be clever. 'Cause I know you are, and it cuts no ice with me. I'm clever too, you know. I can tell you've been talking with Juanita."

"I surely talk with our dear ma." He rubs his palms together as though anticipating a good argument. In Pop's brown robe, that close-cropped hair, he looks like a sly monk, an abbot—patrician and smooth-jawed. Ma claims she named him Franklin because he had that snobby air, an upward thrust of chin that made her think of FDR in his heyday. She said that even as a baby Franklin could look supercilious. Knowing he's her favorite doesn't rile me anymore. I take it as a given, the way of mothers and their sons.

"You've been discussing me and Reece. I heard your little crack about the peanut butter candy."

"That was just being funny. I wasn't trying to put him down. I never met the guy. Why would I want to put him down?"

"It's your own fault you never met him."

"Ah, here we go." Franklin's smile, truly sad now, might melt a warmer heart.

"Here we go."

"You won't let up?"

"I won't give up on you like *she* has."

"She understands."

"I think *she* is the cause."

"No. That isn't so. It isn't fair." Franklin is pacing now, testing the boundaries of this place he's made his world. The room looks as it did when he was in his teens—plain oak furniture, a double bed that leaves scant room to move around. Shelves in every likely corner hold his books. The walls are drab off-white and bare except for two school pennants, crossed like swords—the blue and gold of the Bethesda–Chevy Chase High School Barons, the red and white of the University of Maryland Terrapins. That is the sum of Franklin's life.

Juanita raised us on disaster tales. When we were kids, she told us about the *Titanic,* the *Hindenburg,* the sinking of the *Lusitania.* Those were our bedtime stories.

Franklin stops pacing. "You turned out healthy," he says, almost accusingly.

"I'm a mess. And I'm getting scared for Paulie."

"That kid is great. Just stop calling him Paulie, and he'll be fine. As for me," he smiles, smooths the heavy robe that still bears odors redolent of Pop, tobacco, printer's ink, "the problem may be biochemical." He's watching me now, slyly (a hint of cruelty in the look), waiting for what I'll say.

"I've begged you to see a doctor, to consider therapy."

"Ah, no. You know the way I feel." He's laughing, happy that

I've fed him the desired cue. "The body is a temple. Don't want no drugs messing it up." Before I can reply to that, he deftly switches to another subject. "You hear from Buddy lately?"

I'm on my feet, the rocker still moving behind me, as though the spirit of a long-gone Linda has taken over. "He's somewhere on the West Coast. His mother won't give me his number."

"No chance of child support?"

"Zip, if I can't find him."

"Sorry, keed," says Franklin, who with his chin thrust up looks bored as though my troubles are too banal for his contemplation. He is sneaking covert peaks at the TV. The Frugal Gourmet is frying kippers on PBS, and Franklin once liked to cook.

"Listen, what did you want with all that banging on the floor? You're driving Mama crazy."

"A drink, baby? A ginger ale? A Tab?"

"Goddam you, Franklin! Why don't you go straight to hell?"

"Hey, babe. What did I do?"

"The kitchen is straight down the hall. Try hard; I'm sure you'll find it."

"Nah, baby. I don't wanna."

"Don't tell me it's too much to leave this room."

"I hear people downstairs."

"It's her television!"

"Well, I couldn't tell if it was someone there or not."

"God, Franklin, you're not that crazy! You're not!"

"Told ya, babe. It's biochemical."

"Then go and get examined. Let us bring someone here."

"Not that again. Oh, no."

"Franklin, they work miracles today. You take a pill, you're out there giving speeches."

"No, Linda. I don't want to."

"That's it exactly. You don't want to. You like things the way they are. You've become addicted to despair."

Surprising me, Franklin guffaws. "De spare. De spare." He is clowning now, mimicking the dwarf on "Fantasy Island," one in the long array of TV reruns he watches through the day. "De spare is in de trunk."

"Oh, can it!"

"De plane is in de air."

He's sick all right; maybe Juanita and I impede his cure with what we mistakenly think is kindness. We're like those keepers in gothic tales, hiding our guilty secret in a stuffy room. Perhaps that's too melodramatic. I'm not Jane Eyre. God knows, Juanita isn't Rochester. But here sits Franklin, cackling in his brown monk's robe, "De plane. De spare." He is weeping tears of laughter. He stands up, fumbling in his pocket for a Kleenex.

"Go ahead and laugh over your little puns," I tell him stiffly. "It's not so funny for Juanita, four years of this. First you won't drive on the Beltway, then you won't drive at all. Then you won't take the bus. Then you won't leave the house. Now you're scared to tiptoe to the kitchen. What's next? You crawl into bed and pull the sheet over your head and wait to die?"

"Can't help it, babe." He hasn't found a tissue in his pocket. He shuffles to a bureau drawer and pulls out a new box of Kleenex. I watch him as he presses in the perforated cardboard lid. He discards the top tissue, selects another, mops his eyes.

"If the house burned, would you leave this room?"

"Linda, gimme a break."

He *is* crazy, I think, but clever, armed with his little strategies for passing time. He spends mornings in the Boston rocker sketching sparrows. He devises recipes he'll never cook; works out acrostics; fools with coins, perfecting magic tricks. He's begun reading our old encyclopaedia, the '68 Britannica that Pop bought through a special deal for *Star* employees. He's still muddling through the *A*s, studying *alewife* and *Alexander.* He's always been this way, hungry for facts, organization, preternaturally neat (maybe *that* was crazy), maybe the thirst for information, and the sweep he made through college majors (history to astrophysics to computer science), were all part of his lunacy. He was eager for new experience in his student days; then something fizzled. Now he sits for hours watching birds in the white pine. The waste just slays me. "You know, you say Pop's death made Mama worse. Maybe it isn't that. Maybe it's you, breaking her heart."

"Can't help it." He is still dabbing his eyes.

"Can't you try? Please, Franklin, can't you try?"

"Can't do it. Can't make waves." The tears are falling free now. He discards the sodden Kleenex, lifts the robe's hem to his face and wipes. He is wearing green-and-white-striped pajamas under the brown caftan. "I'm sick, babe, that's no lie. All of it, biochemical."

I'm fed up with pointless argument. I feel wiped out, breathless, as though some newly ominous virus has got me by the lungs. "I've got to go. Paulie's late for his swimming lesson."

"Thank you for stopping by." That courtesy strikes me as the ultimate absurdity. Still, I respond, reaching to kiss his wet cheek. He is still weeping softly. Before I leave the house with Paulie I bring Franklin a ginger ale liberally dosed with ice and topped with lemon and a sprig of mint, the way he likes it.

When Franklin and I were little we had a swing in the backyard: two benches shaded by an awning canopy. You sat facing one another with your feet set on a wooden "floor." You couldn't swing too high that way, which was the point. Juanita said this type of swing was safe, but Franklin thought it was too tame. He'd stand up (he wasn't much older than Paulie) and grasp the poles that held the canopy in place and tug with all his strength, and pump his body, till the swing moved higher, higher. As we swung, there was a phrase he'd chant because he liked the rhythm: "We're going to Cali-*forn*-ya. We're going to Cali-*forn*-ya." On that third syllable of California we'd be flying, laughing, not afraid, swooping toward the branches of a maple tree my father swore a squirrel had planted. There was tall grass in the yard that sometimes grew as high as our knees. To cut it my father had to use a scythe. You can bet we didn't own a power mower (dangerous to store the gasoline; besides, in one misguided motion you could cut off all your toes), and the old-fashioned, hand-driven mower just got stuck in clumps of grass.

One day when we were swinging my father came out with his scythe resting on his shoulder. He was a sweet, sad-looking man, already going jowly. His chest was narrow, but he had a hefty paunch, a beer belly that made him look a whole lot older than his years. He had small feet for a man his height, an almost dainty walk, like a dancer concentrating to be sure each step was right.

That day he was wearing a khaki T-shirt and old army fatigues that had gotten way too small. When he hefted these over his gut the trousers looked like flood pants. I think I started giggling at that. Franklin, oblivious, was singing: "We're going to Cali-*forn*-ya." My father listened for a while. Then, very deliberately, he set his scythe down in the grass. He caught the swing as it was on the rise and hauled it to a sudden stop. He was glaring straight at Franklin, almost mean. "What's that all about? That thing you were saying?"

Franklin shrugged. "It's just a song."

"*She* tell you that?"

Franklin shook his head. "It's just something to say."

"*She* planning to take you kids away?"

Franklin stared at him, not answering. He had a snotty look all right, like it wasn't worth his trouble to explain.

"All right," my father said as though he'd learned all that he had to know. "You kids go play inside."

We stepped down from the swing and marched single file through the tall weeds. Franklin led the way with shoulders set, back very straight; although he'd been accused of some mysterious disloyalty he meant to keep his dignity. "He's crazy," Franklin said when we were back inside the house.

"Franklin," I asked, "*are* we going to California?"

"Don't be so dumb!" Disgusted, he had stalked off to his room and closed and locked the door. All my crying, all my pleas wouldn't get him to open it. Juanita was in the cellar with her ladies, and there was no one there to intervene.

Later, I watched my father mowing, swinging the scythe with slow, smooth strokes. Soon the grass was heaped around him in thick clumps, and he was standing in a field of tattered green, pressing a handkerchief to his wet forehead. He looked abandoned, as though the thing he'd feared had happened and we'd scooted off to California.

I don't remember that they fought that much. Not like Buddy and me. In the place we had in Hyattsville our quarrels got so loud the neighbors on one side (who were no angels themselves) threatened to call the cops. Paulie got so he slept through it, like music you no longer hear if it's always blaring in your ears. If you turn it off, the silence wakes you.

I'm thinking of this as we straggle toward the pool through heat so fierce it hits us like a wall. There's sweet ligustrum growing near the entrance gate. "Don't ever, ever eat the berries on that hedge, because they're poison," I tell Paulie, as though he didn't have enough to worry him. He's lagging a step behind me, wheezing a bit, a breath away from tears. He's lost a flip-flop in the parking lot. Now he's hobbling, setting his bare foot on the burning blacktop, then shifting quickly to the foot wearing the sandal. "Go find your flip-flop and come on. We're already ten minutes late for your lesson."

"Don' wanna lesson."

I could've guessed that this was coming. Juanita, who is paying for his lessons, brings him here when I'm at work. If I ask her how he's doing, she says he's "making sufficient progress for his age." If I press, she gives me a version of the drop-dead look and says, "Go yourself and talk to Monte if you want more information." I think she's vague because she doesn't pay attention, just

14

dumps Paulie in Monte's care and goes to swim her laps. "Swimming is fun, Paulie. Every little boy should learn to swim." I hear that phony rapture in my voice that adults use when they want their kids to do something unpleasant.

In the sun, the black macadam of the parking lot shimmers like a tarry sea. Paulie hobbles back to get the sandal. He pokes it with his toe, as though it were some poor, dead animal. He moves it an inch or so towards me, then stands there staring at the ground. He has Buddy's coloring—fair hair and pale, almost translucent skin already turning freckled from the sun. "If you don't put on that flip-flop and come on, I'm gonna smack you."

People say my marriage wasn't all a waste, because there's Paulie, and I can thank Buddy for that. To this, I'm sure to answer, "Yes, indeed. Oh, yes. Oh, isn't that a fact." The truth, which I wouldn't say to anyone, is that I'm not always convinced I love my son. I know I would protect him. See he eats well. Has his shots. But in many ways he is a disappointment—a sickly, timid kid, not the feisty sort who'll make it in this world. Even when I was carrying him, I thought, this baby's movements are too tentative. No hearty kicks, no thrashing round *in utero,* just sudden nervous flutters, as though he knew he'd be unhappy—as though he already was.

"Paulie, I'm really losing patience. Now, come on!" There are circles under his eyes from loss of sleep, so dark against his skin that it looks as though he has two nasty shiners. Turning from me, he starts his hobbled movement toward our car. "Paulie!"

"Gotta get my fins." He is so thin his shoulder blades protrude like pointy wings. His Speedo trunks are drooping. You can see the sharp crease that divides his skinny butt, no flesh at all to pillow him.

"You leave them in the car and get yourself moving or I swear you won't be sitting for a week. Now, I've never hit you hard, Paulie, but there's gonna be a first time, and you won't like the surprise!" So we finally make it past the dangerous wall of sweet ligustrum—with me threatening and Paulie, sniffling, shuffling, kicking the sandal ahead of him as though he's practicing for soccer—into the pool.

It's nice here for a city pool. There are wide grassy areas where people have spread towels and blankets, and there are chaises set up all around the pool's perimeter. There are three pools really, the big one where today it seems a million kids are playing happily, a separate wading area for tykes, and a lap pool where the serious swimmers, like Juanita, work out daily.

Monte is standing at the big pool, near the shallow end. I've known him since we were in high school. He was a year ahead of me, in Franklin's class, a pesky kid who laughed a lot but never got the point of jokes till ample time had passed. You could tell him something funny and, for sure, he would guffaw, but his eyes would have this puzzled look, like you were talking to him in a foreign language. He was bright enough, I guess, just saddled with a literal mind. Try a Henny Youngman monologue on Monte, say, the one that starts: "Take my wife. *Please.*" Monte would ask you, "Take her where?" Then, maybe an hour later, you could be in study hall or sitting in the cafeteria and you'd hear this awful whooping, like the clamor of a lovesick whale. Once, in the lunchroom, some girl new to the school heard Monte bellowing and asked Franklin and me, "What's that?" Franklin, unwrapping his tuna sandwich, flashed her his superior look. "Monte's having an epiphany."

Even as he's greeting Paulie, Monte eyeballs me. "Hey, kiddo, we've been waiting for you."

I tell him it's my fault we're late. "I lost track of the time."

"That's okay." He forgives me with his sappy grin. "Linda, it's so good to see you." He checks out my outfit, cutoffs and a halter top that doesn't leave too much to the imagination. "How ya doin'?"

"Hangin' in there, Monte. How're you?"

"Good. Good. You're lookin' great."

16

"Thanks. So're you." He looks the same, not much taller than I am, a stocky frame, a swimmer's robust torso. His hair is crinkly brown, cropped close. He wore it short even in high school when the style was long. His eyes are milky blue against his tan. They still seem puzzled, a little wary, like he's frightened I'll crack wise and he won't understand.

Bending to Paulie, he says, "Take your shower, kiddo, and then hop in the pool. The class is waiting for you."

"I'll take him to the ladies' locker . . ."

"Oh, no. He knows the drill. He can manage it himself. Can't you, sport?"

Paulie has closed his eyes—the way kids do, the way they think if *they* can't see, that makes them safe, invisible. I tell Monte, "I guess he's just a little shy."

"I noticed that this week. We're workin' on it, aren't we, sport?"

"So many changes in his life."

"I heard about you and Buddy. Linda, I'm sorry."

"Well, it wasn't in the master plan."

"It happens so much nowadays. It's like an epidemic. You gotta pick up the pieces, though. Learn from it. Move on."

"That's true." I'd forgotten that he was this boring, full of gung ho talk and righteous platitudes. "The body is a temple" is one of Monte's lines, which Franklin is forever quoting.

"I'm not married myself." Monte is wearing khaki trunks with a senior lifesaver's emblem sewn on them. There's a whistle dangling from a cord around his neck.

"Well, lucky you."

"I wouldn't say I'm lucky. Just scared to take the plunge."

"You haven't met Miss Right."

"Time's passin'. I hope I do. I hope she likes the things I like and feels the way I do about living right, 'n proper diet, fitness, everything. 'Cause when it happens, I want it to be permanent. Forever."

Well, dammit, don't we all? "I wish you luck." He tugs the whistle on his chest as though he means to underscore my wish for luck with a good, hearty toot. Or convene a team of proper girls, all hell-bent on permanence and healthful swimming. Suddenly, I don't see Paulie. "Where's my son? Hey, Monte, where'd he go?"

"Taking his shower like I told him. Don't worry, Linda. He's just fine."

"Well, what if he fell in the pool?"

"If that happened, he'd let us know, I promise you. He's not too keen on the water, but we're gonna change that. We'll have him swimmin' like his grandma in a while." Monte's grinning now as though he's caught on to a joke. "Y'know, Linda, that Buddy must be crazy. You're prettier than you ever were, if such a thing is possible."

He had a crush on me in high school. He used to hang around Buddy and me, trail us at parties; at BCC, he'd loiter near our lockers waiting to intercept us. Once, he found us on the bleachers back of school. It was spring, late March I think, still winter in the air. We were watching track practice, just killing time, too happy with each other to go home. Buddy had handed me a joint, my first, and said give it a try. I'd told him I'd be killed, if my mother found out. I'd be dead meat. But I took it, inhaled, and then gave it back. Buddy took a long, slow drag, then placed the joint between my lips again. This time, when I inhaled I started coughing. "Easy," Buddy said, nuzzling my face with his lips, his cheek. "Easy." We passed the reefer back and forth, and we were giggling a lot. Buddy asked, well, what do you think; and I told him, it's nice, but it doesn't affect me, affect me, affect me. Then we were rolling in each other's arms, half falling off the bleachers, laughing too hard to kiss. Buddy's hands were cold; he put them up under my sweater to get warm; then he reached out for the joint. I remember how the sun was very bright, so bright I had to blink away the glare. But it was cold.

18

There were puddles on the bleachers edged with ice, and gray ice patches on the field. The team was running like they were inspired. I never saw those guys run better. They were moving with such graceful strides, it seemed as though their track shoes never touched the ground. They were like athletes in a Grecian frieze, long-legged and oh so beautiful. "Should boys be beautiful?" I asked Buddy, who answered, "Hell, I am." Which again got us hysterical. Then, out of nowhere, there was Monte, watching us with stricken eyes and pleading, "Don't do this, Linda Jo. Oh, you shouldn't. You shouldn't. Don't you know the body is a temple?"

"Here's my man," Monte says to Paulie, who's standing on the concrete apron of the pool. There's water dripping from his hair, and he is shivering. "Jump in," Monte says.

Paulie shakes his head no, and suddenly darts close to me and rams his face hard against my thighs. He must have showered in cold water; his skin feels clammy. I bend to him to whisper, "What is it, sweetie? Are you scared? You shouldn't be, because you've done it all before, haven't you, and you know you won't sink. Just close your eyes and jump and you'll bob up like a little duck, I promise you."

Monte's fiddling with his whistle; he wants so much to blow it, get things started. There are kids splashing in the water just below us, playing Marco Polo. That's a game Franklin and I played too, here in this pool. The kid who's "it" closes his eyes and calls out, "Marco." When the other players answer, "Polo," he swims in the direction of their voices, trying to tag whomever he can catch, a kind of floating blindman's buff. I never really saw the point of it, but we used to play till we were waterlogged and ready to drown from sheer exhaustion. "Look at the fun those kids are having, Paulie," Monte says. "Don't you want to play?" Paulie rams his face into my body till it hurts. I feel his head shaking, no. Monte says, "Okay, Linda Jo. I tell you what you oughta do. You oughta get yourself a chaise over by the lap pool and just leave this young fella here with me. We'll work it out."

Paulie screams "No!" loud enough to be heard over the cries of "Marco," "Polo."

Monte puts his hands on Paulie's shoulders and tugs on him till Paulie's hold on me gives way. "Just go wait by the lap pool, Linda, please."

I hesitate. "You're sure?"

"I'm sure. We had this little problem yesterday. We solved it though. I'll tell you how. I sat down just like this." He lowers himself to the pool's edge. "And Paulie climbed onto my lap. C'mere, kiddo," he says, and Paulie, as if he's in a trance, moves to Monte's arms. "Then we closed our eyes. Close 'em, Paulie. You got 'em closed. You sure? Then we just sort of fell . . ." The kids playing in the pool must be used to this. They separate to give Monte some space as he topples to the water, hauling Paulie with him.

The water in the lap pool is a chemical blue-green. Sun splashes the surface with gold lights, like a spill of flashing coins. The swimmers paddle back and forth as purposeful as robots. When they touch the far edge of the pool, they dip to racers' turns, kick off. Their feet raise little flurries of white foam. Their arms lift like the arms of dancers. Their bodies pitch to one side as they breathe; then they turn their faces back into the water as though craving sustenance. It hypnotizes me to watch them, calms me after the ordeal with Paulie.

There's a group of girls I knew in high school lounging on chaises, a full pool's length away. Thank God, I don't have to talk to them. They smile at me and wave in languorous slow motion as though the heat has got them weary. I wave back, aping their grins, the languid motion of their arms. I can guess the subject of their conversation: That's Linda Jo Merceau, used to be Linda Jo Burke. Her brother, Franklin, was senior class president and ran the literary magazine and won a Chancellor's Scholarship to Maryland. Then something happened, he went crazy; now he never leaves the house. *She* eloped with that cute Buddy Merceau who quarterbacked the Barons the year they almost made it to the championship. Her kid's old enough for *elementary* school. Isn't that dumb, having a baby right away? No chance ever again for having fun.

One of the girls stands up, and I can see she's very pregnant. Lila something or other, somebody Franklin dated. I think she went to UVA. She's wearing a bathing suit for expectant mothers that I don't believe. It fits her like a monstrous bubble and the front is printed with a face. Wide eyes over each breast, a cute dot of a nose, and at the point Lila's belly projects the farthest, a monstrous gaping mouth, open as though ready to expel the baby. I can hear Juanita saying, "That's obscene." Different, for sure, from how I dressed when I was carrying Paulie. I'd wrap myself in Buddy's shirts, or his BCC team jacket. When I got big, I wouldn't show myself. If we went out, it was in deep cover of darkness, maybe to the Dairy Bar at U of Maryland where they make their own, terrific ice cream. I was hung up on their black bing cherry, my only craving.

All during that time, Juanita spooked us. When she learned we were expecting she made us promise not to buy a stitch of infant clothes until the kid was safely born. "Not a diaper, not a bib. You got to swear. And no painting the room. No setting up the crib. Nothing. All of that gets taken care of later," Juanita said. Buddy asked her, did she think the kid would come out with two heads if we stocked up on Pampers? She told him don't be smart; it doesn't hurt to take precautions. It got so she would call us in the night, armed with some witchy prescience. "He's assembling the crib, isn't he? He's bought the bassinet." One night, Buddy blew sky-high, not at her, at me. "I can hang a goddam mobile for my kid, if I want to. Can't I? I can paint his room a fuckin' yellow, without her butting in. Can't I? Can't I?" I hollered that he'd better shut his trap. The unborn child can hear, I'd read this in a magazine. The unborn child is sensitive to the mother's voice and the sound of pleasant harmonies. It reacts to songs sung calmly, the temperate counterpoint of Bach played upon the clavichord, the dulcet measures of the harp.

I think the child unborn is like a swimmer drifting in a dangerous sea. The very lifeline that sustains it can be a source of harm, transmitting fear and anger. I think our fights affected Paulie, just as Juanita's gloom marked me and Franklin. Something of Pop has touched us too, his odd preoccupations, his need to wrap himself in arcane memories. After the *Star* folded, he wandered in a fog, and that's what killed him finally. Depressed and self-absorbed he stepped into the street only a block from home. A Metro bus, speeding to make time, plowed into him. Franklin said it wasn't so much suicide as a willed absence of vigilance. Juanita thought the years of nicotine and printer's chemicals had sapped his brain of its acuity.

It's too hot in the sun to sit still comfortably. I meander to the big pool to observe the class. The other kids are floating under Monte's tutelage, but Paulie's clinging to the wall, kicking dispiritedly. When he sees me he begins to cry. His look suggests, *Do you think this is worth it?* Juanita says it is. He might be stuck without a lifeboat on a transatlantic crossing. He might be on the Pan Am Shuttle and crash into the drink. The Potomac might overflow. Picture us, treading water over by the Tidal Basin, blessing Juanita's foresight.

"Okay, Paulie, you ready for the dead man's float?" He hollers no. Monte persists, "I'm here to catch you. You won't sink, I promise you. Give it a try." But Paulie is fixed tight to the wall, stubborn as a barnacle. "All right, kiddo," says Monte. "You win this time. But here's what I want you to do. You come here tomorrow with your grandma, and you practice. You get her to show you how. At lesson time, I wanna see you kick off and glide to me on your own, face in the water. That's all I want. You do that once, the rest is easy, I promise you. Is it a deal?" Paulie shakes his head, no deal. Monte grins without a trace of humor.

"You mull on it, okay? 'Cause I'm not gonna give up on you. No way. You're gonna learn to swim, and I'm gonna teach you. Know why? 'Cause I got tenacity. Ask your mama what that means." He gives a soft toot on his whistle. "That's it, guys, lesson's over for today." Some kids, little brownnoses, say they want to continue. Paulie's trying to scramble up the side of the pool wall. His struggle has me mortified. *My son. Take him. Please.* Monte hefts him to dry ground, then lifts himself out of the pool with a single, easy motion.

Paulie speeds past me. "I'll be at the wading pool."

I yell, "No. There isn't time."

"Oh, let him. He needs to think things over." Monte has drawn abreast of me. His hair is wet and gleaming, and his eyelashes, longish, curly, are dabbed with drops of moisture, like tiny pearls. "We're gonna lick this, Linda, don't you worry. I mean it when I say I'm tenacious. Bulldog Monte Morris, that's who I am."

"I appreciate your efforts, Monte."

"No sweat. He's a spunky kid. He'll come round."

"Paulie? Spunky? I don't think so."

"Sure he is. Say, Linda, maybe one night you and I could go somewhere and grab a bite of dinner? Talk about old times?"

"I can't do that, Monte."

"Ah, look. You gotta take a break from the responsibility."

"It's because I'm seeing someone."

He absorbs this with a funny motion of the mouth, like a fish gulping in the thinner reaches of the air. "Well, I didn't think . . . it seems so soon."

"Buddy took off eight months ago. Should I be living like a nun, do you suppose?"

He ponders this as seriously as though it were a punch line he's trying to figure out. "You do what you gotta do, Linda Jo."

"Well thanks. I will."

"See you around, then?"

"Oh yeah. See you, for sure."

He starts for the men's locker room, hesitates, turns back to where I'm standing, lead-footed, amid darting bodies diving to the pool's cool depths. "You *will* come out to cheer our team, won't you?"

"What team is that?"

"You know. Juanita swims with my prime timers at the Y. She's our star performer."

"I know she likes to swim. She never mentioned that she'd joined the Y."

He seems amazed at this. "Why, she's the best we got. Competitive, as well as quick. Those little ladies like your ma do best, you know. They skim over the water like a leaf."

"She never said."

"Will you come out to our first meet? Two weeks from now? Right after Labor Day?"

"I guess I will. If Ma's your star, I guess I have to."

"Bring Paulie too."

"I will."

"And Franklin, if he's willing."

"I don't know about Franklin."

"You gotta keep at him, Linda Jo. You gotta let him know there's nothing to be afraid of. That his friends are with him all the way."

"Thanks a bunch, Monte. I think I've got that figured out."

"Yeah, well I don't mean to be buttin' in. It's just, you're all part of my past. I cherish that, those days at BCC. And your ma, well, she's my best prime timer."

"I should get Paulie now. Thanks for helping him with swimming, Monte."

"Anything for you, Linda. For you the world." He looks as though he's steeling himself to hear laughter. He won't face me directly.

"That's nice to hear." I just want to be rid of him. "Gotta run, now. Thanks." As I head back to the lap pool to collect my stuff I can feel his pale eyes tracking me, full of solemn accusation. That naughty Linda Jo dating another man. He'd drop dead if he knew the half of it. Screw him! Screw his buttinsky looks. And not just him. I'm pretty fed up with Juanita. She never said word one about the Y, never mentioned she was Monte's star performer. She's quick enough to give out bad news; come up with something pleasant, and she'll sluff it off, repress it like it was a shameful secret.

Lila, the pregnant girl, is waddling toward me with her face set in a smile that duplicates that bizarre grin she's sporting on her belly. Quickly I grab my pocketbook and keys and head off to the wading pool. There's nothing I can think of that I want to say to her.

Two

Reece, pondering what we'll have for dinner, asks, "Chinese okay?"

"Chinese is great."

"Then I'll go in and get things started."

"Don't rush on my account. This is so nice. Just sitting quietly." We're lounging on his lawn in slant-backed chairs, sipping gin and tonics in the soft night air, cooler here in Ashton, an hour from the city, the section people call "up county." To get here you tool casually down curving roads, past century-old oaks and red ramshackle barns and horses grazing quietly in stubbly fields. You swing by country stores, with spinning wheels and cradles set outside, as lures to passing travelers. You pass a boarding kennel and a private school. Reece's house sits on a hill that slopes to a back pasture and a little brook. The property covers a pleasant acre, no neighbors near.

Reece doesn't mind the long commute. He claims that when he's driving he can tell the actual moment when the air turns sweet and the stale fumes of the city dissipate. He'll roll the windows down and sing old show tunes loud enough to scare the cows. He has an okay voice, not great but passable. One season he played summer stock, not due to any blazing talent, he is quick to say. Mainly, the costumes fit, and he could sing on key. When we're alone, and he is in a happy mood, he'll belt out these old chestnuts. "Bali Ha'i." "If I Loved You." "Stranger in Paradise." Stuff Juanita owns on 78s.

Now, humming in the August dusk, Reece seems content. We've pulled our chairs to the side lawn near the fancy birdhouse he put up to attract purple martins. They don't nest here, scared away by sparrows. The birdhouse, high atop a pole, is an architectural marvel Reece built from a kit, with a steep pitched roof and a dozen or more rounded openings, entries for the absent martins. ("Birds of the swallow family," says Reece, quoting a nature guide.) Too bad they won't take residence, because they eat mosquitoes, and their presence augurs happy times. "Where they most breed and haunt, I have observed the air is delicate," Reece recites; his bookishness surprises me. I don't perceive him as a reader; he's more the brilliant tinkerer concerned with high-tech toys. The study near his bedroom is a trove of modern gadgets, winking, buzzing, recording, as though they had a mission without him.

"Your drink okay?"

"Oh yes."

"You're goin' at it kinda slowly."

I study the wedge of fresh lime floating in my gin. The clink of ice against the glass is pleasant, like the calming play of wind chimes. "I've got to drive later, remember?"

"You could stay."

"I know. But I should be home for Paulie. And then I don't have to give explanations."

He nods, extends both arms, his glass held high as though he's offering a last enticement to the swallows. "Let's finish these inside, and I'll start on the food."

Feeling the gin, I get up cautiously. "What can I do to help?"

"Just watch. Save your energy."

I trail him silently across the lawn, heels sinking in the spongy grass. In the lush light of the moon his shirt gleams coldly white; his hair picks up the radiance of silver. In chinos and white sneakers, the laces casually trailing, he looks the part of the romantic lead. Breathless and dizzy from the drink, and the tension Reece invariably provokes in me, I follow him onto the porch, sensing something worrisome under this roof, some spirit of reproach.

Reece's house is all one-story because his mother had MS and spent her last years in a wheelchair. When her condition worsened, his father split. For six years before her death, Reece cared for her. When he speaks of this, his voice takes on the stilted tone of a recording, emotion banned. When he says he merely did what was required of an only son, it sounds stilted and out of character.

The house has big rooms, extra-wide doorways and halls, and ramps, covered with indoor-outdoor carpeting, that slope to the outdoors. When Reece's mother was alive he had the whole place wired with an intercom, so he could track her movements, page her, know she was okay. There are lots of special touches—the screened side porch, a terrace off the master bedroom, and a dreamboat of a kitchen at the house's hub, with work islands and all the counters adjusted to the proper height for someone in a wheelchair. There are railings everywhere. Some nights as I follow Reece along the cushioned ramps I feel as though I'm on a ship, cruising somewhere strange and quiet. I always talk in whispers when I'm here, always walk on tiptoe. Sometimes I feel a sharpness in my chest and realize I've been waiting, scared to breathe lest I upset some careful balance. The indoor air smells antiseptic—some freshening spray his cleaning woman uses. When—if—I become the lady of the house, I'll switch to floral scents, or fling the windows wide and let in buffets of fresh air.

As Reece works, I pace the kitchen, admiring things. He asks, "You don't mind garlic?"

"Never have."

Thoughtfully, he surveys a clove of garlic, adds another to the chopping block. "Chicken and broccoli? How's that?"

"Perfect."

"I want this evening to be perfect," Reece says softly. "So drink up."

Something has told me we were moving toward a new arrangement. Although it's been only two months that we've been dating regularly, something gave me the hunch. He's going to ask me to move in, Paulie and me. It's too soon to mention marriage, but marriage is a possibility. He's told me he's been lonely since his mother died. He says I've brought him joy he couldn't have imagined. "I want it to be perfect too, Reece."

His smile of pleasure makes my knees totter. I've always flipped for handsome men. Buddy is twelve kinds of cute, everyone agrees; but Reece has the craggy-jawed perfection of a model, someone you see on ski posters, or hawking menthol cigarettes. His hair is whitish blond, his eyes a true glass green—cold sometimes. He doesn't show a lot of spark unless he's fiddling with his high-tech toys, or cooking. Chinese is his favorite since he can wield knives with a flourish, indulge his bent for showmanship.

"Won't be long now, Linda Jo." He's got oil sizzling in the wok. He adds onion and garlic, sherry, soy sauce, stirs in chunks of chicken, already diced and seasoned. I love to watch his hands, long white fingers, the nails trimmed short and manicured. When we met in the computer store, I was turned on by his hands, the way they skittered on the keys, called up commands as though

29

they had some independent intelligence. All the time his hands were tapping, he was chatting with me about RAM and DOS and hard disc versus floppies. Gibberish to me then. Finally, he sat me at the keyboard and commanded me to type. His eyes were distant, green; I didn't think he was impressed with me. He was just doing his job, not flirting, acting courteous. When I tapped the usual message on the keys, "Now is the time for all good men . . ." he interrupted. "Don't type that."

I asked why not.

"Type your phone number," he whispered. And I felt this sudden surge of joy as though the bad times since Buddy left were finally over. "I live in Hyattsville. But I might be moving to my mother's when my lease runs out."

"Then give me her phone number too."

Two months since we met. It *is* too soon to talk of marriage, but I sense it's on his mind.

"I need the broccoli. Get it for me, please." He can sound distant, imperious when he requests something, as though he's still with his machines, all programmed to serve him. There's a model that's been developed that responds to voice commands. I imagine Reece confronting it. *"Achtung!* Backspace. Delete. Insert decimal tabs or die!"

"Almost done," Reece says.

"Shall I light candles?"

"Don't bother. We're not gonna linger, are we?"

"Not if you don't want to."

"Would you like to watch a movie after?"

"Not that blue stuff, please."

"Only to set a mood."

"It usually does just the opposite for me. I guess you noticed."

Reece lowers the flame under the rice. "You could think of it as art, you know?"

"It's gross."

Reece finishes his drink with a long, noisy swallow and sets the glass down on the counter. "Don' know what's so diff'ren' about doin' it and viewin' it." He's trying to sound funny, pretending that he's drunk. I've never seen him actually get high, turn silly or sloppy like Buddy did. The most that happens, color floods his cheeks and his eyes glisten warily like he's concerned he might say something dumb.

"We do it, Reece. Isn't that enough?"

"You never"—fumbling for the tactful phrase, he pulls me to him—"lose composure." Resting his lips against my hair, "I want to make you crazy. Is that bad?"

"I just don't get that way. I don't think Buddy expected it."

"My women get that way."

Should I be optimistic that he sounds possessive, or put off because he's lumped me with this vast unseen sorority—his women—moaning in the sack? Like this babe we watched one time on VCR who was all implants and phony screaming, diddling the houseboy on the kitchen table—all of it so false, her gestures as phony as those bobbling boobs. "Reece, I enjoy being with you, but it's just not in my nature to be . . . noisy."

"This new cassette will flip you out, even you Miss Cool and Quiet."

"Is that the rice I smell burning?"

"Even you, Miss Married and Refined." He slips his hands under the blouse that Ma ironed so carefully.

I place my arms around his neck, both of us laughing now, the gin helping some. "C'mon, Reece, let's eat and then we'll both get crazy."

"With or without the flick?" asks Reece.

"If it means that much to you, I'll watch. But I might doze off, I warn you."

Reece's eyes bright with secret knowledge. "Trust me on this one, Linda Jo."

Sometimes *he* is so quiet, detached, almost depressed, as though sad memories weigh on him. We'll eat dinner in silence, and if I compliment him on the food, he'll pull up from some revery and look surprised as though wondering who I am and how I turned up in his house. Other times, he's almost chatty, as he is now, flushed from a second drink, and plying me with questions as we eat. He's interested, intense, charged with this keen, cold curiosity, but only on one subject, getting down, and the more I get embarrassed, the more he seems charged up. "When you were married, did you have good sex?"

"Sure. You shouldn't ask me things like that."

"When was it better? Before you had the kid, or after?"

"Before. Oh, maybe after, once he started sleeping through the night. I don't know, Reece. It varied. We were pretty clumsy at the outset, but I guess I'd have to say we were fast learners."

"When was it best?"

"I can't answer you."

"Can't? Why not?"

"I don't want to. That's private; it's between me and Buddy."

"Did you ever have wild parties? When you were at Maryland?"

"What is this, please? Are we on 'Nightline'?"

"Did you mess any with drugs?"

"We couldn't afford drugs or parties. The ones we went to were pretty tame, mostly married students."

"They don't get high? Play switch?"

"Some of them do. If I'd caught Buddy playing around, or spending our money on drugs, I'd've left him just like that." I snap my fingers in the air.

"So, what did you do at parties? Drink? Dance? Talk?"

"Drank beer. Talked. Mostly about finding day-care. After we had Paulie, that was almost all we thought about. Buddy got a little drunk sometimes, a little happy. Reece, why the third degree? What did you do when you were at school besides fiddle with computers? When you played those musicals, did you make out with your leading ladies?"

"Was there a time you knew things changed between you? Did you start losing interest or did he?"

"I didn't notice any change. His leaving was a big surprise, I'll tell the world."

"What would have made him happier in bed?"

"I don't know, Reece. I didn't think he was unhappy. I thought he was. Happy, I mean."

"What would have satisfied you?"

"Nothing. I mean, it was fine. Sometimes, I'd be too tired, and I'd put him off, and then he'd lose his temper. Buddy could be a brat, because mostly as a kid he got his way. His blowing up, that was the worst of it."

"How many times . . . ?"

"Hey, Reece, I'd rather see the movie. What's this one called?"

He grins, *"College Girls in Hawaii."*

"Oh, brother!"

He is moving to collect the dishes. "I like to know these things because . . ."

"Because?"

Shrugging, as he scrapes our plates, "I like to know."

He's working up to the big question about our moving in, I know it. There's a lovely room for Paulie, lots of space for him to play outside, enough land to keep a pony. Paulie should have a dog, some shorthaired breed that wouldn't make him wheeze. I like the kind that looks just like a lamb, a Bedlington. Maybe he could keep a rabbit in a little hutch out back. I don't know if Reece cottons to animals.

"Gettin' to know you," Reece sings, carrying dishes to the sink.

I gather up our empty glasses. "There's not that much to know. You're the one whose life gets interesting." Women coming to the shop don't hesitate to hit on him—guys too, which certainly offends him. If he wanted, he could party every night, go to gallery openings and benefits and chic dinners in Georgetown, hang out at sushi bars and restaurants where the "in" crowd gathers. People meet him once—rich ladies craving window dressing for their parties or something more—and want him on the scene. He hates that, relishes his privacy, wants time to putter on his hobbies, wants a solid, warm relationship with one attractive gal who'll concentrate on him. He needs that after his sad situation—his mother sick so long. He hasn't said this in so many words, but having spent a fair amount of time with him, I can put two and two together.

He's rinsing dishes carefully before loading the dishwasher. There's an odor in the air of cooking spice, pungent and sweet. On a shelf above the sink there are pots of flowering plants, glossy-leaved begonias all in perfect bloom. The first time I stood on tiptoe to inhale their scents Reece told me, "Don't bother. They're plastic." Pretty to look at and they need no care save an occasional dusting. Reece says his mother enjoyed them. I've peeked just once inside her room. It seemed pleasant, ordinary, no sign that she was ill save for the ramp leading to the little terrace, but I sensed her presence—long suffering and calm, the steely resignation of an invalid with a death grip on her son. I thought her disapproving spirit must be watching us that night, unhappy that I shared his bed. All mothers alike in that regard.

"I'll just wipe out the wok," says Reece. "You ready to see the flick?"

"Sure thing." *College Girls in Hawaii?* I just don't know. Franklin, who is my captive audience and confidant, says it's not exactly kinky, guys get turned on viewing porn (it doesn't make them Jack the Ripper or the Boston Strangler), and they think it gets women excited. He muses, "Maybe it does." When I tell him that's a crock, he frowns, big brother getting worried, after all. "What do you know, really, about this guy? Aside from making it with him, what do you know?" I tell him that he sounds like Ma, and there is no perfect guy, and Reece has all these super qualities. He just wants me to loosen up, and that is hard after putting trust in Buddy and getting burned, and I regret that I told Franklin anything.

There is a dimmer on the light switch in the study, which Reece adjusts according to his mood, sometimes flooding us in brightness, sometimes wrapping us in shadows. Tonight the room glows in a silvery twilight. The gray computer screen looms like a watchful eye. The TV set, the VCR, the compact disc player, are lined up on a worktable, like silent spectators. I've settled dutifully on the couch, which is a chrome and leather import that is murder on the back. Reece inserts a tape into the VCR and fiddles with some buttons on the set. A title flashes on the TV tube, accompanied by the mocking plink of ukeleles. Reece sits down beside me and drapes his arm around my shoulder. "This one is a corker."

These college girls have been around since Pearl Harbor, at least, and the only school they have attended is the College of Hard Knocks. I sense Reece watching me. He does this when we are in bed, something I hate. I hate men gauging my reaction as they diddle this and that, like engineers adjusting levers, hoping to raise steam. To tell the honest truth, Buddy's conscientious foreplay often left me irritated, like he was concentrating on some how-to manual and had forgotten me. When I got pregnant with Paulie, Buddy changed and got so loving, as though he'd proved something important and could relax and just be sweet. Sometimes he brought me so much pleasure—just the bulk of him, the strength, the youth, the sober concentration on the task at hand aroused such tenderness in me—I would have died for him. *Those* were the best times with Buddy, the months before Paulie was born.

Laughing, Reece is nudging me, "Well? What do you think?

Is that fantastic scenery, or what?" There's a long shot of mountain peaks with tiny figures struggling toward their summits, then the not-so-subtle parallel, fingers roam the contours of twin, naked breasts, inching over cones of silicon toward nipples firm as bullet casings. Pan to a woman's face, the star college girl, her mouth gone slack in what's supposed to be a daze of passion. She looks to me like she has just been decked, and the sense of what has happened hasn't hit her yet. She's lying on a beach, her chums and their admirers nearby, a bareass luau taking place. Drums beat. Waves break. Bodies roll and tumble in the sand. The camera flashes to a man's rapt face (this tour guide who got lucky with the star). He pokes his tongue into the woman's navel. She flutters phony eyelashes and murmurs, "Ah," which absolutely breaks me up, she sounds so much like Paulie when he gets his tonsils checked and the doctor tells him, "Open wider." The guide moves southward down the woman's belly and worships for a time. The woman parts her legs to the camera's dreamy probing and the studied catlike flicking of the tour guide's tongue. Overhead shot now. The woman thrashing—no surprise to me. I'm thinking how that sand must itch, besides being alive with creepy crawlies. The college girl moans, "More. More. I can't get enough of this."

"Oh, Reece, honestly. The dialogue!"

Fires burning on the beach. Frontal views of males trying to look satanic in the light of flames. "How do they stay that way, the men? They can't be acting."

"They get aroused."

"Is that so." I close my eyes.

"Linda, you're not asleep?"

"Resting."

"You're missing all the fun."

To placate him I watch it for a time. When it's apparent he is totally absorbed, I duck free of his arm and hightail it out of there.

No lights on in the hall. The doors to his mother's room and the guest room (the one I want for Paulie) are tightly closed. Using the railing as a guide, I make my way down the long ramp, past the spicy-smelling kitchen, the formal dining room we rarely use, the living room with its aura of antiseptic. A burst of noise blares out of nowhere, a rumble of ferocious drums and a clash of female voices shrieking what passes for ecstasy. Reece must have turned the volume up and then switched on the intercom. Mean-spirited, to say the least. Annoyed, I make my way outside via the porch, letting the screen door slam behind me. Passing the side lawn and the purple martins' house, I head for the backyard, hoping Reece won't follow all that soon.

A lover's eve. The night breeze bears the smell of moss and sodden leaves. I slip out of my sandals and wander barefoot toward the brook. Insects are singing in the weeds. Meandering toward the sheen of water, I think I feel their frail wings fluttering, ticklish against my toes and sort of nice. At intervals I hear the gravelly croak of bullfrogs. Above a line of trees, the moon shines implacable. Stars, big as phony diamonds, glitter out of reach.

There's something of a nasty streak in Reece, that business with the intercom. The big deal that he makes about my so-called cool, when he's the one hog-tied by self control. He needs those raunchy flicks, not me. Cross him and he turns mean, malicious in a childish way, something I blame on his past troubles with his family. Imagine all the afternoons he toodled home, speeding the country lanes and singing songs, to find his mother dozing in her chair, a little paler than the day before, a little closer to her death. She liked a stiff drink before dinner, so he'd fix her scotch and ice and wheel her to the terrace where they'd both sit drinking calmly in the fading light, and she'd tell him soap opera plots. He'd nod, nursing his gin, and ask appropriate questions. "Did Fiona marry

Dr. Bob? Was the brain tumor benign?" She'd ramble like an elderly Scheherazade, keeping the young, bored caliph close in check. "Did that interest you?" I've asked him, and he flashed me this disgusted look: What do you think? Once I questioned if he ever saw his father and he answered with a little shrug, as though the matter had no consequence. "I talked with him after her funeral. We went out for a drink."

When I asked, "What did you talk about?" Reece answered, "Nothing much."

"But what?"

"He wondered if I was taller than him, and I said I was. He said, no way. So we stood up back-to-back, in this bar downtown near the Willard, and asked the bartender to measure us." Reece smiled in icy triumph. "I was taller."

"That's all of it? Nothing about his walking out? His being sorry?"

"Nothing. Why dredge it up?" He's that detached and cold, mysterious at the core. I'm clueless how to reach him, but I will. Sex is the route we go for openers. At some point he will talk. At some point, he'll unbend, and show a loving, generous spirit. I know it's there because of how he tended his dying mother: fixing her drinks, and listening with pretended interest to her stories.

A hand touches my arm, like the soft brush of a sparrow in the leaves. I jump a mile. "Oh, God!"

Reece, bare-chested, tugging on his belt, complains, "You got away from me."

"Oh, jeez, Reece, you frightened me! Why did you sneak up like that? What are you doing? Why are you undressing here?"

"Why not? No one to see. Why did you sneak away?"

"The college girls got boring."

"Boring? I thought it was a gas. What's happened to your sense of humor?" He's kicked his sneakers off.

"Sorry to be a party poop."

"You think I'm a," he searches for the word he wants,

"voyeur?" Swift pull of the zipper. He lets his pants fall to the grass and hastily steps out of them. Slim in white jockey shorts, he has the pale grace of a Grecian statue. He pulls off his shorts impatiently, the lingering thrill of college girls apparent.

"I wish *I* was as big a turn-on as that stupid film."

"Forget the film. If all that you can say about it is 'it's stupid,' don't bother to mention it." The cold voice of command, profoundly distant, curt. So odd to hear the cold gestapo voice in the young slim god, aroused.

"I'm sorry, Reece. I didn't mean to criticize. I know it's just a way to have some laughs . . ."

He interrupts, placing a finger on my lips. "Must we spend this evening arguing? That's such a waste."

"You're right."

"Of course I'm right." He fiddles with a button on my blouse. "So take this off, 'cause one of us is overdressed."

"Well, that's for sure. Let's go indoors."

"Too nice a night. C'mon back to the terrace."

"But Reece."

"No one around. C'mon." He plants a firm grip on my arms as though he fears I'll cut and run.

"My shoes are somewhere. Help me find them."

Reece, pulling me toward the house, and not inclined to hunt for sandals, "Come *on.*"

The terrace, nothing but a slab of concrete set flush with the grass. The furniture not fancy. A round glass table where they must have had their drinks and two white metal chairs, both peeling paint. On one chair I have placed my blouse and skirt, each item folded decorously, and I pray they won't be wrinkled when I dress. Bronze bells, slung from a low tree branch bong dolorously in the breeze, like sea bells. The night air smells of mint. There is a hammock wide enough for two, suspended on a metal frame—the kind they sell in Bloomie's. One year I wanted to buy one for Pop, but the yard was such a jungle it would have been lost in the weeds. The damn thing cost too much, too, the mesh sling of the hammock and the metal frame priced separately. . . .

Reece, pulls me down, croons, "Come to blue Hawaii."

"Not here, Reece. Are you kidding? The way this thing swings, I'll be seasick."

"How does this bra unfasten, front or back?"

"Front. Reece, we'll fall."

"Shush. Hold still. Whoever designs these, why can't they be consistent? Here we go. Move just a little, will you? That feel good?" His lips, under the loosened bra, tickle so much, I gasp to hide a giggle. His hands exploring everywhere won't light. "Help me with these pants. Hips up, that's it. Just ease 'em off. Linda? You're so tense. Relax, will you. Just lie still."

"I can't help it. The hammock jiggles." And I think I'm getting rope burn.

His hand, traveling my thigh, like the tour guide's busy fingers charting strange geographies. "Do you like this?"

"Well, yeah. That's very nice. But, please. Let's go inside. I feel stupid out here."

"Inside. You betcha. In a bit."

"In bed, dingo!"

"In a minute. Linda, pretty Linda, you could participate a little bit, you know? That big thing there, it doesn't bite. That's it. You like the feel of that?"

"Sure." Ferocious stars above our heads, blinking like signals. Franklin told me something once about these scientists, who are sending impulses to outer space, hoping to contact life in other galaxies.

"Linda, don't just lie there."

"You said I shouldn't move." They're going to flash a certain number of impulses skyward—1,679, which is a product of the prime numbers 23 and 73, and they hope someone will find a universal language in the math and understand that there is life on Earth. It seems farfetched.

"See why I wanted you to watch the movie?"

"I must've missed the best of it." Franklin says the sky is full of radio waves right now and if we journeyed far enough in space we'd catch up to broadcasts of past events, like the royal wedding in London and the landing on the moon.

"Linda, are you daydreaming?"

"Just thinking about things." If a man and woman astronaut made love in outer space, would they bounce and bob like this and feel like fools, or would they merely float serenely, having flown free of gravity, and finally when they linked, like twin craft docking in the dark, would it be possible to say in earthly terms how that would feel? It could be wonderful, I think, or maybe weird. "I'm wide awake, Reece, honest." Seeking his pale face as a point of ballast. The hammock swinging as we move. Lovemaking impossible, because we're going to fall.

"Did your husband ever do this? Tell me how it feels."

"Swell."

"Swell? That's all? That's it?"

All I can think of is the college girl batting her eyes and bleating, "Ah," as though she needs her tonsils checked. Instead of giggling this time, I'm overtaken by despair, sadness so deep I want to press my face against Reece's smooth chest and weep. He is so serious, so intense, and I am feeling downright spacey, out of it, plain bored, posing riddles to myself to use up time. Buddy declared I was a prude (as though that was a point of pride), and Reece complains he's dealing with a snow maiden, which isn't fair. I can lose myself to pleasure well enough, given some patience and a solid mattress. "I'm just uncomfortable, okay? If you want me in the mood, let's go into the house and get in bed." With a last-ditch show of strength I push him off, then I roll out of the hammock to my feet. "Are we going in or not?"

Reece lies there like a fish encumbered by a monster net. "Okay."

I grab his arm and pull to get him to his feet, as though I can't wait anymore, as though the stupid movie got to me. "We'll play ex-college girl in Ashton, all right? Once we're in bed. Please, Reece. I promise you, you won't be sorry. Let's go."

"Have it your way." He's looking small-boy sullen, not intrigued. If getting me revved up is in the plan, you wouldn't guess it from his face. He's standing now, unsteadily, heading toward the entry to the master bedroom. "Come on."

"Reece, not in there."

"We're going inside. Right?"

"Not through that room." Both of us naked. It isn't right.

"Are you crazy, or what?"

"I'm going through the porch. I'll meet you inside."

"What is this, Linda? Are you mocking me?"

"No way!"

"Then knock this off. Right now!"

"Don't get so mad. I know that it sounds funny, but I feel strange in that room. We shouldn't be there naked. We just shouldn't." Both of us circling the terrace like twin dolts searching for the gate to paradise. Now it's Reece who's looking anxious, like he thinks he's stuck here in the boonies with some crazy kook. Wait till I tell that to Franklin. "So humor me a little, please?"

"That's all I've done tonight."

He's mad all right. Assumes I'm trying a delaying tactic. I can't help that. To saunter through her room, brazenly nude, bare bosoms jiggling, seems like a desecration. "For God's sake, Reece, bear with me just this once. It's her room, isn't it? Your mother's room!"

"I don't need you to tell me that."

"I'm sorry!"

For what seems like an age he doesn't speak. Somewhere

above us in the tree the bronze bells clamor woeful sounds. The wind lifts Reece's hair into a kind of crown. His face is pale, impassive as a mask. Moving to me, he grasps my arm. "We'll go in through the porch."

"You think I'm being stupid?"

"If that is what you want, that's what we'll do. It doesn't matter."

It's what I want, and yet it isn't—Reece, gripping my arm, not tight enough to hurt, but strong enough to let me know who's taken charge. He leads me from the terrace through the grass, smiling a bit as though he's humoring a child, and childlike I feel tears of disappointment burning behind my eyelids. Nothing tonight has happened as I planned.

After one when I get home. Lights are on in Franklin's room and in the kitchen. Juanita is sitting at the kitchen table, bundled in her old blue flannel robe, blue ski socks on her feet. She's sipping lemon and hot water, sadly, as though it's something she's been given as a penance. "What is it?" I ask. "Indigestion?"

She pounds a balled fist to her chest. "Heartburn. No biggie." She takes the cup and saucer to the sink, spills out what's remaining. "Your pop swore by this stuff. It doesn't do a thing for me." She looks bad, dark circles under her eyes, worse than Paulie's, and her skin is yellowish, almost jaundiced. Her hair, which was always reddish, curly, her best feature, is mostly gray. One side— she must have been sleeping on it—is squashed flat; the other curls in springy tufts, like Brillo.

I ask her, "Paulie?"

"Dead to the world."

"Was he any trouble?"

"Nothing I couldn't handle."

"He got pretty worked up at his lesson today."

"Monte'll bring him round."

43

"Monte says you're some kind of swimmer. I didn't know you were a hotshot."

She leans against the sink and sighs, as though there's something painful she must tell me. Her eyes are fixed at a point on the refrigerator. "I was shopping in his store. He owns this place on Georgia Avenue, Fit for a King. The swimming lessons, that's a hobby, and they bring in business. He sells equipment you would not believe. Nautilus machines. This space-age stuff that monitors your heart, your body temperature. You gotta be loaded to afford it."

"What were you doing there?"

"I was looking at a stationary bike for Franklin. Well," she turns defensive, "he doesn't get a bit of exercise in there." She gestures with a motion of her head toward Franklin's room. Our house is small. From where I'm standing at the kitchen counter I can see into the darkened hall. The light from under Franklin's door spills out like a golden puddle. "He just sits and stares at the TV all day. That can't be good for him."

"Oh, Ma, I'm begging you, don't make Franklin so comfortable."

"That's why I didn't want to tell you. I knew you'd carry on. If you must know, Monte told me the same thing. Don't encourage him. Make him want to get back in the world. Monte's no dope."

"If *I* say it, I'm a pest. If Monte says it, he's smart!"

She waves that off, shaking her head as though a pesky fly were buzzing round her ears. "Monte says that I'm a captive too. That I need some respite from the worrying. About Franklin and you. Everything. He told me about his team, and I figured, what the heck, it could be fun."

"I think it's great."

She is still ramming her fist against her chest, as though she's hit upon a pleasing rhythm. Maybe the motion calms her. "Sometimes . . . sometimes, I kid you not, I get so tired of having to be . . . vigilant."

"Ma, I understand. I'm all in favor of you swimming. When it comes time for your meet, Paulie and I will be there, cheering."

"Well, thanks." She stares at me with some suspicion, as though she can't trust my goodwill. She shrugs, signalling the subject closed. "You have a good time tonight?"

"It was fine. I'm dead tired, though. Can't wait to hit the hay." I'm edging toward the kitchen door, sensing whatever brief détente we shared is soon to crumble.

"Did he propose yet?"

"Would you be happy if he did?"

"Would you?" That's my cue to vanish. "You got your blouse all wrinkled, didn't you?" she calls to my departing back.

Franklin must have been poised to intercept me. The minute my footsteps hit the hall his door flies open. He's still wearing Pop's brown robe. It doesn't look as though he's been asleep. "Home at last," he grins. "I waited up."

"What'sa matter? You still thirsty?"

He shrugs off my sarcasm. "What was the main feature tonight?"

I turn around to see if Ma is following. I can hear her puttering in the kitchen. She must be testing the gas burners to see they're all shut tight. "None of your business, Franklin."

"Look, Linda-bean, you were the one who brought the subject up. You can't blame me for wondering. This whole affair, it sheds some color on my dull, drab life."

"I didn't watch."

"You went cold turkey, huh?"

"Screw you, brother dear." I leave him standing (he's pretending to be awed), and duck into my girlhood room, which I share with Paulie. It's furnished as it was when I was little—a plain white dresser, a "sweetheart" chair, the back shaped like a pink valentine heart, narrow twin beds. Juanita has left Paulie a night-light shaped like Jiminy Cricket, though I protest this is a bad idea (he should accept the dark) and I can't sleep in the greenish glare.

Paulie is sitting bolt upright in bed. His breath is fast and shallow, and his eyes are open wide the way they get sometimes when he's dreaming. He's dead asleep, I know, even though his eyes are round and staring. "Paulie," I whisper. "Wake up, Paulie."

He answers, "Noooo," a long, high scream.

"Baby, you're dreaming. Please wake up." I sit beside him on the bed and touch his hair; it's wet, matted with sweat. I tap his shoulder lightly. His whole body is tense. If I try to hug him, he'll react as though I'm cutting off his air. He'll arch his back and fight me off. "You're dreaming, hon. Wake up."

"Noooo," he's trembling.

"What is it, babe? What's frightening you? Tell Mama, and I'll make it go away. I will, I promise you." In spite of my better judgment, I try to pull him toward me. He begins to kick and thrash.

"Noooo. Leggo of me. Leggo. No Marco Polio! No Marco Polio!"

"Oh, Paulie! Oh, please wake up, hon. Please."

"No Marco Polio!" He's crying now, such deep heartbroken sobs I can't believe his body can contain them. I take his hand and hold it to my lips, trying to kiss the poor clenched fingers, the tiny palm. There's nothing I can do when he's like this, no way I know to calm him or myself, nothing for either one of us to do but sit and hang on tightly, wait it out.

❧ *Three* ❧

Buddy was *it* for me, from the time we were sixteen. The first time I ever saw him ambling down the hall at school with a gaggle of his football cronies, I knew he was the one. The way he moved—he and his friends— there was never anything so sexy. These guys, they had this macho walk. They held their torsos rigid, and their arms hung loose, half-bent. The motion started from the hips, a kind of easy shuffle that advertised, "We're cool. Catch our act, folks. There's nothing that will faze us."

Buddy wore jeans torn at the knees and a sloppy denim jacket with a sheepskin lining, the collar turned up high against the back of his neck, the jeans skintight, and sneakers with the laces trailing. He had this husky laugh, secret and rich like he was chuckling at a private joke. And he spoke this funny patois—all of the team did—part ghetto black, part Southern redneck, part nasal Maryland; Marylanders do things with their *A*s and *O*s that I can't stand, can't even replicate. You either have the accent or you don't.

Every time I looked at Buddy my reactions would speed up, like I'd been plugged into fast forward. I'd hear my voice, high-pitched, talking about nothing. I'd laugh too loud, too often. I'd tap my heels or shuffle through some silly dance step. I couldn't stop. If I felt him glancing toward me, I'd toss my head to make my hair fan out. I knew he loved the look of it, so long and silky dark. I knew he itched to touch it. Every schoolday I was up at 5 A.M. to shampoo it and douse it with conditioner.

In an exercise of high-level negotiation worthy of a Kissinger, his friends and mine set up a date. Word was brought to me that Buddy might be interested in going out. Would I be interested in turn? If he phoned, could I be counted on to be receptive? Was I seeing someone else? Since neither one of us would countenance the horror of rejection, nothing was left to chance.

Our friends discussed the best time for a call, even reviewed the nature of our maiden date. Would we be happier doubling with another couple? Should we have time alone to talk, or was small talk, all that mannered prattle, more than we could stand? Would we chance being seen together at a high school dance or did we relish privacy? Should a dinner be Dutch treat? If Buddy squired me to a party, could I be trusted not to flirt with other guys? Would he ogle other girls? By the time discussions were concluded, we were drained, and the partisans in our respective camps had turned plain mean. Buddy's friends let it be known that he was a prime catch—cute-looking, rich, athletic. Did I really measure up? My girlfriends circulated word that I was on the A list, college boys dying to date me. Wasn't Buddy a bit young?

Our first date was a movie at the Baronet. We spent the time fooling around. Buddy kissed nicely, never got too fresh. By the time the final credits rolled, I knew I loved him.

Once, in a fit of abject boredom (it must have been in algebra, doing time and distance problems) I began a list of places in the county and the District of Columbia where Buddy and I made out: in cars and in the choir room at school, in dark back booths at Shakey's (our pizzas going soggy as we kissed), at rock concerts and on the Mall during the Fourth (the music of the Beach Boys amplified around us), in the new East Building of the National Gallery and on the steps of Air & Space, beside the C & O canal, and in the Sylvan Theater, on the terrace at the Kennedy (the noise of big jets zooming low over the river), in the Music Barn at Shady Grove before they tore it down, and the little park back of the Air Rights Building in Bethesda. Most of it grunt and grope and paw and kiss. Nothing heavier. Buddy said I was a sexual *retard* who had yet to hook up with the modern world. Juanita said if I lost my virginity she'd know it by the way I looked, the way I walked, the way I held my chest.

My reluctance to experiment was not entirely Juanita's fault. Instinct told me that Mr. Burton Paul Merceau III, who quarterbacked the Barons, and played golf with his folks and their rich cronies at the Chevy Chase Club, and loped around the halls at school like "Mr. Stud," retained an ideal about female innocence that was Victorian, perhaps because he was an innocent himself. I don't know how I knew this. Juanita claims most gals have ESP about such things, wisdom she gleaned during the days she did electrolysis.

Nonetheless, Buddy pushed and pleaded; I refused. We fought and broke up, kissed and reconciled, broke up again. Buddy said he was obsessed with me; I'd gotten in his blood like a disease. Near the end of our senior year, with his place assured at Dartmouth (in the tradition of the Merceau men) and me enrolled at Maryland (on scholarship like Franklin), we got into a fight over

Buddy's mother's cashmere sweater and finally broke up, *forever.* A week after our graduation Buddy showed up with his class ring and a brave offer of marriage, because, as he said glumly (in what turned out to be an accurate prognostication), the only way he could forget me was to take me on for life.

You don't need a blood test to get married in Montgomery County—just proof you are of age and twenty-five dollars for the license. The clerk at the courthouse in Rockville flipped through our birth certificates without much interest and then asked for the fee. When Buddy flashed a VISA card, she shook her head. "Cash only." I knew Buddy was thinking, nasty bitch, but he gave her the full impact of his dimples and asked could there ever be exceptions, since we were trustworthy, and his father was a power in the county and a pillar of the medical establishment. She fixed her mouth in a just-sucked-on-a-lemon pout, and shook her head. "No way."

Her rancor hardened us. If she'd been only a little nice, we might have headed home and, given time to think, acknowledge we were being hasty. Stupid, in fact. I saw the stubborn set in Buddy's jaw. "You got any money on you?" he asked.

I searched my pocketbook. "$8.50."

He sifted through his wallet. "I got fourteen bucks." He assailed the clerk again. "I don't suppose you'd trust us for $2.50?"

"Certainly not."

Buddy said to me, "Wait here," and went loping off before I could collect my thoughts, and ask him not to leave me. That cute, lean butt of his vanishing around a corner was all I saw.

He was back in maybe twenty minutes with the $2.50 in hand. When I asked him how he got it, he whispered, "Saw my broker."

"C'mon, Buddy. What did you do?"

He winked. "Panhandled."

"You're not serious!"

"Well, yeah, sort of. There's all these nice people in the lobby waiting to be called for jury duty." He'd gotten five of them to kick in fifty cents apiece, in homage to young love. I could understand why they would do it, seeing how Buddy was sweet, clean-cut, polite. He had a way with older people; Pop and Juanita had noticed that about him early on.

The clerk looked meaner than ever when we showed her the cash. "There's a two-day waiting period," she said, as though that gave her pleasure. I was already brooding, two days to reconsider; but Buddy was busy calculating. His folks were leaving on the weekend for a trip to Hilton Head; mine would be driving Franklin to a waiter's job in Ocean City. "Friday," Buddy whispered. "What do you say to Friday? Lucky thirteen?"

"Friday the thirteenth! I couldn't, Buddy. I wouldn't dare."

"Okay," he grinned. "Just kidding. It isn't the thirteenth. Just a little wedding humor there." He knew he was taking on a world-class worrier, Juanita's kid. He knew it would be no pink tea party if we went through with the plan. He *knew* it, didn't he?

Abandonment can be like death. When Buddy split, leaving a dumb note fastened to the fridge with mushroom magnets about his need to find out who he was (he was Linda's husband, Paulie's Dad, but he wouldn't cop to it), I reacted like someone in mourning; there was rage, denial, fear and finally resignation, an almost philosophic calm. We'd lasted longer than our folks predicted, had a kid. We'd weathered being ignorant of sex, broke, pregnant, weary, cut off by the Merceaus and plagued by the Burkes' all enfolding pessimism. We'd seen Buddy through his bachelor's at Maryland and most of graduate school. We'd found out we had *character,* tenacity that kept us hanging on through part-time jobs and backed-up pipes and weevils in the flour and roaches in the sink and Paulie's bouts with enlarged tonsils. When Buddy split, we'd already gotten through the worst, which is such a stupid irony—it's part of what keeps me awake, pacing the space between my bed and Paulie's as he whimpers in his sleep and hollers no to "Marco Polio."

After I found Buddy's note, I phoned Juanita. "Is it safe to refreeze hamburger?" I asked. "On accounta there'll be just the two of us for dinner, and I think Paulie and I can make do just as nicely with canned spaghetti." I was babbling nonsense stuff like that, the tears streaming.

"Well, I surely wouldn't chance it," Juanita said. And then, catching the terror in my voice, "Where's Buddy?"

"He's gone. He left a note."

Juanita said, "Ooh boy."

"I don't think it's another woman, Ma."

"Did I say it was?"

"What should I do?"

"Cook Paulie's supper. Don't refreeze the meat."

"Do you think he will be back, Ma?"

"I can't say that, unless I know the reason why he left. I never thought this marriage had much chance. You were both too young."

"It's not my fault."

"Well, it takes two to tango. I know that much."

"I didn't think you'd take his side."

"I'm certainly not taking sides," Juanita said. "Call me later when you're calmer." And she hung up so firmly, I could tell that she was mad, but I don't know who she'd fingered for the culprit, Buddy or me.

After I'd cried and carried on, I settled into a routine. Dropping Paulie at the day-care, going to work, the laundromat, the Giant, visiting Ma and Franklin every weekend, because they both needed distraction, and so did I. All that time, going through the motions of a normal life, I tried to dope out what had done us in. In spite of all our fights, we had seemed like rock, immutable. Maybe that's the wrong analogy. Rock buckles under constant pressure. Mountains explode; the very templates of the earth shift and crack. I learned that in freshman geology before I quit school to have Paulie.

These girls I knew at work wanted to set me up with guys. Forget it. The world is full of weirdos that make Reece and his blue movies look like Mother Goose. Finally, when the loneliness got overpowering I wrote a want ad for the personals in *Washingtonian* thinking I could specify the kind of guy *I* like: "Pretty, lively señorita seeks handsome, loving compañero for long walks, sweet talks, good times." I thought I'd struck the perfect tone, a casual plea for a good buddy (no pun intended there). I wasn't that high on sex. I missed male company, the way Buddy would stroke my hair or tilt my chin up toward the light and murmur, "Pretty." Before I mailed the ad, I checked it out with Franklin for a man's opinion.

He read it through and frowned. "Technically, you're not a señorita, Linda Jo."

"I know that, Franklin. But my status is unclear. I can't say Divorced, because I'm not. And if I say *S* for Separated, they'll read it to mean Single. So what's the difference?"

"Spell it out. Separated."

"Too expensive."

"It's the same length as señorita, more or less."

"I don't care."

"All right. What's with compañero? It sounds like some gay code."

"It means comrade, life's companion. I like the sound of it."

"Well, they're going to think that you're Hispanic."

"Let 'em. It just seems right. I don't know why."

Franklin warned, "Don't run the ad. Too many kooks out there. Too many oddballs and perverts and outright morons. Don't, I repeat, don't do it, Linda Jo. You don't know anything about the singles scene. You got married right out of high school and you don't know anything about real life."

I'll be dipped if I can figure out what Franklin knows living barricaded in his room, scared of voices on the television, pan-icked if a package arrives COD. In four years he's been out once to see the dentist (Ma says they had to put him under for a filling), and he used to go for short jaunts in the car (Pop or Juanita driving) till he decided that was pointless. Still, he has a vision of the world that seems to be on target. He's unhampered by details, the distractions of responsibility. He slouches on his bed like royalty and takes things in and hands down weighty opinions, on politics and world economy and pop psychology. Sometimes I think the life he lives in fantasy is richer than the one I live in fact.

Reece saved me from the singles scene, the stilted meetings over wine, and movies in art theaters where the audience is into chains and leather, and Sundays in the zoo with grouchy divorced fathers taking their snotty kids on outings. Reece likes my having Paulie, but wouldn't want another kid. A pregnant partner in his bed would kill the mood. Reece may be cold, and a bit peculiar; but he's handsome and attentive, and well off with that property in Ashton. Reece is my ticket to a pleasant life: so screw Juanita's judgments on my not-so-hot morality, screw Franklin and his jokes, and Paulie's nighttime dreams that keep me wracked with guilt; and screw Buddy for splitting—him, most of all, for losing faith in us, for turning the sour warnings of our elders into prophecy.

Four

In the morning all of us are bleary-eyed from lack of sleep. Paulie keeps blinking as though trying to clear his eyes or change the picture in front of him. "Don't do that," I snap at him, worrying that he's acquired a nervous tic. Franklin, who'll venture from his room when the solitude becomes too overpowering, is dressed and begging for black coffee. Juanita, who still looks frazzled, is pretending to be perky. She wants to discuss Paulie's birthday, which falls before the start of school. Even though he hasn't made friends in the neighborhood Juanita thinks that he should have a party. When I ask, *"Whom* would he invite?" Juanita points out most of the tykes in swimming class are Paulie's age. If they come to a nice party and start feeling a bit more chummy, Paulie will have a leg up in first grade. If we plan the celebration for a Sunday, Monte will help, bring equipment from his store—exercise mats for tumbling, soccer balls. He'll supervise the games, Capture the Flag and Pin the Tail on the Donkey, a scavenger hunt, maybe, if we can keep the kids out of the traffic on Wisconsin Avenue.

When I ask, why would Monte want to help, Juanita comments it should be apparent that he's fond of kids. Besides, he's lonely. He was orphaned very young; the foster parents who raised him died just recently.

Pouring milk on Paulie's chocolate-flavored cereal (Juanita is casting dark looks at the box), I say, "Poor Monte," without sincerity—a knee-jerk reaction that has nothing to do with sympathy. Lonely, or fond of kids, he's just a fool.

Franklin waits till Ma heads to the door to get the *Post*. It's not the paper of her choice, not as sprightly as the *Star* was, but now she takes morning delivery and fears Pop will berate her for it from the grave. "The simple truth is, Monte's the designated hitter." Franklin winks.

"What are you talking about?"

"The heir apparent. The new prince consort. Once you divorce Buddy."

"Franklin!" I roll my eyes toward Paulie. "Everything gets noted and recorded."

"I doubt he gets my drift." Franklin leans to Paulie with an air of mock concern. "Do you understand your uncle, little Paul? Does anything he says or does make sense to you?" Giggling, Paulie shakes his head. Franklin grins at me. "You see?"

"I hate it when you act affected, Franklin. And, you're talking nonsense."

"My *life* is nonsense, Linda Jo. My *talk* is always on the mark, lucid and clear. Articulate. Affected, maybe, but not without the ring of truth."

"Oh, can it."

"Don't mind it, little Paul, if your mother picks on me. A prophet in his time is heard, but rarely." He turns to me. "You better listen. She's picked him out. He's everything she wants for you. Faithful, a good provider, a worrier. Hell, if I liked guys, she'd pick him out for *me!*"

"You are ridiculous."

"Not ridiculous. If Monte was a vegetarian, he'd be perfection in her eyes. She'd have him bronzed. As it is, he worships her—and you." Franklin bends to whisper in my ear, "He's hot for your body, kid, although I doubt he'd have the guts to act on it. I'm not the only coward," he says aloud.

"Franklin, shut up!"

"Don't fight, kids." Juanita, looking flushed, is back, fanning herself with a section of the newspaper. "When you fight, it makes my heart pound." She's wearing her old nurselike uniform, which she hauls out when she plans a day of cleaning. After countless washings, bleachings, the fabric has turned ivory yellow, but the outfit still fits trimly.

"Your daughter doesn't want to hear some simple truths." Pretending to be hurt, Franklin sips his coffee with his little finger prissily extended. That's a new role he's assuming, simpering fop, as though these years without a girlfriend have sapped his manhood.

Ma ignores him. "What about it, Paulie? Should we have a party?"

With his head bent to his cereal, Paulie shivers, "No."

"Anyone for scrambled eggs?" asks Franklin. *"Omelettes aux fine herbes?* I feel the need to keep my hand in, *à la bonne cuisine.* Forget cholesterol for once!"

"What kind of six-year-old kid doesn't want a party? Birthday cake? Presents? Make-your-own ice cream sundaes?" Ma starts out pleasantly cajoling; by the time she gets to ice-cream sundaes she is sounding edgy.

"Sharing toys, having to wait your turn at playing games,

having to be polite and say 'thank you' for presents you really hate. Don't do it, Paul," Franklin advises. "I was never one for parties as a kid."

"Sure you were." Ma turns to him in disbelief. "You had some great ones. Remember, we put brown paper on the floor so the kids could trace the outlines of each other's bodies?"

"Yeah, Ma, and we were seventeen."

She will not be distracted by his jokes. "Remember, we rented movies? One year Pop took you ice skating at Wheaton Park? And Linda Jo twisted her ankle?"

"I remember the year we had the chicken pox, and Pop took us to the Spanish Ballroom," Franklin smiles.

"That wasn't a birthday," I tell him.

"Sure it was," says Franklin. "It must have been mine, sometime in winter."

"It was just some place he took us, Franklin. You remember it, because it was . . . unusual."

"Unusual, all right," Franklin laughs. "Pop was looney tunes."

"None of that," Ma warns. "I will hear *none of that.*"

"Talk about the pot calling the kettle black." My hands are trembling as I pour my coffee. I have a mean stiff neck this morning, the consequence of lying on that hammock with my head turned at a funny angle. Reece surely wasn't thrilled with me last night. I never did get in the mood. When I left he seemed withholding, glad to see me go. "It's because I was uncomfortable," I said to him. "Next time I'll be more 'into it.'" He'd pulled his chinos on to walk me to my car. Lithe as a young god, he'd stood bare-chested in the drive. "Sure hope so." He'd looked beyond me to the road. "Man," he'd yawned, "I'm beat."

"If craziness is in the genes, I'm nothing but Pop's victim," Franklin declares.

"I won't have this," says Ma.

Paulie has placed his spoon down in his bowl and is looking

from Ma to me to Franklin, like a kid watching a three-ring circus. Only, he's not amused. I know that fearful look, the pupils of his eyes dilated till there's almost nothing of the iris showing, and his pale lips hanging slack. There's a dribble of spilled milk on his chin. I dab it with a paper napkin. "What do you want to do for your birthday, Paulie? What's your secret wish?" He shrugs and casts his eyes downward again. "Come on," I urge. "There must be something you want. Is there?" He nods. "Well, tell me, hon. I'm not too good at guessing games." He murmurs something I can't hear.

"Teach the child to speak distinctly," Juanita says.

"What do you want to do, Paulie?"

He mutters loud enough this time for Ma and me to grasp that he wants to go to work with me. Today.

"Well, he knows he can't do that," Juanita says. "That's just a silly wish."

"Paulie, you can't." I try to stroke his hair, but he's already stiffening, pulling away from me. "Mr. Fowler wouldn't like it, and I might get fired."

"Plus, he'd miss his swimming lesson," Ma says, as though the poor kid needed a reminder.

Franklin suggests, "Stay with me, young man, and I'll dig out my *Boys' Book of Famous Trains*. We'll read about the Trans-Siberian Railroad and the Orient Express."

Paulie starts to whimper, building momentum for a tantrum; his whining drives me nuts. Both of us are grouchy after a restless night. "Honey," I grasp at straws, "I tell you what. Maybe you could visit the office on your birthday. I'll come for you at lunchtime and drive you back with me and give you the grand tour. Would you like that?" He answers no. He wants to go with me today. "You can see Mr. Fowler's brand-new car, that has the steering wheel on the wrong side . . ."

"The *right* side, to be accurate. A nonfunctioning Jaguar." Franklin remembers everything I've ever told him. Ma says he's gotten jokier, more chatty, since Paulie and I moved back home. "The locking mechanism sticks, and he has to pry it open with a wire hanger. Don't you love it?" Franklin asks of no one in particular. "The great and glamorous executive, having to break into his own car?"

"You can see the helicopter. Would you like that, Paulie?" I've told them how my boss commutes to the branch office in Phillie in his latest plaything. How the pilot brings the aircraft in from National and sets it on a grid of yellow lines painted in the parking lot. How the sun is briefly shadowed by the spinning rotors, when the copter hovers in the air at rooftop like a bright blue bug. When it lights, my boss, Cal Fowler, strides across the pavement in a silky suit, fancy Hong Kong tailoring—the jacket and the trouser legs flapping in the gusts whipped up by the whirring engine. How he radios to me when he's aloft, his voice crackling like an astronaut's, about suddenly remembered memos and missing files. How covertly I sit in his big chair (he'd raise hell if he saw that) and jot down notes, a link between safe terra firma and the frail "bird" bobbing between wisps of clouds. How the pilot, T.J., promises to take me up one day, but we both know I won't do it. I'm too scared. Full of Juanita's warnings: "You know how many rescue helicopters crash in any given year? How many traffic reporters flying in those babies 'buy the farm'?" She saw it on "Sixty Minutes."

"The helicopter," Franklin gushes. "I'd go for that, if I went anywhere."

"Franklin can come with us."

"Thanks, babe, I'll pass."

"Well, Paulie?" I sneak a quick peek at my watch. Already late, I'll have to drive like gangbusters to get to work. At least I'm spared the long commute from Hyattsville, which was another topic of contention between Buddy and me. When I suggested we move nearer to the office, Buddy said no way. We'd be too close to my crazy family. "And your folks?" I shot back. "From what I have observed, they're not the Brady Bunch! But you go to see them every Sunday." And so the screaming started, and our neighbors hit the walls with broom handles, to add their two cents to the action.

Paulie says he wants to stop his swimming lessons. That can be his birthday present. Nothing more.

"I'll think about it, Paulie."

Juanita sputters, "Swimming is not negotiable."

"You heard him last night, Ma. He's scared to death of everything. He doesn't need the added pressure."

"Swimming is a survival skill!"

"He can learn it when he's older." It's no picnic to contradict her. There's her look, coupled with an air of certainty that implies she knows something we don't. It's like she scoots behind her turquoise curtain in the rumpus room and consults some gloomy oracle. The prophecies she makes sometimes come true. But not always. "What about the bomb that's supposed to blow us all to kingdom come, Ma?" I want to yell. "What about the viruses at NIH getting spread around an unsuspecting populace?" Some of Ma's worst fears spring from a too-fevered imagination, too many horror flicks and TV serials. "The Twilight Zone." "The Outer Limits." And yet, there's always some tough nub of truth in what she says that gives her power to frighten us.

Ma drops the *Post* on the kitchen table, sending coffee spoons clattering to the floor. "Sometimes I wonder how you think, Linda Jo. How your so-called logical and clever mind, that your poor Pop was so proud of, functions? No party and no swimming lessons? That's a damn fine plan for Paulie! He can grow up to be a recluse. And if he goes fishing or on a ferry and the boat goes down . . . What's with you, Franklin? You sit there smiling, like you think it's all a joke. Sometimes I think this family is completely crazy, everyone is nuts, including me, because you drive me bonkers!"

"It's in the genes." Franklin evokes the full fury of her look.

61

"Crazy, crazy, crazy," murmurs Paulie, sensing he's won the day.

"From the mouths of babes," says Franklin piously.

Franklin believes Pop was looney, paranoid at the end. Pop thought the *Star* had folded just to take away his job. He thought no paper in the world would hire him again, and that this time, for sure, our ma would leave him. It's funny how he conjured the right plot; only the characters were wrong. It's Buddy who took off for California. It's me who was abandoned. Pop would have grasped the irony in that.

I think of Pop as diffident, whimsical, impish sometimes. He'd be the first to poke fun at himself, grin at his quirkiness, then include us in the joke. He didn't mind being the butt of laughter. Our laughter counteracted Mama's gloom. He was happiest when the three of us—he, Franklin, and I—were giggling at some made-up entertainment. Maybe Pop was looney, but he had a way about him that was charming, a solemn and inspired silliness that enchanted us when we were kids.

It was a Saturday in February (gray slush in the streets, a mean wind blowing) when he took us to the Spanish Ballroom. I was nine; Franklin was ten. We were getting over chicken pox, both of us spotted with red scabs. My case was the worst. I had a watery cough and runny eyes; I still felt itchy, antsy. Franklin had been tormenting me, calling me "Speckled Cow" and "Dotted Swiss," "Miss Insect Bite of 1971," cute stuff like that. I was chasing after him and screaming bloody murder. Finally, Mama came upstairs complaining we were interfering with her work. She told Pop to take us out. "Not in any crowds. They still have a low resistance. Just drive them around somewhere. Give me an hour's quiet."

So Pop cruised with us around the county, up and down the pleasant streets, pointing out houses he liked. That didn't interest me or Franklin; pretty soon we were at war in the backseat. Pokes and prods and dirty looks, more nasty names, and finally I flung myself on Franklin in a rage, lunging for his neck. I meant to squeeze the last breath out of him. Pop hollered, "Cut that out, you two." And then promised, "If you will behave, I'll take you someplace interesting."

Franklin was barely holding me at bay. "Gifford's for hot fudge sundaes," he panted.

"Maybe afterwards," Pop promised. "It depends on how you act."

Franklin said, "That's a bribe."

"Shut up, stupid," I yelled, backing off. "What difference does it make?"

Somewhere off MacArthur Boulevard Pop veered onto a rutted road that led us to a vast, deserted parking lot. On a steep hill near the entrance to the lot was a sprawling, shingled house, bordered by twin black turrets. Pop told us, "That's the Clara Barton House, built by the gal who founded the Red Cross."

"Jeez," Franklin said. "It looks like the place in *Psycho*. It looks like the Bates Motel."

"Well, take a gander at it, will you, so you can tell your ma I showed you someplace educational."

Pop sped us past the house, clearly not bent on giving us a course in history. We slowed down in the lot, zigzagging over broken pavement marked by pot holes and debris. Ours was the only car. Pop parked beside a dirt path sloping upwards. On a ridge above us were the ruins of buildings, some caved-in barnlike structures and a gray stone tower that loomed above the shambles like a castle keep. "You guys behave now," Pop said as he got out of the car. He opened our door with a flourish. "C'mon," he told us happily, "let's look around."

He led us single file up the muddy path. We stopped at what had been some kind of kiosk papered with blurry posters. "Do you know this place?" Pop asked. "Glen Echo Park?" He ushered us into a ruin. Burned skeletons of buildings, and upended trees and picnic tables flung onto their sides, some of the slats missing, wrenched out to feed fires. A carousel, almost in tact, horses adorned with ribbons of flaked paint, their hooves poised in mid-gallop. A crumbling wall bounding the confines of the Crystal Pool, the pool itself an immense concrete pit choked with up-rooted bushes like a grave dug for tumbleweeds. A ruined mid-way, signs hanging askew, great timbers fallen, theater seats flung every which way on the frozen ground. "This was a lovely place, once," Pop whispered. "This was a grand amusement park."

"Well, it's a dump now," Franklin said.

"Not very long ago, people were coming here in summer. It had got a little seedy, but you could still have a good time."

"What happened to it?" I asked.

Pop whispered, "The park closed down three years ago, in '68. One summer there'd been riots over integration—so much rage and pain, people stopped coming back. And before that, there were fires. I don't know how they started," Pop added sadly.

"Well, there's not much left to see," Franklin complained.

Standing between us, Pop grasped our hands. "Come on with me. I'll show you what was once the best of all." He led us past the sad wreck of the Crystal Pool and up a little incline to a white stone edifice, hardly touched by fire, a graceful Moorish palace, with archways like a touch of the Alhambra and many narrow windows at the upper level, screened by ornamental grilles, as though captive maidens languished there. Propped against one wall was a duo of romantic cutouts drawn in profile, a faded señorita in a lace mantilla with a dark fan tilted to her chin; facing her was a leering gaucho in a wide-brimmed hat. In the shadow of a corner tower a phony palm tree, with a trunk of heavy-duty cardboard ridged to look like palm bark, cast bogus shade. Pop chuckled as though he'd found things as he'd hoped. "This is the Spanish Ballroom." A sawhorse, in place of absent doors, blocked the entrance. Blithely, Pop climbed the barrier and motioned us to follow. Franklin cleared it with a jump; I scooted underneath. Pop walked us down a littered hallway to a room big as an airplane hangar. Under the thick grime on the floor we could see the mellow hue of brown-gold wood. Sun filtering through the chain of windows at the second story bathed the room in dusty light. A long distance away, maybe a mile it seemed to me, was a great raised stage shielded by a dark blue curtain spangled with silver stars. Pop pointed to the stage. "The bands sat there when we came to dance." Pop rubbed his eyes, as though in disbelief. "Wonderful summers in the Spanish Ballroom."

"How come this place didn't burn?" Franklin asked.

Pop shrugged. "Fortuitous. Simply fortuitous. Do you want to look backstage?"

At that I balked. "I bet there's mice back there."

"Then wait here, scaredy-cat." Franklin followed Pop the distance to the stage. I watched them climb narrow side stairs and disappear into the wings, engulfed by the blue curtain. I settled on the dirty floor, heart pounding, dust filling my throat. After what seemed a terrifying lonely space of time, Franklin rejoined me. "Nothing back there but old sofas and rags and paper bags and brooms and stuff. He's sitting on a sofa talking to himself."

"What's he saying?"

Franklin sat on the floor beside me, and dropped his voice a register trying to emulate the sound of Pop. "Didn't they just play the nicest music in the world? Didn't they just have the finest bands, not bands, really Franklin, but orchestras. You know the difference, don't you? Bands have brass and drums, and orchestras have fiddles." Franklin leaned toward me and twirled a make-believe mustache. "Well, my dear, they fiddled while the whole park burned."

"Franklin, I don't like this place. When are we going?"

"It's a big nothing," said Franklin. "It's a big, dirty old room. Just an old dance hall somebody forgot to burn."

"Go get him and tell him we want our sundaes."

"Better wait, or he'll change his mind. Look," said Franklin. "There he is. There's Pop, on the stage."

He had stepped out of the darkness of the wings, still talking as though he meant to give a lecture to his audience. "Didn't they just have the prettiest girls coming here to dance? And handsome boys, soldiers and sailors spiffy in their uniforms. Some with medals, battle ribbons. Doin' the fox-trot, and the lindy hop, and all those complicated Spanish numbers. The Latin bands with bongo drums and guys in ruffled shirts and the leader sitting at this white, mirrored piano, and the beat so strong you had to move to it, even if you didn't know the steps. Didn't it just get in your blood?" Pop stepped to the apron of the stage and peered at me and Franklin as though he'd only just realized that we were there. Suddenly he spread his arms parallel with the floor. He snapped his fingers once, waited, snapped them again. He shuffled his feet in what looked like a dance step. Then in a tinny, quavering voice, something we didn't recognize, he began to sing:

> *I started out to go to Cuba,*
> *Soon I was at Miami Beach.*
> *There, not so very far from Cuba,*
> *Oh, what a rumba they teach!*

Arms outstretched and fingers snapping, he moved in a circle on the stage, singing, *"Dum de de dum, da da dum, da da dee, de de dum, de de dum, da da dum de dum de dee."*

Franklin had clasped both palms over his mouth and was struggling to contain a rush of laughter that was erupting with the sound steam makes when it escapes a radiator. *Whoosh. Whoosh.* I had fallen to one side and lay stretched out on the dusty floor, head cradled on my arm, muffling the giggles in the thick sleeve of my jacket. Pop continued to circle on the stage, oblivious, dancing a hoppy little step, snapping his fingers, and singing his dum de dees. Suddenly, he became aware of our reaction. "All right, you two." He pretended to sound stern. "You're going to learn the dance." Still snapping his fingers Pop descended from the stage. Grinning, he moved toward me. "Stand up, Linda Jo. Up. Up. This minute. You'll never have this opportunity again. And if you don't get up out of that dirt, your ma is gonna kill me and you both when she sees your coat. Stand up I say."

Groggy, I clambered to my feet. Pop stood before me. He placed his palm on my left shoulder and grasped my right hand in his own. "Step back on your right foot," he said. "Now bring your left foot back. Now step to the left with your left foot. Now close the step with your right. Now forward with your left." He was confusing me. "Look, princess, pay attention. No, no, don't look at your feet. It's nothing, just a simple box step. But what you wanna do is bend your knees and that in turn causes the movement in the hips. Pay attention, Linda. Listen to the rhythm." And again he sang, "I started out to go to Cuba . . ."

So we began to dance, slowly at first, then with confidence and brisker rhythm. Pop moved like someone balanced on a drift of air and breathlessly I followed, astonished at the grace with which we moved. Whirling through the gloom of shadows into sunny light and back into a velvet dusk and into light again, we circled the big room. Pop had switched to crooning words in Spanish and when his memory of the lyrics failed, he went back to his dum de dums. When Pop determined I had learned the dance, he sent me off to practice, then he went to work on Franklin who was a quick study, and in no time at all was box-stepping around the hall. "All right." Pop clapped his hands. "Attention! Franklin and Linda Jo together, while I perform the role of Big Name Band." But first he fussed at us because we slouched. "Look straight ahead. Heads up! Up! You gotta have an attitude. You are the gaucho and his señorita! You're very proud." Franklin chirped, "Gauchos live on the pampas, not in Miami Beach." Pop turned mock stern, but his eyes were twinkling with pride at his kid's intelligence. "Enough of that. For our purposes, the name will be appropriate."

Franklin and I stood face-to-face, gazing over one and another's shoulders, the gaucho and the señorita, frozen in the posture of the dance, till we exploded into giggles. Pop boomed, "Compose yourselves!" When we achieved a stance that Pop decreed appropriate, he clapped his hands. "Begin." So Franklin and I danced together with Pop singing accompaniment, and when Pop had tired of that, he yelled, "Change partners!" and he danced with me. When I complained that I was out of breath, Pop ordered me to sit down on the stage, and he took the floor with Franklin, both of them whirling now, faster and faster, with Pop da da deeing the rhythm and pausing between beats to tell Franklin to bend his knees, loosen up his hips. I had settled on the edge of the great stage with my legs hanging free over the apron, my whole body shaking with laughter and the tears flowing down my scabby cheeks into my mouth. "Oh, stop," I begged finally. "Please stop." But Pop wouldn't be stopped. "Dance with your sister, now," he told Franklin, "while I critique this." Pop box-stepped to me and held out his arms and I seemed to float down into them and he set me firmly on the floor. Then I was taking my turn with Franklin, whirling around the slick wood floor, our steps raising little puffs of dust as we turned, in the slim columns of sun streaming through the narrow windows like spotlights tracking our progress. "Hips, hips!" cried Pop, who was growing hoarse. And finally, "Okay, you dancin' fools. The orchestra is pooped. I think it's time we called it quits."

Franklin and I yelled, "No!" We were ready for another trip to Cuba. But Pop complained his throat was dry and he sure was looking forward to an ice cream soda. Even with the lure of ice cream, we begged Pop for another turn, but he stood firm. "I think I got you too excited." On the path descending to the parking lot, Pop, Franklin, and I shuffled three abreast, arms linked like good companions, dancing and humming till we reached the car.

Pop drove us to the old Gifford's in Bethesda where everything was painted pale mint green and they served the hot fudge sauce for sundaes in white crockery pitchers that could be counted on to tip over; the green marble tabletop got strewn with sticky stuff, and you had to run your fingers through the mess and lick them clean. "You havin' a good time?" Pop kept inquiring. We nodded, yes, and went on slurping up the last of soupy ice cream. By the time we'd polished off our sundaes and trekked back to the car, Franklin and I were overtired, flushed, dirty, sticky with chocolate goo. We settled in the backseat in a bleary daze. Pop worried, "You guys are quiet? You feel okay?" Franklin piped, "Real good. I hope I feel this good at least a year!" But I refused to speak, still caught up in the whirl of laughter, golden air—groggy with the magic Pop had spun.

Juanita met us at the door and nailed Pop for the third degree. Franklin and I sped past our parents and scooted into Franklin's room. Once he had locked the door, Franklin kicked off his sneakers and hopped onto his bed. He held his arms out straight and closed his eyes and began bouncing up and down in rhythm, as though the mattress were a trampoline. "I started out to go to Cuba. Soon I was at Miami Beach." Franklin sang in a squeaky falsetto, and I lay on the floor coughing and whooping gales through a new flood of delighted tears.

That night, Ma discerned I had a fever and sent me to bed with a dose of scotch, honey, and lemon juice mixed together for my cough and some vile-tasting red stuff for the fever. No dinner except toast and tea. As I lay itching and shivering under heavy quilts, Pop came in to see how I was feeling. When I told him it felt sad to be alone, he unbuckled his watch and fastened it around my wrist. "Just listen to it tick," he whispered. "The sound will keep you company." After he left my room, I did as Pop had said, and the busy, steady tick began to seem a little like

the rhythm of the dance. I lay there half awake, half in a dream, sorting out the recollection of the day, how odd and wondrous all of it had seemed—Pop, Franklin, and me, fearless and teary-eyed with glee, dancing through swirls of dust and sunlight in the Spanish Ballroom.

Five

Something has ticked Ma off. When she's upset she functions in a white-hot blaze of energy like August heat. At odd hours, she roams the house, routing dust balls out of gloomy corners and batting cobwebs from the air. She gathers Paulie's scattered toys and sets them down in piles, a steely Slinky quivering on a mess of Tinkertoys, a ravaged Nerf Ball and a tattered net, and Matchbox cars with missing wheels and dinosaurs with sawtooth spines of plastic, sharp enough to slice the fingers. She holds her hand up to display a cut, and whizzes past, carting a basket full of spray bottles and household sponges that leave behind a harsh chemical aroma like a residue of jungle war.

Franklin says she had a fight with her neighbor, Mary Lindquist, who dabbles in the necromantic arts and recently claimed to have seen a purplish aura around Ma's head, portending disappointment. Ma says if this has bearing on the coming swim meet she doesn't need to know, and it's mean of Mary to upset her. She's up and out at dawn to swim her laps and practice racing turns. These days, when I come shuffling in to breakfast, I find her hunched over a cup of decaf, her wet hair in red-gray ringlets, her eyes bloodshot from chlorine. She looks beat. When I ask her how it's going, she starts a diatribe about the competition, a woman named Marchetti who is the linchpin of the rival team. Marchetti's the reason for the purple aura, Ma is sure. If the woman would get sick or take a powder, Ma would have it made. She doesn't wish her rival major harm; only a virus that might weaken her a day or two.

"Maybe Marchetti's got a purple aura. You should sic Lindquist on her."

Ma burbles her disgust. "Do you think I believe that stuff?"

One night, when I get home from work there's a wintry smell of chili in the house and I find Ma in the turquoise cellar, pulling dishware and old clothes out of brown cartons. The rank odor of cumin reminds me of sneakers worn too long. The smell recirculates in the frigid air and makes me sneeze.

Ma is wearing flowered, tapered pants (so old they're back in style, though I doubt she thinks of that) and a tie-dyed shirt I owned in elementary school. Her hair is frizzy at the crown, with little sweaty ringlets on her forehead. Her cheeks are flushed.

"Good," she mutters when she sees me. "You got home."

"I usually do around this time."

"Help me with these. But first, you better change outta those clothes."

"What are you doing, Ma?"

"Cleaning out the place. Getting rid of things. There's money in this stuff. We're gonna sell it in a yard sale, maybe Labor Day.

We're gonna advertise it in the *Post* as *objets junques*. You like the name? I thought it up while I was swimming."

"Oh, Ma!"

"Don't start with me, Oh, Ma, because your brother said that, too. He doesn't even want to help."

For once, I am on Franklin's side. "Look, Ma, if you're that strapped for cash . . ."

"If I'm that strapped for cash, what will you do? Float me a loan?"

"I can ask for an advance. We can cut corners. We can surely give up Paulie's swimming lessons."

"When I have to ask my kids for help, I'll pack it in. I'm not that strapped. Your pop was provident. There was insurance. There is a little bit we put away."

"Then, why go through a yard sale? You know Franklin will die, people running up and down, knocking on the door, asking to use the bathroom."

"The bathroom will be off-limits. But we will offer complimentary lemonade. The old-fashioned kind, made with fresh lemons and sugar syrup, like Viv and I made when we were kids. None of that powder stuff in cans. It's nothing but chemicals."

"You'll use up all your profits doing that."

"It buys goodwill. Jeez." She rubs a damp cheek on the shoulder of her shirt. "I'd hoped one of my kids would have good business sense. Or any sense, for that matter." She eyes me, darkly.

"What will you sell?"

She gestures toward a carton. "That's what we must decide. You need to help me with the inventory, because I intend to be extremely organized. I'm gonna make a list of everything we put on sale. Then we sit down together to determine price. Then Franklin helps us with the price tags. I got Magic Markers, poster board for advertisements. Paulie can help you put these up around the neighborhood, but I want you to stay together. He shouldn't wander far without an adult. There's that little four-year-old just got abducted from a wading pool in Silver Spring. And she shouldn't have been left alone anyhow, 'cause a child can drown in three inches of water, any idiot knows that."

"Can't this wait till after dinner? You're overheated, and you look so tired."

"I want a leg up on the inventory. Look at all this muddle packed in here." She starts lifting articles out of the carton and setting them on the floor. "No rhyme or reason. No system at all. I know I didn't do this box. Probably Viv."

"What's that? A tea cozy?"

"Toaster cover. Matching cover for the Mixmaster. Needs laundering. Write it down, would you, if you're not gonna change your clothes. There's a pad and pencil I put down somewhere, I can't remember. Look for it."

"Who buys such things?"

"Shower gifts," Ma tells me huffily, insulted by my tone of voice. She brandishes a toby mug. "Franklin would only drink his milk from this. The first one broke, and I had to dash right out to Woolworth's to replace it. He was so stubborn. Drove us nuts." She lifts out a stack of yellow *Geographics* and begins arranging them by date.

"Oh, Ma. You can't sell those."

She nods and sets the magazines down, reverently I think. "God strikes you dead if you sell, spindle, or mutilate the *National Geographic.*"

"Franklin loved the topless ladies. So did Pop."

"I remember, Linda Jo. No need to harp on it." She wrestles with something stuck inside the carton, hauls out a monster pan, and a domed, shiny cover. "Turkey roaster. They make 'em lined with Teflon now. Easier to wash."

"I never saw you cook in that."

Her grin shimmers with malice. "Oh, sure. Aunt Viv and George came down that one Thanksgiving, and Viv insisted she would do the bird." Ma shakes her head. "Dry as dust. Viv never did get the knack of cooking."

It's not Juanita's strong suit, either. She's far too busy plotting paths through mine fields to focus on frivolities like taste. She does her vegetarian stews, her watery soups, and turns baffled and glum when we complain.

"What in the name of heaven shall I do with these?"

She has plunged into the box again and surfaced, like a diver wresting treasures from the deep, with a jumble of old ties, bright narrow strands and wider painted jobs, adorned with skyrockets and squares. A few sharp regimentals. And some with polka dots.

"You could use those skinny ones as belts. Sew the others in a quilt."

"If I could sew that well," she answers dreamily, "that might be nice. He had good taste. Nothing was cheap or shoddy." She smooths a slim, blue length of silk, reluctant to add it to the list of possibilities. "If Franklin needed ties—"

"Is that the chili I smell burning, Ma?"

"Sometimes your father could be weird. It's probably where Franklin gets it."

"I'll go upstairs and check, okay?"

"You know I caught him with another woman once?"

"What did you say!"

"That's right. I did. Purely by lucky accident. I'd gone downtown to do some shopping, and I stopped into this People's Drug, where I knew he went for lunch, thinking I'd surprise him and we'd grab a bite together. Well, I surprised him sure enough. He was sitting at the counter with this woman from the *Star,* and both of them were sipping Cokes and laughing, fit to kill. Pretty innocent, you'd think. Only, I knew right off, the way their heads were bending toward each other, the way they laughed—not your normal kind of laughing at a joke, but giggling, like they had this dirty secret—something was going on between them. I saw him hand this woman a fresh straw, and I knew, right off, the way she took it, and popped it in her mouth, they had been intimate." Ma pantomimes taking a straw and placing it between her lips. She has her mouth pursed in a ghastly simper.

"Ma!"

"She was nothing all that special, just this skinny little snip he worked with at the paper, not pretty at all. I walked up to him and told him hi, and he answered, 'Hi, honey, isn't this a nice surprise?' without missing a beat, and he gave me this big smile and told me, 'Join us.' And I asked him, 'Why? Are you coming apart?' And everybody laughed, till I stopped smiling and said, directly to his face, making sure that she heard everything, 'Listen, I don't know what is going on, but I'm telling you it better stop as of this minute or the kids and I are history.' I promise you, that was the end of it, right there. He acted sullen for a while, but I know he toed the mark, and I never had to mention it again." The message isn't lost on me. When *her* man strayed, she dealt with it. Savage and swift.

"It sounds so harmless, Ma. What were you thinking of?"

"You think I couldn't tell? You think I was imagining things? That shows how much *you* know, not all that much for all your carrying on. Look, help me with this other box. I know what's in this one. It's all children's books, moldy probably, so I can't let Paulie have them. I figure we can sell 'em for a dime apiece."

"No!" From the stairway comes an anguished bellow. That sneak, Franklin, eavesdropping in the shadows. He bursts upon us, pasty-faced and trembling. "Not the Oz books. Not the Brothers Grimm. You can't sell those. No way." He begins digging through the carton, pulling out old storybooks, the lot of them in disrepair. "There's a *Bob, Son of Battle* here. A *Scaramouche.*" There's an annotated *Ivanhoe.*"

I add, laughing, "And *Nancy Drew*s. Come on, Ma. Have a heart."

Franklin says, "Those are expendable."

"Oh, no, they're not!"

"Don't argue now, you two! You make me dizzy." She is still holding Pop's ties, streamers of red and blue, a gaudy paisley job we bought for him one Father's Day. She fingers the silk strands like worry beads. "Let's eat," she says, after a time. Nudging the carton with her toe, "Leave these for now. I'll decide about 'em after dinner."

It's a vegetarian chili no one likes. Paulie enrages Ma by taking teeny-tiny nibbles and washing down each bite with great swallows of water. He has spent the afternoon next door, helping Mary Lindquist bathe her cockapoo. Ma views this as treason. I feel equal despair, knowing he will wheeze all night from the dog hair.

Ma glares at me as though I am responsible. "Tell him he is excused. Perhaps, when he gets hungry, he'll remember he has table manners."

Franklin presses palms together, importuning, "Me too? My manners are awful. May I be excused?"

When I laugh, Ma turns the full force of her wrath on me. Wait, her stare implies. Wait, till your kid grows up and disappoints you. Franklin looks contrite, as though he wishes he'd stayed silent. "You two think you're funny, but you're not," Ma says heatedly. "Eat or don't eat, I don't care." She slides her chair back from the table and rises to her feet, wavering, as though anger has afflicted her with vertigo. "I'm going to my room, because the hassles that I get from both of you have ruined my appetite. Linda Jo, when you finish, please clean up."

"I will, Ma, but I think Franklin should help. I work all day . . ."

"I helped, all the nights you lived in Hyattsville. Remember that."

She zooms from him to me in a pantomime of disbelief. "Infants. I raised two infants. Two kids who have superior intelligence, who act like brats. Look here, I have all kinds of troubles.

Franklin isn't well, Linda is abandoned, your father's hardly resting in his grave, and you two bicker, bicker, *bicker*. How can that be?" Ma lets her napkin flutter to the table. Scowling, she marches off. Her face is flushed as though she'd hovered too close to the stove. Her curls bob on her head like coiled, bright wires. It's cold in the kitchen, but we feel the heat of Mama's rage, like a pale fire consuming her. Paulie has scampered off, his small feet thudding barefoot on the floor. Ma must be in a state because she didn't warn of puncture wounds. Franklin is practicing his sleight of hand, toying with a quarter as though it's life or death to show off his dexterity. "Stop that," I hiss at him. "Can't you ever do something constructive?" He palms the coin and gazes at me, hurt. I stand to gather up the dishes, feeling edgy and guilty, as though I alone have caused the tension in this house.

Later, I find Juanita busy in the cellar, putting all the stuff that she unpacked back into boxes. She's changed her mind. It's all too much a bother, and she doesn't relish strangers trampling on the grass. Why give them lemonade? If it's as good a treat as she remembers, we can have it for ourselves. When I reply that this seems wise, she calls my name as though I've faded from her vision and she needs to get a fix on my position. "Linda? Linda Jo?"

"Right here, Ma. Shall I help you with these things?"

She shakes her head. "What I told you before dinner about Pop. Don't make too much of it."

"I've already forgotten it."

"Because, no matter if we fought, we were fond of one another."

"Of course you were."

"It was a love match, don't you know. It really was." Her eyes meet my own, the serpent's look, daring me to challenge her.

Six

It's pouring on the night of Ma's big race. Rain slicks the roadway with the sheen of hard, black plastic as we head toward the Y, driving at the snail's pace Ma requires. Some wiseguy trailing us complains with long blasts on the horn, so Ma gives him the finger. "Mama," I remind her, "Paulie," but she merely shrugs, content to set a bad example. She does her share of posturing in front of Paulie, playing to his dazed attention, as she does with me and Franklin. Her "tough guy" act is hardly new, but I remember times she could be downright prissy. She wouldn't go to Lord & Taylor without donning girdle and hose. She said gals shouldn't jiggle their behinds. She believed bare legs were tacky, even in the hell of D.C. summer, and she deplored women in slacks. A simple skirt, a plain white blouse, could take you anywhere, could gain you entree to the realms of potentates and nobody would look askance. Tonight she's decked out like a bag lady in floppy jeans and Pop's blue satin bowling jacket, an artifact she's donned for luck, as though Pop was bountifully endowed with that.

I need a dab of luck right now, as the headlights approaching out of darkness blind me. When I flick my brights the drivers dim their lights, but the sudden switch from glare to low beams leaves me dizzy. Suddenly, a siren screams behind us, and I veer from harm's way to the curb in nothing flat. The turkey who was tailgating roars past, followed by an ambulance. Both drivers cut a swathe through standing water, drenching my car. My wipers sweep the flooded windshield with a sound like clacking tongues. The noise sets my teeth on edge.

Ma is nervous, babbling. "Marchetti's the only competition. Marchetti's good, but I think I've got more staying power. If I can get ahead, I can outlast her."

Squinting in the blur of rain, I ease us back into the flow of traffic. "Marchetti's on what team?"

"Colonial Health Club. I told you that."

"Sorry, Ma, I forgot. I've got a few things on my mind, you know?"

Paulie, listening from the back, sits with head tilted, judging whether this will be a quarrel. He's had four days of school, which haven't gone too badly. He has a nice enough young teacher, moon-faced, sleepy-eyed, too bland to be a screamer. He's made a friend named Hilary who sticks with him at recess and prods him to play games. I've put his swim lessons on hold until next summer, although Ma disagrees. She hopes her race this evening will inspire him.

"If I can pull the center lane," Ma says. "I'm in like Flynn. 'Cause you don't get any wake there to slow you." She tilts her head to the back. "Do you know that, Paulie?"

Watching his reflection in the rearview mirror, I see him shrug. "Answer your grandma, Paulie."

"Why won't that child talk to me?" Juanita asks before Paulie can speak.

"Because you don't give him the chance. You ask a question, and before he can collect his thoughts, you're already complaining he won't talk to you."

"He should be quicker on the uptake."

"Says who? Do you want conversation from him, or snappy patter?"

"One or the other would suit me fine. You and Franklin were so bright. You read everything you got your hands on. You talked a mile a minute, about any subject. Pop called you the Fast-Track Kids."

"Ma! Paulie is damn bright."

"Did I say he wasn't? And don't use *damn* so freely. Children imitate. Maybe it's better that he doesn't talk so much. If he imitated his mother, every other word would be profanity."

"Oh, thanks, Ma. Thanks a lot. First you pick on him, and then you criticize me in his hearing. Do you think that's right?" She's got me so riled I almost miss the turnoff to the Y, although the parking lot is brightly lit and there's enough traffic converging to call attention to the place.

It's a boxy red brick building in a pleasant parklike setting. The entry drive slopes sharply downward. When I brake too firmly on the incline, my car slides in a skid and caroms to a stop against the chain-link fence that rims the tennis courts. For once, in synch, Ma and I turn to Paulie, who has crossed his arms over his head as though fending off blows. Ma tells me acidly, "Nice going." She releases her seatbelt and flings open her door. "When you get this thing parked, meet me inside, okay?"

"Let me drop you at the door."

"I think I'm safer on my own." She stomps away in disgust, clutching an Eastern Airlines bag stuffed with her suit and towel.

She looks like a vagrant moving on a zigzag path toward warmth and light. I watch her weave across the lot, sidestepping to steer clear of cruising cars. By the time she hits the entrance to the Y, she's soaked. Before I have my car in gear, ready to back up cautiously, she's disappeared through the glass doors.

When we find her in the lobby, she seems calm amid a turmoil of excited kids in dripping slickers and harried-looking women like myself clutching wet umbrellas to their chests. A gaggle of boisterously alert prime timers mill near the doors. Through a window in the lobby wall we can peer into the pool. A fat man, the only person swimming, lumbers in a wobbly sidestroke, doing laps. A string of plastic pennants dips above the surface of the water. Someone, a pool attendant, is fiddling with the dragging line, trying to pull the pennants taut, but the bright flags (little orange triangles, like the bargain signs you see at Safeway) droop and bob over the man's bald head, almost beaning him.

Juanita pokes an elbow in my side. Finally, she's smiling, though she looks half-drowned. "We made it in pretty good time."

"Do you want me to help you change?"

"No. You and Paulie go inside and get a seat. You make me nervous. You're so uptight."

I nod my head, defeated, and walk away, framing a retort in my head. Maybe I'm tired, Ma. Maybe a day of pushing papers in a boring office and rushing home to tend to Paulie and racing through a makeshift dinner has me tense. Maybe I'd like to be with Reece, in the quiet kitchen up in Ashton, eating stir-fried beef and chatting amiably about the week's events. Maybe a quick trip into sexy "Let's Pretend" is preferable to this overheated room full of swimmers and their agitated relatives.

The only way to get into the pool from the main lobby is through the locker rooms. Paulie and I pull off our boots and enter through the Ladies, moving cautiously across the slick tiled floor. Two prime timers are taking showers behind skimpy curtains. We catch glimpses of them turning, bending—slack breasts, saggy bellies, pasty white behinds showing like moons through clouds of steam. Paulie lags a moment and I prod him, "Just keep moving, Mr. Big Eyes."

It's jungle-damp inside the pool. There's a smell of Jell-O powder and chlorine. Juanita says some of her fellow swimmers eat dry Jell-O just before a meet for a quick energy fix. Juanita prefers Snickers bars except the filling sticks between her teeth. She says eating dry Jell-O is like eating perfumed bath powder. Grape isn't so bad, but the other flavors make her sick.

Bleachers rise along one long wall of the room. At the finish line are folding chairs for the judges and the timers. People are arriving pretty fast. I see Monte, dressed in a black T-shirt and khaki slacks, the omnipresent whistle dangling from his neck. He clutches it from time to time as though it is a rabbit's foot. When he sights Paulie and me, he waves and smiles, a big, silly grin wreathing his face. "Hey, Linda. Hey, Paulie." He clasps both palms above his head in the classic winner's stance. "We're gonna cream 'em!" I nod and smile through frozen lips. Paulie and I settle on the first rung of the bleachers, poised for a speedy exit when the meet is over. We're still holding our boots; our feet are soaked. In the dank, close air I feel woozy again. Facing us are sliding doors that open to a stand of hemlocks, bending beneath the weight of rain. It's like we're on a boat, water at our feet, water at the sliding doors, pummeling the glass. I nudge Paulie, "Water, water everywhere, and not a drop to drink." Predictably, he says he's thirsty. He wants to find a drinking fountain in the lobby. "You stay put. You can't go through the locker room again." He starts to whine. He's thirsty, thirsty, thirsty. He can't stand it. His throat is dry. To prove it, he starts coughing, working up to a surefire attack of wheezing. I still owe $200 for his allergy tests, and another $150 on his tonsillectomy. "Paulie, knock it off, or I'll take you home and make you stay in your room, and no TV all weekend." Now he begins to wail, building to a major scene. People look up from their chatter to stare at us. Juanita, emerging from the locker room, looks good in a modest tank suit, widow's black. Not an ounce of fat on her except her upper arms, which are going a bit flabby. She eyes me bleakly, questioning: Now, what have you done?

"Look, Paulie. Quiet down. There's Grandma. She's going to swim in the first race. Now you hush up, or you'll distract her. You save your energy to cheer when Grandma wins."

A voice above us, amplified as though this was a stadium, tells the swimmers to find their marks. Paulie wants to know what that means. I tell him to watch and learn. Juanita has a center lane. I know she must be pleased. In the lane next to her is a tiny woman in a sky blue suit, pinkish blonde hair topped by a blue bathing cap that sits above her pale curls like a pudding bowl. That must be Marchetti. The other swimmers, pudgy, earnest grandma types, don't seem to pose a threat. Juanita nods a greeting to Marchetti, who answers with a brusque half wave. Juanita and the other swimmers assume the diver's crouch. Marchetti stands with eyes closed as though praying, then bends into position. A gun pops with the blurt of a dud firecracker. The women dive amid commotion, clapping. Marchetti hits the water cleanly, barely stirs a ripple in the pool. Ma lands with a splash, harder than I like, but then she takes off swiftly, plowing down the pool's length in a solid freestyle. Not exactly pretty, but workmanlike.

It's clear Marchetti has the edge. Dainty as a doll, but strong, a natural swimmer, Marchetti takes an early lead. Ma, following, looks off her rhythm—kicking up a storm, expending so much effort in the chase, I fear she won't have steam for the return. She's said she needs to get in front; but her rival, who's a healthy length ahead, shows no evidence of tiring. Ma should be getting angry, which would stand her in good stead. Anger always beefs up her adrenaline.

Now, swimming like it's life or death, Ma starts to gain.

"Watch Grandma, Paulie. Cheer for Grandma. Look, Paulie, she's catching up." He says he's thirsty and doesn't want to see. He even slaps his hands over his eyes, so he won't have to watch. I think, there's a lot of Buddy in this kid. A lot of nastiness that doesn't show itself right off, but zaps you when you get up close. What can I do to counteract it? Is it something he's inherited that will make him turn on me someday, as his father did?

Juanita and Marchetti reach the wall at the same moment. Both dip to pretty racing turns. Ma pushes off as though she's jet-propelled. Marchetti seems to hesitate before starting to stroke, and it's just possible she's flagging. Now Ma moves to the lead. If she can keep the pace, she'll pull it off. "She's going to do it, Paulie. I think she's going to do it." I can't hear my own voice because of voices all around me calling, cheering. Monte's crouching at the finish line, talking Juanita home. He's wearing thick-soled sneakers that make him look off balance. When he walks he's like a sailor moving on a pitching deck. I suspect he wears the sneakers to look taller.

Suddenly he's yelling Mama's name, loud enough to sound above the clamor of the crowd. "Juanita! Juanita!"

Almost near the finish, Mama has stopped swimming. She's bobbing up and down, treading water, looking around her at the other swimmers as though she's suddenly confused. She dips under for a moment, pops up again, her gray curls plastered to her head like a dark cap. Her eyes are open, scared. She waits until a laggard swimmer has pulled past her. Then she ducks under the rope that separates the lanes, and bobs up like a cork. The crowd is cheering Marchetti's strong finish as Ma bobbles her slow way to the wall. Monte scoots to meet her at the ladder. I can hear him calling, "What? What?" Ma extends an arm, which Monte grabs and holds, as though he means to push her back under the water. Finally he helps her mount the ladder. For a time they stand engrossed, their heads bent close, talking like conspirators. Monte shakes his head from side to side and tugs the whistle on his chest.

At last he shrugs and gestures to the women's locker. He looks disconsolate.

"Wait here, Paulie. You stay right where you are and you do not move. Is that clear? I'm going to see what's wrong with Grandma." I suppose she got a cramp. Bad luck but there's nothing to do for it, but cut our losses and go home. "Do you understand me? You are not to move." He still has his eyes covered. "Look at me. Look at me when I talk to you!" I pull his hands away, so I can see his face. It's like a mask—no tears; no spark of sympathy or recognition. "Did you hear me? I'm going to see what's wrong with Grandma. You're to stay here and not move till I come back. I want you to tell me that you understand."

The briefest flicker in his eyes. Fear. Maybe contempt. Imperceptibly, he nods. I leave him staring at the rain that pelts the wide glass doors.

In the locker room Ma is sitting on a bench and gazing calmly at her toes. There's a mess of towels and tangled clothing on the floor. She nudges someone's tote bag with her foot, gingerly, as though certain it contains something alive. Seeing her composed, almost regal in the chaos of the place, I almost blubber with relief. "You're okay, aren't you? Why did you quit?"

She shrugs. "A leg cramp. No biggie. Killed my momentum, though."

"Is it better now?"

"Like it never happened." She still stares toward the floor.

We can hear the clamor from the pool. "Do you want to change and watch the outcome of the meet?"

"No way." She motions with her head in the direction of the noise. "Is that still for Marchetti?"

"I don't know. Ma, you almost had her."

"Oh, I'da done it, Linda. I was holding back, you know? Saving for my big spurt at the finish." She sighs, "Monte's disappointed."

"You'll swim another time. You'll win it. Shall I help you dress?"

"Yeah, help me, please." She's stuck there like a block of wood.

"Come on, then, Ma. 'Cause I left Paulie alone." I can't help the impatience in my voice. She acts as though she's in a stupor.

"Is Paulie upset?"

"Yeah, 'cause he wants a drink of water."

"Go get him one, then."

"After you change."

"I can manage by myself. Go look after Paulie. I'll meet you at the car."

"You're sure?"

"Sure I'm sure," she flares at me. "I'm just a little bushed. Am I entitled to be bushed? I almost won the race, remember that."

Almost is no cigar, she likes to say. If it was me who quit a hair's breadth from the finish line, she'd never let me hear the end of it. "I'll pull up to the main entrance so you don't get soaked."

"I'm already soaked," Juanita tells me dreamily.

"You're sure you don't want me to stay and help you?"

"Go tend to Paulie."

"Because I will . . ."

"I was dressing myself for a long time before you were born. I think I can still manage it."

"Look, Ma . . ." Anger chokes me like an errant bone, so sharp and mean I have to gulp for air. I'm the good kid who performs whatever crazy task she asks, and I get nothing for my pains but her contempt. "Look, Ma." I settle on the bench beside her. Up close, she's pale. The loose flesh of her arms is paper white. "Before I go, something I need to say. Maybe it's not the greatest time, but I have to say it. I don't know why you have to get so mad. I know you're disappointed, and I'm sorry. I want to help. But I'm stuck out there with Paulie and he's being such a brat . . ."

"I fail to see the relevance."

"I'm trying to be a conscientious mother, and a loving daughter, but it's hard. Sometimes I feel so pulled, you know? I know I disappoint you. I know it's tough, having me home again with Paulie. I appreciate your help, with baby-sitting, with the bills. I don't know why we have to fight."

Juanita, acting startled, "Do we fight?"

"All the time, Ma. If I say boo, you jump on me. Nothing but angry, nasty words. Why does it have to be like that? Why can't we have a truce?" I reach to touch the loose flesh of her upper arm; it's clammy like cold dough. She's looking old tonight, a pouch of saggy flesh under her chin, deep lines around the mouth. I calculate that Ma is somewhere in her middle fifties, no blooming rose, exactly, but not a stretcher case. Right now she seems played out. That seeming calm must be fatigue. I know she ought to dress—she's shivering—and I ought to get her home, but I don't know if I'll get this brave again. If we could talk things through right now, that cramp that robbed her of her victory could be . . . fortuitous.

She glares at me, the serpent's look, the cold, bone-chilling gaze that sours milk at twenty paces and grips the heart till one feels strangled. "Can the chitchat wait? Because I'm beat. And I thought you had to check on Paulie."

On the drive home we don't talk. In the backseat Paulie's making buzzing noises, acting out a flick he watched with Ma, *The Killer Bees.* He's performing swooping motions with his palm, insects dive-bombing their helpless victims. The buzz builds in intensity as he poises for the kill. Then it softens to pianissimo as the insect swarm regroups. He swoops in for another kill, louder buzzing now.

Paulie's play is better than the silence between me and Ma. Gauging her bad mood, I presume she's building up a case—all the disappointments she has faced in life, thanks to Pop and me and Franklin, Paulie too. When she cites her aggravations, doubtless, I'm in the vanguard: times I missed the mark, a whole life's history of thwarted chances and wrong choices. A string of races lost for never trying them. If I get her talking now, she'll tick off my transgressions one by one. Some stuff is not my fault. Am I responsible for Pop walking in harm's way toward a speeding bus? For Franklin cowering in his room? My troubles are my own. She blames me for bringing them home to roost again.

The rain hasn't let up. Ahead of me a traffic signal flickers in a blur of amber, transforms to a wash of red like a bloodstain spattered in the wet black night. I pull to a cautious halt, pumping the brake this time so we won't skid on the rain-wet pavement. Traffic is picking up; the usual weekend crazies getting an early start. I can't wait to get home, to put this night behind us. Tomorrow, Saturday, Paulie and I have a date with Reece at the computer store. Reece is going to show Paulie some new computer games. I take that as a favorable portent.

Ma says, "Turn right at the light."

"That's not the way home."

"Do it," Juanita says.

"That's the turnoff to Suburban Hospital."

"I know it. Please turn right."

"What's wrong with you, Ma?" Instinctively, I feed to the right lane, not especially alarmed. It's in Juanita's character that she would panic at the slightest pain. I suppose she's diagnosed the leg cramp as phlebitis. If she had a headache we'd be talking killing tumor.

Juanita says, "I'm having intermittent chest pains, moderate to severe. They came on when I was swimming. They stopped awhile, and now they're back."

"You said you had a cramp."

"Sue me, I lied. I didn't want to start a fuss."

"Well, do you think it's serious?"

"That's just what I would like to find out, Linda Jo."

"Well, damn it, you should have said something before."

"Kindly don't swear in front of the child."

"Maybe we should have called the rescue squad."

"It's quicker to drive directly, isn't it?"

"Are you having trouble breathing?"

"Not at all."

"Maybe it's nervous tension. Do you think it's tension, Ma?"

"I'm sure I wouldn't know."

"Is it hurting now?"

"Indeed it is."

"A little or a lot?"

"Quite a lot, Linda Jo."

"Quite a lot doesn't tell me anything. On a scale of one to ten, with ten being the most, how much is it hurting?"

"Seven and three-quarters," Juanita says.

"Mama, that's quite a lot."

She surprises me by uttering a little giggle. "As long as it's not eight, I'll be okay."

We drive the two blocks to the hospital in record time. She seems strangely composed. She is breathing softly, steadily, a pleasant sound like a child breathing in sleep. In the backseat Paulie has stopped humming, and is sitting quietly.

The doctor in the ER is Indian, bearded, balding, the smell of onions on his breath. He does not look at me directly, but keeps his gaze fixed at a point above my head. He blinks furiously as he talks, as though he's trying valiantly to keep awake. The waiting room is jammed, typical of Friday night. Accidents have been arriving, victims of crashes on the Beltway are rolling in on gurneys; one woman in a pink silk evening dress has black eyes and a battered face, the blood caked on her cheeks like excess rouge. The doctor's attitude implies our troubles are unimportant. "Mrs. Burke will be all right. You're not to worry." He steps forward, so that we're almost touching; if I breathe deeply or sway the least bit toward him, my breasts will graze his chest, the frayed white coat, the stethoscope draped casually around his neck. "Your mother's EKG is normal."

"Then, what was wrong?" I'm looking past him for a sight of Paulie who's vanished to the men's room in the lobby. Normally, I wouldn't let him go alone, since I've been brought up on my mother's warnings: "You ever heard of perverts in the stalls? Little boys who are never the same again?"

"Insofar as we can determine, her general health seems excellent. The pain could come from tension."

"I thought that's what it was!"

"We'd like to keep her overnight for observation." He's advanced half a step. We're really touching. I'm positive that I can feel his heart beating under the floppy coat. His breath could knock me out. If I step back, I'll bump into a row of chairs set against the wall. With no retreat, I sit abruptly. The doctor settles down beside me, bending toward me as though he still wants the pleasure of our chests colliding. "Maybe you want to call your family doctor. Ask him to look in on her. We could order some more tests."

"If it isn't serious? I mean, it's Friday night, and if it's only nerves, I hate to bother him."

"Surely. You can let it wait until tomorrow. Talk to him in the morning."

"You really have to keep her here tonight?" I'm nervous about Paulie, who still hasn't appeared. I wonder if the doctor would consent to make a quick tour of the men's room, weed out lurking sickos.

"Just to be cautious. We'll check her vital signs all night." The doctor smiles without much warmth. Since there's no more danger of our touching, his interest in our case has waned.

Instinctively, I prod his near leg with my knee. "I wonder if I could ask a favor . . ."

"You want to see your mother. Of course." He motions toward a cubicle draped with gray sheets. It's like the old examining room down in our cellar, without the warming touch of turquoise. "She's in there. As soon as we free up an orderly, we'll have her moved upstairs." He's wearing a name tag on his coat. Shanti? Shantar? The words swim out of focus. He's a blur because I'm crying. I suspect he's been looking beyond me because my tears embarrass him.

Propped in the gray-draped cubicle, Juanita seems alert. There's a sheet drawn to her chin; her color has returned. Her hair is still damp from the pool. An IV bottle is suspended near her bed, and the tube is running liquid to her arm. That startles me. "What's that for?"

"Search me. Did you talk to the doctor?"

"Yes. He says everything looks normal."

"Zattafact?"

"We'll take you home tomorrow. You'll stay the night; just as a precaution."

"He said that?"

Does she think I made it up? "Yes, Ma."

Juanita contemplates the IV bottle. "That thing shouldn't get empty. Air bubbles in the blood. Not such a good idea. They killed someone that way on 'Alfred Hitchcock.' "

"Don't worry, Ma."

"I'm here. You're there." She points to me with her free hand. "Easy for you to say don't worry."

"The doctor says you get too tense."

She answers with a grunt of disgust. She's eyeing the IV as though the slow drip of liquid has her hypnotized. I wonder if she's noticed I've been crying. "I want you to get Franklin here, tonight," she tells me suddenly.

"Ma! You know I can't do that. Plus, there's no need."

"Don't tell me there's no need. I want to see my son tonight. Paulie, too."

Oh, God, I still haven't found Paulie. "Paulie's in the bathroom, Ma. I'll bring him here the minute he comes out."

I wait for her to chew me out about sending Paulie to the men's room on his own, but she seems to take no notice. She must be feeling punk. "If you call up Franklin, and tell him I got sick, he'll come. I know he will."

"Mama, you're coming home tomorrow. Can't it wait?"

"Tell him to call a neighbor if he has to. Mary will drive him here."

"Mama, much as he loves you, you know he won't go out. Not for anything. He wouldn't go to his own father's funeral."

"Tell him if Lindquist isn't home, to call a cab. I got Barmark's number in the drawer under the kitchen phone. He'll find it right on top. You wait outside and pay the cabbie. I doubt Franklin has any money on him." She lets me have the look. "Do it, Linda Jo."

"I'll try, Ma, okay? I'll go out right now and call him. I'll do my best."

"Do better than your best."

"It's the way he's lived for years. I don't know how to change it in five minutes."

"I didn't say it would be easy. Just get him here."

"You have to steel yourself, in case you're disappointed . . ."

"And for God's sakes, will you go find Paulie! How could you let him go to pee alone?"

The phone rings maybe ten times before Franklin answers. I might have known he'd take his good ole time picking it up. I can hear the TV blaring, so I know he's in his room. There's an extension on the table near his bed. All he has to do is reach for it; but even that effort dismays him.

Responding to my news his voice is calm. "I take it it's a false alarm."

I'm calling from a phone booth in the lobby because the

phones in the ER are all in use. "It seems so, Franklin, but she wants you here tonight."

"Even if I could, it sure seems silly. You know how Ma cries wolf."

"I know it, but it wouldn't hurt to humor her. If you could do this, she would be so happy. So would I."

"Well, I can't."

"If you could get Lindquist to drive you, I'd be waiting outside. Or, if you got a cab, I'd be here to pay him."

"Don't be stupid, Linda."

"Look, Franklin, none of this was my idea."

"Tell her I'll see her in the morning. I'll have her breakfast waiting . . . those banana muffins that she likes."

"Listen to me, brother. She's as mean and crazy as she ever was, but I think she's scared. If only you could manage it, it would do a lot to calm her."

"I'm scared too. Story of my life."

"Get over it, goddammit! Make the effort, would you!"

There's silence for a moment, nothing but the sound of breathing, like an obscene caller building the suspense. "Understand this, Linda," Franklin finally intones. "Wishing doesn't do it."

"Well, what am I gonna tell her? She's counting on it."

Franklin sounds remote as though something on the TV screen has caught his eye. "Give her my love. Tell her I'll talk with her tomorrow."

"Your love! Oh great. Oh, that makes everything just dandy . . ." There's a soft click on Franklin's end of the line. The bastard. I'm furious, digging in my wallet to find another quarter so I can call him back and allow myself the luxury of screaming, when mercifully, across an island of ungainly sofas, positioned back-to-back, I get a bead on Paulie. He's standing at the gift shop window absorbed in the display. Before I can consider chiding him, I'm at his side, knees wobbly with relief. "Paulie, where have you been? Do you know I've been worried about you?"

He's staring at a teddy bear dressed in a yellow raincoat and a wide-brimmed hat. "Paddington," he says. "Paddington Bear."

"Is that who that is?"

"She reads the story to me."

"Who does? Your teacher?"

"Grandma."

"Then he must get into lots of stuff, Paddington. Grandma likes action stories."

Paulie shrugs. "Did she die?"

I bend to him, but he won't face me. He's gazing raptly at the bear. "Paulie, she's fine. She's coming home tomorrow. She's staying here tonight, just till she feels stronger. She wants you to say goodnight before she goes upstairs."

He presses both palms to the window glass and shakes his head.

"A quick kiss and goodnight? Just to make Grandma happy?"

Paulie begins kicking at the wall under the window glass. His boot leaves greasy marks on new tan paint. I grab his shoulder hard. "Don't do that!" I can hear the hoarse rales in his chest, the wheezing starting. He shakes free of my grasp and goes on kicking. Suddenly he looks directly at me. His eyes are palest blue, the pupils large and dark. "You could buy it for her," he suggests and gestures to the bear.

"She wants to see you. It's you she loves, not Paddington." An idea strikes. "Suppose I buy the bear for you? If you go to see your grandma?"

"No," Paulie says firmly. "No." I can see his father's look, sullen and firm. The Merceau stubbornness in which I once took ample pride is going to do me in.

"All right. Go sit on that sofa over there. Do not move. I'll tell Grandma goodnight for you. If I find that you have moved, you are going to get a whipping you will long remember. Is that clear?"

I wait until he's settled on a sofa, hunched low in a corner as though he wants to disappear; then I go to confront Mama with a dual lie. I tell her Paulie has nodded off in the lobby and it would be a sin to wake him, and that Franklin says he'll try. "He's scared, but he's gonna make the effort."

"He'll do it." She's staring fixedly at the IV as though the frail tube represents some kind of lifeline. Given her genius for presentiment, she has to know I'm lying through my teeth.

Wishing doesn't do it, Franklin says. Sometimes it's all I know, my talisman against the blahs and black depression, anger and fear, and worst, the cold gray funk that moves in like a cloud over the sun and scares me worse than anything, because it saps my will, my energy. Wishing that Franklin would get up off his ass and saunter to the corner, buy a paper, hail a bus. Wishing Buddy would send a check, a letter of apology. "Maybe we can't make it as man and wife, anymore, but I'll always love you, Linda Jo, and I'm aware of my responsibilities." Wishing Reece would propose marriage, adopt Paulie, buy a pony and a Bedlington, throw the porn tapes in the trash. Tomorrow, before I go to pick up Mama I will stop at the computer store to tell Reece Juanita's latest caper. Listen while he clucks in sympathy and pats my hair and murmurs, "Poor Linda Jo. Poor kid." He'll be wearing his gray suit, a stiff white shirt, a tie striped blue and green that makes his eyes shine bright as emeralds. He'll whisper, "Can't you stay a minute?" And I'll reply, "Ah, no, I must get my mother home from the hospital." And he'll nod and press my hand and blow a kiss, soft as the flutter of a moth, from his pale lips to mine. I love being with him in the store, love being seen with him in public. He stands so tall and straight. His hair is the color of white corn. He speaks so softly, walks so elegantly, like a member of old-world nobility, a Hapsburg or a Windsor; Reece could be authentic royalty.

Franklin has the house ablaze with light when we get home. He's sitting at the kitchen table, very calm, eating pudding from a foil container, something I bought to pack in Paulie's school lunch box. He's wearing stiff new jeans and a starched blue shirt and sneakers. He's shaved and slicked the bristle of his hair down flat with water. "Don't you look great?" I say. "Expecting company?"

"Just you and little toot. How is she?"

"Disappointed not to see you."

"Get real, Linda Jo." He takes a taste of pudding, licks the back side of the spoon, surveys the residue of chocolate. "Monte called. He was upset when he heard you took Ma to the hospital. I told him she was fine, but he wants to talk with you. He left his number. He says call him when you can."

"Monte can wait." Turning to Paulie, I let him have my sergeant's tone, "Get changed and into bed." When he starts to holler "No," I cut him off. "No arguments. None of this whiney stuff tonight, or your backside is raw meat!"

" 'Night, sport," Franklin calls as Paulie vanishes. And then to me, "You're rough on him, you know."

"Don't tell me how to treat my son."

"Excuse me for living," Franklin says and takes another taste of pudding.

"Put that down."

"Put what down, sweeting?"

"That pudding that I bought for Paulie. That's for his lunch box, not for your midnight snack."

Franklin holds the silver cup aloft, examines it as though admiring the way the light shines on the foil. "There's plenty in the fridge. Don't be so chintzy."

Half-crazy with fatigue, I knock the pudding from his hand. Both of us watch it hit the table and clatter to the floor. Chocolate spatters Franklin's shirt. He stares at me. "What is wrong with you?"

"Don't you dare sit here at the kitchen table and eat my son's chocolate pudding! Don't you dare! You miserable, weak shit. You're good for nothing. You won't help me with anything. You won't do a thing, but sit and make your stuck-up comments and crack your lousy jokes and call us funny names. You won't go see your old sick mother when she needs you."

"You know I can't!"

"I don't know if you can or can't. I don't even give a damn. What I do know is you're not gonna sit in this kitchen and eat my son's dessert that I bought with my hard-earned money. That I worked for. Work, Franklin. Remember work? Remember the last time you lifted a finger?"

"That isn't fair! That's damn mean of you, Linda."

"Don't you dare call me mean. I'll tell you what is mean. Mean is that woman lying on her back, staring at an IV, waiting for you to come and see her."

"She's coming home tomorrow. You told me that."

"I don't care when she's coming home. She asked for you tonight. *I* asked for you. I needed you. I needed your support. I needed someone there to keep an eye on Paulie who managed to disappear and scare me half to death."

"Did something happen? Did someone hurt him?"

"That is not the point. It's not the point that Ma's got nothing wrong with her but nerves. The point is, we are stressed. We're all nervous as cats. And we can't depend on you . . . for anything, except talking like a smartass, and eating up the pudding."

"All right." Franklin holds up his hands to show he'll humor me. "I won't eat anymore."

"Damn straight you won't."

He gestures to the floor. "I'll even clean the mess you made."

"Big deal!"

"Well, what else do you want, Linda Jo?"

"Stop being crazy!"

Franklin laughs. "Okay." He snaps his fingers in the air. "Poof. I'm not crazy. Everything's cool."

"And don't you mock me anymore. Not about this, not about Reece, not anything."

"May God strike me dead if I mock you."

"You're doing it now."

"You're paranoid."

"Right. Just like Pop. He thought you were malingering, and so do I."

"I can't help what he thought, or what you think. I'm not."

"Then prove it. Go outside and take a walk. Call a cab and go see Mama. It's not too late. She'll be happy for your company. I doubt that she's asleep."

"I tried to, Linda Jo. I did." Franklin is standing now, holding the table edge as though he needs it for support. "Look at me. I did get dressed. I shaved. I got the taxi number. Go look; it's in my room. But I couldn't get myself to dial it, so I thought I'll go next door and ask Lindquist to drive. I lit the house up first—it looks like Christmas, doesn't it—just to keep things cheerful. Then I couldn't find my key, so I looked for Ma's, and when I found that, on the hook in the broom closet, I practiced some deep breathing, and I said, 'Okay, Franklin, old sport, this is it. This is your moment of truth. Go, be a man and a good brother, and a loving son.' But I couldn't, Linda Jo. I couldn't make it out the door."

"Am I supposed to pity you for that?"

"I don't want your pity."

"Good. 'Cause there's none left in me. I'm fed up with you all. You, Juanita, everyone."

"I just want you to let me be." Franklin tears a long sheet from a roll of paper towels hanging on the kitchen wall. He wets the paper at the sink, then bends to clean up the spilled pudding. I watch him for a time. "Have you thought what you would do if

I moved out, and something really happened to Juanita?" Franklin grunts but won't respond. He is concentrating on the wet lino-leum, scrubbing at a clean place as though all his pride depends on getting a high shine. "Have you thought about it, Franklin?"

He gets up, crosses to the garbage can, and throws the crum-pled paper in the trash. He tears off a clean towel and wipes his hands, examining them studiously. He won't look at me. "I'd make out."

"Just tell me how."

"As long as there are stores that deliver, I'll do okay."

"You've got it figured out?"

"Get off my back, will you, Linda Jo! Go marry Mr. Fun 'n Games and have a life. I want that for you, hon. Peace, security, stability; every night another screenplay. Go for it. Enjoy."

"You leave those movies out of this. Things I told you, things I said in confidence, I don't expect to get thrown in my face."

Franklin bends in a mocking bow. "Your secret dies with me, madame, I swear. You and Reece wanna play Rhett and Scarlett in the sack, that's your affair. Just don't be so quick to call me crazy. 'Cause everyone's a little crazy. Everyone's got something a little twisty in their lives that they'd rather keep quiet. Look at Ma and her catalog of horrors. And Pop. What pushed his button, do you suppose?" Franklin does a quick tap-tap upon the floor like a flamenco dancer. He snaps his fingers in the air. "Olé?"

"Don't make fun of that day. You loved it as much as I did." I'm sidestepping the wet place on the floor. Franklin has some-how turned the talk around so that he's the injured party, and the rest of us look crazy. Knowing that, I don't feel guilty hitting him where he's most vulnerable. "Don't you miss being with girls, Franklin? Sex and all that 'twisted' stuff?"

He grins as though he were expecting that. "Depends upon the girl. You remember Beryl Blackwell?"

"The phobia counselor lady? Sure."

"I don't miss her."

"That's not what I mean, but it doesn't matter anyhow." I'm too bushed to see straight and my taste for argument has vanished. As usual, when I talk with Franklin, I end by throwing in the towel. Let him have the last word if it pleases him. He is slipping from our grasp as though he had a terminal disease. Since we don't know what to do, we always end by humoring him. "I have to get some sleep. I'm beat." I leave him slouched against the kitchen sink, staring at a smear of chocolate on his sleeve.

"Ho, Linda," he calls after me, "Will chocolate stain?"

"Probably. Unless you wet it with cold water."

"If it does," his mockery trails me down the hall, "I'm gonna tell Ma it was all your fault."

It pours all night, the stubborn rain that hits us every fall like a monsoon. Awake, I listen to the pounding on the roof, steady, like someone driving home a point, over and over and over. From time to time lightning illuminates the room with a swift, flashy explosion; that subsides, leaving an eerie green glow, the color of Paulie's night-light. There's no sound but rain and Paulie's breathing. My little guy's out cold, exhausted by the rigors of the day. I pray he'll have a dreamless sleep. Sometime toward dawn I have a nightmare. Buddy and I are in his parents' ritzy house in Chevy Chase in Buddy's boyhood room; the only furniture is a bunk bed. He's in the upper bunk, and I'm stretched out in the lower one. Buddy complains that this isn't his idea of fun. I keep telling him to hush, please hush, and let me sleep, *just let me sleep,* I want to forget, I want to close my eyes and forget everything.

The phone's ring rouses me, saving me from a replay of Buddy's droning that by God, the way you go around protecting it, you'd think the thing was made of Steuben crystal. I swim up out of sleep, thinking that must be Monte, and does he have to call so early in the morning?

It's just a little after six, the cold gray of a day that follows rain. Franklin is in the kitchen, talking softly to whoever's calling.

Telling Monte off, I hope. I sleep another minute, a blessed, dreamless, dozing, till Franklin's knock jars me awake. I struggle out of bed, still in a fog, but annoyed that he would bother me for Monte's sake. I open the door softly, trying not to wake Paulie. "For God's sake, Franklin. Couldn't you tell Monte to get lost?"

He's in his green-and-white pajamas and beat-up loafers. He needs a shave and his hair is standing up in prickly bristles, as though something has really scared him. He's holding a wooden spoon that's coated with muffin batter. "Linda," he whispers. "Linda Jo? That was the hospital. They moved Juanita to Intensive Care."

"What's wrong? What happened?"

"They said she had a heart attack."

"Franklin! That couldn't be! They said her tests were normal."

"A heart attack," he enunciates, as though he thinks I have a hearing problem. A blob of yellow batter falls from the spoon and beans his shoe. Like an idiot, I stand staring at it, thinking that is just so gross, that sticky goo spattered on his loafer. "Linda," Franklin asks. "What happens now? What are you gonna do?"

Seven

"**W**hatever needs doing," I told him, staring at the sticky batter on his shoe. Thinking, what a slob he is cooking breakfast in that getup—soiled pajamas and those beat-up shoes that look like rejects from Goodwill. Cruddy batter on the toe, some of it sure to dribble down and stain the rug. "Whatever needs doing I'll do," I said, pretending courage, as if courage, in this family, wasn't something of a rare commodity. He asked, "What will you do?" Putting light-years between us as though he occupied another planet. Franklin, who, early on, displayed executive potential. Class president and editor of *Chips,* the high school magazine that won all the awards. The editorial "we" would have been welcome just now. The offer, "Come, let's cope together" (empty as that would have sounded, given the extent of Franklin's helplessness) would have posed some comfort.

Fear and bleak contempt for Franklin's woeful presence made me boast, "Whatever needs doing I'll do." Dry-eyed, I went to the phone and called the hospital to ascertain Mama's condition. "Guarded," a voice said, sounding annoyed, as though I had some sweet nerve asking.

I called Aunt Viv, Ma's widowed sister, in New Jersey, who cried, "You know I'll come at once if you all need me, but my vision has got so bad from the glaucoma." (That's true. When she was staying over for Pop's funeral, Ma found her spraying the furniture with oven cleaner, thinking the can was Pledge. Ma said it left a so-so shine, but the odor was ungodly.) I called Mary Lindquist (who wanted Mama's birth date to consult the stars) and Monte, who was silent for the longest time (waiting for the punch line, maybe) before saying he'd meet me at the hospital, and Cal Fowler, who told me to take Monday off, and then put me in touch with a cardiologist named Greeley (a huge man, Lincolnesque, with a low-slung jaw that looked like Marfan's syndrome). I called Reece, who sounded distant. Tension, I thought. My God, he's been through it, hasn't he? I called some of Ma's old clients who sent their best love and their prayers; then I called Buddy's folks, who were "elsewhere for the day," Monroe, the houseman, told me, as he always does, but said he'd see they got the message. I doubted that; since day one he has disliked me, his face a black mask of contempt. I started to call Paulie's school to tell them he was staying home because of illness in the family, before remembering it was Saturday. I called the internist, the one I didn't want to bother Friday night, who huffed, "Greeley's okay, but you might have asked me first. There are plenty of other good men in the area."

"Are you telling me Greeley's no good?"

"I told you, he's okay. I just think, considering Mother has been my patient, you might have asked me first, just as a courtesy. I haven't seen her in a year. I didn't have a clue that she was having problems."

"Sorry," I whimpered. "Sorry, if I was discourteous. Getting her well has got to be my first priority." Because *I* have to *cope.*

"Franklin," I yelled when I got off the phone. "Franklin, it looks as though the stupid doctors are gonna have a turf war over Ma. Can you believe it?" But he had disappeared into his room, and wouldn't answer when I pounded. It reminded me of the old days when Pop got mad at him for acting snotty. "Franklin, can I rely on you to keep an eye on Paulie? I'm going to the hospital." Franklin, lying low, refused to talk, hoping to be wakened when the whole dreadful ordeal was over, I suppose.

Nothing to do but dress, hightail it to Suburban, fake out a babe with diplomatic license plates who was vying for the last apparent parking space, hurry through the lobby (noting Paddington inside the gift shop window, looking cuddly but somber). The elevators, marked Express, stopped woodenly at every floor. "Hurry up and wait," Pop told us of the army. Hospitals, the same. The worst is ICU, nothing there but waiting, dead time, sluggish, boring, where we totter on the brink of crazy . . .

Someone says experts planned these colors—the cool blue of the walls, the flowered sofa covers, muted blossoms, blue and white, green strands of vines. Experts chose a quiet corner, windows looking to a dead-end street far from traffic noises and the sirens' screams. Experts analyzed the play of sun (stippling the nylon grayness of a rug that melds blandness with durability) and hung opaque white shades which I, when I can manage it, keep raised, though others pull them low for coolness, soothing shadows. Experts picked the paintings, perfect in their vague banality.

The picture facing me is of a forest—evergreens divided by a path which wanders upward to a blurred horizon. Not art, but artful. I gaze at it and dream. I feel the cushion of pine needles underfoot; sense the drift of breeze mingling wood scents and hidden flowers. I amble amid fuzzy boughs. Experts provided this.

As the moments pass—each moment seven years in length—I set myself upon that painted path, again and again heading to a picnic, near a rushing brook where I can bend to drink, or sit, toes dangling. I'm clever at this game, vanishing to pleasant places. Sometimes I stroll with Reece or Franklin, even Buddy. We saunter, hand in hand, as we used to in the corridors at BCC. Sometimes I walk with Pop who's happy, humming "Green Eyes" or his "dum de dum" rumba about Miami Beach. Pop and I are skilled at quick escapes, slippery as two Houdinis.

When I grow bored, I mark the clock's slow ticking—seven years to the minute. Four centuries and a score before the hands complete their circuit. Five minutes before the hour I stand and stretch and venture past the double doors of ICU where patients lie sleeping, wheezing, groaning. That part's the worst; I don't blame Franklin for hiding. Five minutes, bordering on half a century, and I'm back, grateful for my territory on the squishy sofa, grateful for the paintings and the shades hanging askew (too many of us making adjustments).

Stuck here against our will, we have become a tightknit clan, privy to each other's stories. The family Kaligyros. Dark hair and deep black eyes. The women in silk dresses and high-heeled pumps. Lumpish earrings big as walnuts, solid gold. Soft leather purses. The men in dark blue suits and painted ties. When their men arrive, the women pull out tins of food, spinach baked in squares of phyllo dough, date confections, almond cakes; they press these treats on us as well, cutting the bitterness of grief with sugar glazes. Papa Kaligyros is in a coma. The family nods and prays; the rest of us chew stolidly, wiping lips and chins with paper napkins, thoughtfully provided. One Kaligyros son, Tasso, potbellied and fortyish, but handsome, pinions me with his eyes. I feel I'm floating in a deep black lake, supported by his passion, his hunger and his grief. Alone, I'd take him to that forest and dally with him in the pines. We don't talk much, mostly we exchange curt, guilty nods, or he offers me a piece of honey pie, which I devour shamelessly.

Anita Romulo is pretty, fragile, shy, with the sharp bones of a bird. Full lips and eyes as dark as any Kaligyros, red-rimmed now. Her son, Manuel, was in a motorcycle accident and crashed without a helmet. We don't ask the prognosis.

Yvette Fallon—soft flesh in a flowered muumuu, brassy hair —lolls in an armchair near the lamp and brazenly smokes. Her kid OD'd. Girded in fumes she stares us down, flinging out a silent challenge: Confront me if you dare. We don't complain, because we are forbearing and we know the woman's boldness masks the craziness of grief. None of us is rational. We're marginally here. Part of us behind the double doors of ICU. Part of us in that forest, or whatever fantasy each must contrive.

Really bored or really desperate, I replay past events. Fiddle a little with the truth. If I cast happenings in a different light, rewrite the script, who's there to contradict me? I have topics I can call up, like subjects stored on the hard disc of memory. Buddy and I, contenders in some major fights, our "honeymoon" at Deep Creek Lake, Franklin's escapade with Beryl Blackwell, Reece and me as Nick Arnstein and Fanny, Mick Jagger and Bianca, Katherina and Petruchio. Or me confronting other guys. The one time I ran my ad in *Washingtonian,* a slew of sorry fellows answered. Some potential compañeros sent poems or photographs. Snaggletoothed or droopy-mustached, not a winner in the carload, balding, sad, confused, and lonely, oh so lonely. ("Loneliness is the *primum mobile,*" Franklin says, in that affected voice he gets. "Loneliness spurs people to desperate measures, more than sex or booze." Franklin drones on, mesmerized by his own voice, "God, in His awful solitude, made us in His lonely image and now requires our devotions to make the silent hours pass.") Lonely, too, I met with one or two sorry guys for drinks, no more than that, but Ma thinks I'm a harlot. That's enough to ponder as I sit, dozing. And still the hours drag.

The keeper of the doors to the ICU is a bouncy, blonde-haired volunteer. Someone savvy picked her for this task, for her cute cheerleader face, her darling dimpled smile that imbues us sufferers with confidence. Someone this cute wouldn't usher us toward tragedy. She holds court in the sunlit corridor at a spindly-legged desk and signs us in. Name and Relationship to Patient. She offers us a yellow pen with a felt daisy at the tip. "How are yew today?" His first encounter with this sprite threw Tasso Kaligyros in a tailspin. He arrived expecting Cerberus and found a nymph from Disneyland. He gaped and offered her a diamond-shaped segment of baklava. "Thank yew!" She weighed it in her little hand, then popped it in her mouth and said, "How good." Tasso blinked tears. The slightest kindness gets us weeping, like lost children not secure with sudden fortune.

Near dusk Monte arrives bearing a bucket of Kentucky Fried. "Gotta make sure you eat," he tells me with a smile.

I say that's all I do, but I settle for a drumstick, and pass the bucket to the others. The smell of cold grease permeates the place. Mrs. Fallon lights a cigarette, inhales. The gray smoke mixes with the odor of rank crumbs and secret herbs.

"Should she be smoking?" Monte asks.

"Let it alone."

Monte holds up a packet of french fries. I shake my head. "How's your mom?" he asks.

"How could she be? She's here."

"The next session, could I see her? Spell you a little bit?"

"It's only next of kin."

"Say I'm your brother Franklin."

"I can't do that." In the past week Franklin has become a shadow holed up in his room. Rocking, reading, sketching, practicing his tricks with coins, he won't come out for meals, won't ask how Mama's doing. He's thin and ghostly pale. More than ever, I'm afraid he's fading, blending with the gray-white of the walls. If Monte takes his name, Franklin may vanish in a puff of dust. "Don't you dare tell them you're Franklin."

"Then I'll say your mom adopted me. I'm practically an orphan, anyhow, so it's not so big a lie."

"If it means so much to you," I shrug. "You won't like it in there."

I'd thought it would be silent, simon-pure, a vast white space divided into cubicles—each section organized and nasty neat. Instead, it is a sorry mess of lines and pipes and hardware, TV monitors. And noisy, all these drips and gurgles, buzzes, bleeps. It's a body shop, spare parts. A crowded domicile of cottage industry, the enclave of a looney scientist concocting monsters. Ma's flesh is draped in sheets and all I see to tell me she's alive are bottles emptying and filling. Her face is gray, dark purple circles underneath the eyes. Sometimes the gray lids flutter to show me she's awake. Something in ICU reminds me of Reece's den, maybe it's the slick high-tech machinery. Is this the price I pay for acting trampy? The first time I bent to kiss her, feeling my way between the plastic tubing, Ma asked me, "Is it curtains for Juanita?"

"No way. You're doing fine."

"Franklin here yet?"

"Not yet."

"Did Pop come by?"

"Pop isn't here, Ma."

"He has this tendency . . . to disappear. Doesn't he?"

"Sometimes."

"Franklin will find him."

Regardless of her firstborn's craziness, Ma invests him with special powers. If Franklin came to visit, doubtless she'd leap up healed.

I confess to Monte, "I could use a breath of air."

"Go on then, Linda Jo." He looks as though he's getting

psyched up for a contest, concentrating on a pep talk, inhaling and exhaling noisily. I half expect he'll make a circuit of the waiting room, slapping high fives with the patients' relatives and yelling, *"Dee*-fense."

Tasso follows me into the corridor and offers me a box of yogurt-covered raisins. I shake my head, "Too sweet."

Those wondrous eyes look stricken as though the worst has happened. "Coffee?" he asks.

"Maybe in a while. I have to make a call."

Nodding, he pops a raisin in his mouth. I sense him watching as I shuffle past our perky volunteer. (*"How are yew?"*) There's music piping through the hall, a Stevie Wonder song that gets me thinking about Reece. In the phone booth near the elevator I stop to dial his store, guilty because he's taking precedence over Franklin and Paulie.

A miracle, he answers right away as though he has been waiting for my call. "Linda! This is a nice surprise. How is your mother feeling?"

"Still no change." I add, "Long time no see."

"You know you're in my thoughts. I don't want to intrude."

When I called to tell him Ma was sick, he turned remote as though the prospect of another ailing parent was more than he could bear. He listened quietly, no exclamations of regret, no pitying sighs. I'd pictured him, eyes clear and cold and harshly distant, gauging the movement of the clock as I assailed him with fresh pain. It was more than he could handle; he owned up to that at once, charged me to keep in touch (I, who'd just played Daisy to his Gatsby), and rang off softly. Later that day, a basket of exotic fruits and jams from Neiman Marcus arrived at my mother's house. His card said, "Forgive me."

"You wouldn't be intruding if you stopped by. Really, I miss you." That isn't what I mean to say. If I slap him with a load of guilt, he'll surely vanish to the privacy of Ashton and cast about for my replacement.

"You know the way I feel, Linda." That's a statement open to interpretation.

"The main reason I called is they play this Muzak in the hospital, and the song that's on right now made me think . . . Can you hear it?" Stevie's bopping through another chorus: "I just called to say I love you."

Reece says, "It's a bad connection."

"Don't you miss seeing me at all?"

"Oh, Linda." His voice falters a bit, enough to give me hope. "If I could wave a wand and change things, make me a better person, I would. At least you know I'm honest. You know why I don't come round. I can't take another sickbed vigil. I just can't."

Tonight that doesn't wash. A stab at courtesy, a little "How ya doin', Linda Jo?" however insincere, might go a long way toward providing comfort. It wouldn't cost. It's not like I'm asking him to empty bedpans. "Well, let's do lunch someday, for old time's sake."

"Linda, you know I'm here. When your mother's better we can pick things up where they were."

If my aunt had wheels, she'd be a bus, Pop used to say. "Sure Reece, take care." This time I hang up before him. I grab the first descending elevator, desperate to quit this place.

At the far end of the parking lot the doctor from ER, the Indian, Devi Shantar, is polishing his car, a squat Volkswagen bug painted lurid orange, a relic. Shantar buffs the car's fat fender with a chamois cloth—long, loving strokes, as though he's fondling a woman's thigh. His mouth is slightly open, eyes intent on the love object. Pausing for a moment, he scans the car's neon-bright hood, searching for imperfections in the shine. When he hears my footsteps he looks up, beckons me closer, flapping the cloth as though shooing off bugs. He's wearing a white lab coat and rubber gloves. "How do you like my car? Terrific, yes?"

111

"You don't see many of those, these days. They're almost obsolete."

"It is a wonderful machine." His smile is radiant in the dark. It's a hot night, more like August. Crickets are chirping in the hedges. We can hear the din of traffic on Old Georgetown Road, muffled like a distant ocean. "It uses very little gas. In snowstorms it is dependable."

I don't know why I rate the sales pitch. He hasn't asked how Ma is doing. Probably he has forgotten who she is. "It's very nice."

"It is the first car I have ever owned." His voice lilts upward like a question. "It's like a dream to me."

So is this night, a strange slow-motion fantasy comprised of humid air and dank, dead leaves and a figure grinning out of shadows, stroking an outsized orange with a square of chamois. Something Pop would cook up as a joke.

"Would you wish to go for a drive?" Shantar's coat gleams ghostly in the dark. His smile seems sinister.

It's the memory of that onion breath and the cold eyes looking past me in the ER that keeps me from bolting for the car and telling him, let's go, let's gun it—just spring me from this dreadful place, which is not where I belong. In all Juanita's stories, the bad news was for other people. "I have to stay with my mother. Maybe another time."

"Another time, then." He turns back to the orange car, my presence already dismissed. I leave him to his strange devotions, a slow and loving guiding of the cloth over the trunk, the compact doors, the sunroof. Passion resides in oddball places, stranger than Reece's fantasies.

Monte says, "They called a code. It was just like on TV. Everyone racing down the hall. The cart with all their instruments nearly turned over."

"Who was it for?"

"I don't know." He pats my arm in a clumsy try at reassurance. "Your Mom's okay. She's conscious, lucid. She wants to know when Franklin's coming."

"You call that lucid?"

"Linda Jo, we have to talk."

I sink into the blue-gray sofa with Monte settling in beside me. The path into the pine forest is beckoning. "Talk away."

"How are you managing?"

"Well as I can. Paulie's in school till three. When he gets home, he has Franklin for company. I'm not sure who's looking after who." I don't describe how Franklin's holed up in his room rereading Conrad, because he's into shipwreck stories.

"Do they hassle you at work for the time you're taking off?"

"I come in at eight and cut out for the hospital at four. Fowler said, 'Take all the time you need.' When I do it, he gets mad. If he cans me, I'll take a temp job, something with easier hours, or turn tricks on Fourteenth Street. Hey, Monte," I nudge him with my elbow, "that last part was a joke. You're supposed to laugh."

"Money's a problem?"

"Sure. The medical insurance won't cover everything; it never does. Ma's got something saved, but I can't get to that." It's in Juanita's nature to be canny about money. I suspect she's got a bundle socked away, though when I was small I always figured we were strapped; the difference between our street of modest ramblers and the glorious manses near the Circle in old Chevy Chase was not lost on me.

"You need your mom's power of attorney."

"No way. Even if she were well enough to sign, she'd think for sure that she was dying if I mentioned it."

"What will you do?"

"I don't know, Monte. Trust in de Lawd?"

"It's wonderful you have your faith, but you need to do something more practical."

Oh Monte, is it any wonder I don't love you! The fact is, I plan to confront Buddy's mother in that big Tudor pile they own out by the country club. If I must, I'll stage a sit-in on her pink chintz pillows, settle down amid the crystal vases and the porcelain bric-a-brac until she talks to me. I think she sort of liked me, before people convinced her I'd ruined Buddy's life. She has to help me contact him, for Paulie's sake. "We'll make out," I tell Monte. Mrs. Fallon, in her smoky corner, is bending to us, listening. Anita is crocheting what looks to be a baby sweater. The Kaligyros women in smart black have assembled on a couch under the forest painting.

Tasso's wife has frosted hair and mean black eyes. She knows about me and Tasso, I can tell it from the way she scans my face as though hoping to find wrinkles or some mark of deep disgrace. Nothing we did was bad, only so oddly sexy I can't stop thinking about it.

My first day here, Tasso saw the terror numbing me and sat beside me on the couch. Under cover of my skirt he took my hand. He has firm cushioned fingertips, callused as though he were a pianist or a tailor. Lately, men's hands turn me on— Reece's for sure, and Tasso's. Tasso touched his fingertips to mine, careful as someone reading braille. When I didn't withdraw my hand, he grew less tentative, raked a swift nail down my palm, only hard enough to tickle, traced the thin skin of my wrist where the blue veins showed and the pulse was beating fluttery and fast. Reading a message in that, Tasso dug his nails into my hand. I responded with my palm spread wide and Tasso laced his firm, fleshy fingers tenderly through mine and held on tight, squeezing till the pain grew overbearing. And there we sat, hands interlocked under the panels of my cotton skirt as I'd waited to hear if Ma would live or die, close to swooning out of lust for him. And he the same. I knew it from the way his chest rose and fell with labored breaths as though he, too, was a heart case.

His wife saw it. She's something of a leader in their family—

short and slim, dark-eyed and tense, with tiny pointed breasts that thrust against the fine silk of her dress like arrows. She likes to give directives, supervises distribution of the treats, can't light in one place for too long, moves in a buzzing funnel of energy like a hummingbird. She watches me and Monte now, her tiny nostrils twitching as though sniffing the rank air of scandal.

Monte, searching the inside pocket of his jacket, digs out a checkbook and a flashy fountain pen. "Linda Jo," he uncaps the pen importantly, "I want to make you a small loan." He snaps open the checkbook with a flourish, waits for my reaction before setting down the date.

"Thanks, Monte, but I can't afford any more loans. I'm already a candidate for debtors' prison."

"A gift, then. Don't even think about returning it." He scrawls something quickly, tears out the check, flaps it in the air to dry. After he hands it to me, I fold it quickly and stash it in my purse, without looking at the amount. I think that disappoints him. "You're a good guy, Monte. Thanks."

"Oh, listen." He waves away gray plumes of smoke. "In a way, I feel responsible, you know? For Juanita getting sick."

"You shouldn't."

"Think of the check as an early Christmas present."

"Okay. But I'll have to get you something."

"If you want. But there's no need of repayment, remember that."

"Well, great."

Tasso is watching from the doorway, his face set in a scowl, as bitter as the mask of tragedy. He stares at me as though in disapproval that money has been exchanged. Tears gleam on his cheeks. "Papa," he says. "Papa . . ." There's a low moan from the couch under the painting and then a kind of stirring as we move to Tasso at the door, the black-garbed women first, Anita, Mrs. Fallon, me. It's like we're in a boat and we're all crowded to port and listing. The room tilts with the weight of our collective grief.

"What is it? What happened?" Monte calls to us from the blue-gray sofa, still the pained intruder, still missing the point.

Eight

The Merceau house looks the same—a sturdy Tudor fortress held secure by double doors. Casement windows mullioned into diamonds catch the morning sun and glitter hard-edged lights. The lawn is dense and soft, lush after days of rain. The bushes are so slick, so boldly green, they could be artificial, like the plants in Reece's kitchen.

Lingering at the base of the front steps, I fiddle with a branch of prickly holly just to see if it's real. The mean edge of a leaf grazes my hand and leaves a faint bloody streak, a lousy omen. Nervous about that, I burrow in my purse to find a Kleenex and press it to my palm. Tense, blatantly stalling, I sink onto a slim wrought-iron bench set on the grass (decorative, not meant for sitting) to think things through.

If I hadn't sorted out the pros and cons and figured Buddy's mom was my last hope, (if I hadn't made that boast to Monte vowing I could handle things in my own way), I'd cut and run so fast, no one would see me for the dust. As it is, I will be late for work, and Cal Fowler has a luncheon date in Phillie, which means he'll want the full drill with the helicopter, all the fuss of that departure, with me, posted in his swivel chair, taking last-minute orders as if our fates depended on it. It strikes me that all the men I know are jerks—Reece, Buddy, Franklin, Cal Fowler, Monte for sure—all pompous posturers, hung up on how the world perceives them. Maybe not Tasso, but I'll never find that out. Maybe Adele and I, in the full warmth of sisterhood (females against the world or some such rot), can work out answers to my situation. There was a day she sought my help, though it's doubtful she remembers.

Someone has picked up the morning paper; that would be Dr. Merceau on his way to early rounds. No sign of movement in the house. If I rouse Adele from sleep, she'll act spacey, assume this vague persona that's part ditzy babe, part haughty beauty, bored with everything except her face (how much of this is act, and how much real, I cannot gauge).

The first time we met she grabbed my hand in a death grip and murmured, "Nice to see you," like some phrase she'd had to memorize. That was the week before our high school graduation, a party in the Merceau garden for seniors and their families, a very fancy do—musicians, caterers, the works. (Happily, the rose-bushes were at their peak, and the day was bright and mild with bearable humidity. "The luck of the Merceaus," Buddy had said.) The invitations (to four hundred graduates) had been handwritten by Adele on pale blue paper, a deeper band of chaste blue for the edging. Elegant. No RSVP required. The well-bred know enough to answer without being nudged. So writes Miss Manners in the *Post,* and of course Adele already knew that without out-side advice.

My folks didn't attend because Pop was working weekends at the *Star,* and Ma accepted my bleak dictum that she'd be miserable if she showed up without him. I warned her there'd be no one there simpatico enough to talk to. I'd be busy with my friends, and everyone who'd ever met them said the Merceaus were stuckup. I know that Ma was hurt by what she termed "my crummy attitude." She put a stoic face on it, however, and shifted to Cassandra mode, saying she didn't trust food served outdoors, anyhow. All those salads drenched in mayonnaise and left out in the heat were free tickets to salmonella poisoning. "You be careful what you eat," Ma warned. "I don't care what outfit does the catering, they don't know diddly squat about the first principles of sanitation."

Adele Merceau, heading the receiving line, filled me with awe. "Nice to see you," she had murmured, a gaunt blonde with imposing cheekbones and a model's height and bearing. Hair piled in a sloppy topknot. Flirty wisps around her face and blonde strands tumbling on her neck, sprayed to suggest insouciance. Eyes like clouded plastic, a somber, baffled smile, an iron grip, so painful when she shook my hand I nearly hollered, "Quit it!" What I did instead, to my great shame (operating on some deeply ingrained peasant instinct, the printer's modest daughter bowing to a goddess) was bobble to a curtsey (like an overanxious toddler at her maiden birthday party) and yammer, "Hi, I'm Linda Burke." (In that presence, "Linda Jo" had struck me as tacky, like a name you'd give a country music hopeful.) "Nice to see you," Adele, cast as "point man" for the Merceau team, had wobbled against Buddy's father, who nudged her with a hard jab from the shoulder to jolt her to a more upright posture. Confused, she wavered toward me, gripping my hand. She was literally swaying, bland-faced, sloe-eyed, whispery, and shivering slightly, beautiful, in a stiff pink linen dress with a matching sweater of palest cashmere, draped around her shoulders as protection against errant drafts. When I looked at her up close, I realized she was sloshed or stoned or so pumped full of Valium, she didn't have a notion what was flying.

Since Buddy's father is a plastic surgeon, Adele can have an annual face-lift or tummy-tuck—whatever—as a family perk. That boggles my mind, knowing she plays Galatea to his brooding genius. Whatever imperfection he observes, whatever bump or lump or infelicity of feature or design, he can reshape to an ideal of perfection. He can fake out age, smooth wrinkles, suck out fat, straighten a crooked septum, carve a butt to be as tight and lean as a young boy's. He's the magus; she's his glamorous assistant and his cleverest trick, a showstopper.

She was drunk or drugged that day. "Nice to see you." Squeezing all sensation from my hand, she passed me to the doctor, who seemed charged up in comparison, small hawkish features, neat gray hair, a prissy air that bordered on effeminate, then, suddenly, a voice of startling resonance belying this prim image. He could have been a sports announcer, or the commentator on the weekend opera broadcasts: ". . . and now a pleased sigh rises from the audience as the swan boat glides on stage . . ." That cultured, modulated intonation always gives me goose bumps. The doctor boomed, "What college?" When I told him, "Maryland," some light of interest in his pale eyes faded. He said, kindly enough, "Good show," and passed me on to Buddy's grandmother, Nana Merceau, a blue-haired giantess, nearly deaf, with the posture of a DAR commander. I was miffed because there was no sign of Buddy.

Nana Merceau was sure she knew me. "Aren't you Phil Burke's child? Weren't we introduced at Chevy?" That's shorthand for the Chevy Chase Club, which is how the "in" crowd speaks.

I told her, "My father's name is Joseph, and he's not a member."

Nana absorbed this with a brisk shake of her head as though signaling, "Desist." Buddy had warned me in advance that, although Nana seemed imperious, she was a love, the family character, equipped with all her marbles, but likely to act eccentric. Since she won't wear a hearing aid, she copes with being deaf by cooking up her own scenarios. She'll answer her own questions in ways that please her best. "Phil is so handsome, and you certainly resemble him. Is it true you were accepted at the Naval Academy?"

I told her, "No, ma'am. Maryland."

Nana grasped my hand between tough palms. She had heavy arms dotted with freckles. Her fingernails were painted hooker scarlet. "I think that is outstanding. Lena, would you come outside with me? I want you to meet Tom Crimmons, the senator? He'll be thrilled to know a student who is planning service to our country, and a young woman, at that. That is just so super." Nana's smile revealed an excess of pink gum, plastic I think, but she did seem welcoming, conjuring, out of deafness, an ideal date for Buddy. She steered me from the entrance hall into the chintz-filled living room and through the wide French doors to the terrace, where a table covered in old lace was heaped with mounds of shrimp on beds of ice, and finger sandwiches on Lenox platters, and green bean and garbanzo salads, and bacony slivers of quiche, and rounds of Nova Scotia salmon stuffed with dill, and little moon-shaped pizzas, and three-tiered plates of strawberries and pineapple and kiwifruit festooned with mint, and a sheet cake glistening with slick white icing and a trim of blue and gold, with blue letters proclaiming GOOD LUCK, GRADUATES. A throng of seniors in their dress-up finery were pressing around the table, heaping food upon their plates with the ferocity of cannibals. At a second lace-decked table, a white-gloved waiter was presiding over drinks, shooing black gnats from the punch and dispensing cans of soda. Still no sign of Buddy, who I feared had gone off

121

with the football team to sample something stronger than the Gatorade.

Easy to recognize the senator. He had a perfect tan and perfectly trimmed hair, a ruddy chestnut faintly touched with gray, and a smile that never wavered, showing even, polished teeth. He pressed my hand with perfectly attuned intensity, not so firmly that it hurt, not weakly, like some wimp unsure of his constituency. He zapped me with an eye lock that made clear, "You are the one. You are the only person on this planet who interests me at this moment in time." He was attentive, effervescent, handsome enough to carry all Montgomery County without addressing himself to the issues. He even had a dimple!

Franklin says these guys come to the capital as ordinary citizens, but before they enter Congress they go somewhere secret to get *burnished.* "It's true," Franklin insists. He says the guy who runs the Charm and Grooming franchise, whatever hush-hush place that is (he thinks it's out in Langley near the CIA and it doles out lessons in charisma), must make a fortune.

After Nana told him I was going to Annapolis, Senator Crimmons twinkled. He wondered, was I interested in math and science, and would I like the names of midshipmen he knew who would surely want to meet me because I was so pretty? Nana Merceau had spotted someone she remembered meeting at the British embassy (it was the caterer, I think); before I could collect my wits she'd tooted off. "Those lucky middies," sighed the Senator. He was flirting out of knee-jerk instinct, even I knew that; but it was pleasant, and I didn't mind the sudden status. "I never thought I'd meet a senator today," I flirted back, figuring he'd set the ground rules, so why not. Suddenly I caught a flash of something tall and pink, wavering near a rose-encumbered arbor like a column of pale ribbon. I called, "Hello, Mrs. Merceau."

The senator spun round, "Adele?"

She was posed against a backdrop of enormous blossoms, great, heavy petaled blooms, some as big as peonies, ivory and salmon pink and dusky coral, and deep bloodlike garnet exuding winey scents. She looked frail against that opulence and pallid in comparison. "Get me a drink, Tom, would you? Anything with ice. Ginger ale. A Coke."

"My pleasure." He left us with a little bow and headed for the crowd around the beverage table. Halfway there, a group of parents intercepted him. He stood surrounded, flashing his dimpled smile and shaking hands.

Adele complained, "It'll take him half an hour to get away."

There was a big old drowsy bumblebee suspended in the air between us, the sleepy black-and-yellow kind that people claim don't sting, though I wouldn't want to put it to the test. For a time it simply hung there, like something drunk and dopey. Carefully, I skirted it and drew close to Adele. I asked, "Shall I get your drink?"

"No. Stay with me." She sought my hand. "I feel so woozy."

"Do you want to sit down?"

"I want to lie down. Will you help me get upstairs?" The sweater was half off her shoulders. Gently, I rearranged it, pulling it round her like a cape.

"Sure I will." Instinctively, I grasped her arm under the elbow and began to steer her toward the French doors of the living room. There were throngs of students and their parents everywhere, barring the way. I hesitated. "I think it's easier going through the kitchen, less of a mob." I could feel her leaning heavily against me, stumbling a little as we walked to the rear entry. She was wearing some gorgeous perfume, heavy and sweet, like the winey fragrance of the roses. It seemed to hover all around us as we moved, a cloud of flowers. I asked her, "Can you manage the back stairs?"

"The stairs?" Adele said dreamily. "Oh, I don't know. It's just a bother, isn't it?"

The uncarpeted back stairway was a tactical mistake I knew right off, because Adele was staggering and needed traction underfoot. Haltingly, we ascended, with me warning, "Careful. Do be careful," and Adele bending toward my face as though she meant to read my lips. Each step posed a challenge. She'd lift a pink-shod foot and plant it firmly, pause to catch her breath, then hoist the second foot up slowly as though her shoes were made of lead. She had surprisingly large feet, long and very narrow in pink linen pumps. When we had made it to the second floor she said, "Hurrah," and swayed so hard against me, I thought I'd lose my balance and we'd go tumbling to our deaths together. "Isn't this terrible?" she asked, with all her weight against me.

"Do you want to rest for a minute, Mrs. Merceau?"

"Oh, I just want to go to bed." She sounded like a little girl.

I'd toured the house before when Buddy's parents weren't home—the weight room and the whirlpool bath and the master bedroom with its fireplace and double walk-in closets and one startling mirrored wall that suddenly reflected me and frail Adele, making our way across the soft beige island of the rug. I got her sitting on the bed; then I stood waiting for further directions.

"Help me take my clothes off, would you?" The pink sweater had fallen to the floor.

"Of course." I waited till she'd kicked off the pink shoes. Then I reached behind her to unzip her zipper. She hunched her shoulders in a kind of shiver, and her dress slipped to her hips. I helped her stand till I could ease it down her legs, which were long and tanned and bare of stockings. She had pretty painted toes; on one ankle she wore a fine gold ankle bracelet, which struck me as the sexiest thing I'd ever seen. When the dress was off I laid it out upon a chaise as though it was some residue of flesh, a featureless pink corpse. It was already pretty wrinkled. "Shall I turn down your spread?"

Adele had settled back upon the bed, half reclining like a skinny odalisque, shivering in nothing but a satin camisole and lacey panties. No bra, her breasts so high and firm, they needed no support; I sensed the doctor's handiwork in that, and blushed ferocious scarlet, to be thinking of such things. "Yes, please, get me under the covers," Adele had said. "It's cold in here. He keeps the place too cold."

To turn the spread I had to get her to stand up again. Again, she leaned against me, and I was shocked by how fragile she seemed—nothing but brittle bones, as though the pink linen had concealed a skeleton. Her topknot had come loose during our struggle up the stairs. With her hair down, she looked older, like an actress in her vintage years masquerading as an ingenue. I helped her stretch out on the bed; I pulled up the lace-edged sheet and a pretty summer coverlet of scalloped green, dappled with perky daisies. "Is there anything else I can do for you, Mrs. Merceau?"

She'd settled her head deep into the pillow with a little sigh and closed her eyes, like a child surrendering to the midday nap. Suddenly she opened her eyes wide. For the first time since we'd met she was eyeing me directly, as though having gotten horizontal, she had shaken off the fog of booze or pills. "You're Buddy's friend, aren't you?"

"Yes ma'am." I fussed over the coverlet and refolded the spread till it lay neatly at the foot of the wide bed. I bent to pick up the sweater. "This is so pretty, Mrs. Merceau." Lovingly, I stroked it. "I'll just put it with your dress."

"Do you like it?" She was sounding spaced-out again.

"It's gorgeous."

"Take it as my gift."

"Oh, no. I couldn't."

"Take it. I want you to have it. Really . . ." She had burrowed deep under the covers. Only her face showed, the stiff, beautiful mask, dull-eyed and sleepy. She seemed to have already forgotten who I was. "You saved me . . . from keeling over in the bushes. So take it . . ."

It was so soft and smooth to the touch, so fluid and almost silky, like something alive, like some mythical pink animal, all gentle warmth and fluff. "Well, I sure do thank you. I never expected, in all my life, to own anything like this."

". . . 's my way of saying . . . thanks. Thanks for helping me." She had closed her eyes again. I sensed I was dismissed, but I didn't want to leave. It seemed so magical and different there, the heady perfumed air around Adele, her golden hair spread on the pillow like the tresses of a sleepy princess, the pale rug underfoot, even the jumble of enameled pillboxes strewn on the bedside table seemed lovely and exotic. "If there's nothing else that I can do, I guess I'll go downstairs."

She answered with a yawn and another deep burrowing movement as though she longed to lose herself between the sheets.

"Thanks again for the lovely sweater."

"Hey." I was treading gingerly, as though leaving the presence of an invalid, when Mrs. Merceau startled me by calling out. I thought she'd changed her mind about the sweater. "Hey," she cried. "What's your name?"

"Linda Jo Burke." I'd reverted to my middle name out of confusion, I suppose. Returning to her bedside, I held out the cashmere sweater.

She shook her head with obvious impatience, annoyed that I could be so dense. "Linda Jo, if you see Tom Crimmons, tell him to bring my drink up here."

"I don't . . . I'm not sure I . . ."

"Tell him to bring the drink up to my bedroom. Okay?"

"Well, sure. I surely will."

"Don't tell anybody else." From her lacey perfumed burrow there emerged a childlike giggle.

"All right." I left there in a daze, clutching the silky sweater to my breast. A flowery fragrance rose from it, as though Adele had plucked it from the rose-filled garden before bestowing it on me.

A mourning dove is cooing near the bushes, a somber low-pitched song—perfect expression of my mood. A mild breeze bears the scent of marigolds, astringent, almost chemical. Monroe, the houseman, who never liked me one iota, had Paulie planting flowers here one autumn—daffodils and tulip bulbs. I don't know if they ever blossomed. Today, if Monroe sees me, he'll fling dark daggers at me with his eyes and step around me as though I carry a dread plague. Not the ideal ambience for conversation.

Too much rides on this. Feeling butterflies, I mount the stairs. A lion-headed knocker, heavy brass, has been polished to a high luster. If I grasp it I'll mar the shine and Monroe will have a hissy fit. Steeling myself, I rap twice, sharply. I haven't phoned ahead, fearing Buddy's mom would pull a disappearing act if given ample warning. I know the doctor takes off early, so it will be Adele and me, she, rosy from sleep and fragrant from her shower, her long, lank hair pinned carelessly. Counting on the value of surprise, on what I must believe is her humanity, I mean to pull out all the stops: Do you have any love for little Paulie? Do you appreciate how badly we've been treated by your son?

No one answers my knock. Paranoid, I think they've seen me from an upstairs window and are pretending no one's home. This time I ring the bell; the shrill, peremptory blare startles me, like the bells that go off in the hospital for no apparent reason.

Juanita, finally stable, is in Coronary Care, a semiprivate room, where she sits propped up in bed like a stuffed doll, afraid to move lest she upset the rhythm of her heart. Greeley recommends a bypass operation, but Juanita says, "No way. You ever count how many people die just from the anesthesia?" She's stuck there, gray and tiny, oxygen lines feeding through her nostrils like the fangs of a Komodo dragon. The bills are mounting out of sight, and there's no one to offer help but Monte. I knock again, this time, an angry hammering.

"Keep your shirt on, will ya?" That's not Monroe's grim-lipped courtesy. The door opens and I blink adjusting from bright

sun to softer shadows and there stands Buddy, in blue silk pajamas, rubbing sleep out of his eyes with tight bunched fists, as
Paulie does. "Linda!" His look implies astonishment that I exist.

Oh God, I don't believe it. My heart is pounding like the first
morning we ever met, a mix of fury and some sense that I've been
had. "Hello, Buddy," I manage to say calmly. "This must be my
lucky day."

"Linda, I was gonna call you. Honest. I got in late last night.
On the red-eye. Too late to phone."

"That was real considerate of you, Buddy." Anger has me
almost paralyzed.

Buddy flicks a palm through the blond thatch of his hair.
He's cut it short, almost a crew cut, and the sun has bleached it
brassy gold. His normally fair skin has darkened to the shade of
honey. He looks like a model for Boston Traders. "What are you
doin' here?"

"I could ask you the same."

"Linda, we need to talk. How's Paulie? Franklin? Everybody?"

He makes no move to ask me in. I'm stuck on the front step
taking in his peachy tan, his shiny silk pj's, like he's a rock star
and I'm a humble groupie hoping to grab his sweaty handkerchief. "Paulie hasn't said your name since you walked out. Franklin is the same as always. Juanita had a heart attack and is in the
hospital, over at Suburban."

"Your mother! I don't believe it! Your mother weighs ninety
pounds soakin' wet, and exercises every day, and hasn't had a bite
of meat in fifteen years!"

Besides that, she's not that old. Does he think I don't repeat
the whole depressing litany, every day? "I only give the news; I
don't interpret it."

"Still the same smart mouth."

"That's right. So, up yours, Buddy!" I'd planned to beg Adele
for his address. Now that we're face-to-face I want only to run

back to the shelter of my car (not the spiffy red Camaro Buddy drove when we got married, but a practical Chevette with thirty payments left on it that Buddy stuck me with; it will die before I own it free and clear). I leave him gaping in the doorway and head back down the walk, running, wanting only to escape the place. I was never welcome here. The first time Buddy brought me to this house I said the place looked like a dormitory in some snobby girls' school. Imposing, and off limits to commoners.

"Hey, Linda, wait. Don't run away."

Ignoring him, I scramble for the car. He's following behind me, yelling, "Wait," barefoot and in pajamas. We must be an amusing sight to the morning dog-walkers and joggers; me tottering in heels down the front walk; and Buddy in his elegant pajamas, striding in pursuit. If Doc Merceau were home, he'd have a proper fit, worrying what the neighbors would think. I make it to my car, but Buddy is right behind me. Before I have the wit to hit the locks, he scurries to the passenger side, yanks open the door, and dives onto the seat beside me. "Okay." He's out of breath. "Just calm down, will you. We have to talk. You know that."

We never had that much to say. Our marriage finished the Great Argument, which was, would we do it without benefit of wedlock; and if so, where and when; and if not, why not; and did I have an inkling of the pain, emotional and physical, that I was causing? Our honeymoon at his parents' summer place in Deep Creek Lake solved that. ("The most awaited consummation since *Pamela,*" Franklin said later, the self-satisfied wit showing off his erudition.) In a less literary vein, say that Buddy, the conquering quarterback fumbled at the start, then, having finally scored, grunted, "That's it," and settled on his back, snoring; while I, not sure of what, if anything, had happened beyond a sudden mean invasion of my body, got up and wrapped myself in Buddy's mother's white terry-cloth robe (still thick with her cloying perfume) and locked myself in the john. Settling on the hard edge of the quaint, claw-footed tub, I thought, ooh boy, ooh boy, let's just examine this. Let's figure out what you have done and how best to cope with it.

"Get out," I say through tight-clenched teeth, terrified that, if I give an inch, I'll start to wail like an abandoned baby. "I'm late for work. And I can't get fired, Buddy. You left me with too many bills."

"I know it." He starts to pound the dashboard with his fists. "I'm a shit. But I was desperate, Linda. Just that desperate. Can I at least beg your forgiveness?"

"Sure. Beg."

"Ah, Linda. Don't be bitter."

"Get out of the car, and I'll spare you."

"I can't. Because I love you so much, Linda Jo. I never stopped."

"Yeah? Well, *I've* stopped, Buddy. Quite frankly, after all this time, you don't exist for me. Put that in your pipe and smoke it."

"I don't blame you. I deserve it." Buddy sighs and stops hitting the dash. Folding his arms across his chest, he eyes me with a look of profound sadness. He makes no move to leave the car.

I warn him, "Get out, or I will blow the horn until your neighbors get upset and call the cops."

"I won't. You came here looking for me, didn't you? Well, here I am."

"I came here looking for your mother, hoping for a handout, if the truth be known."

"I don't believe that, Linda. I know you far too well."

"You knew some stupid kid you married. Not the person who's been coping for a damn long time without you. I've changed, Buddy. I'm a real hard cookie now, all thanks to you." I've had drinks with scraggly compañeros. I've fooled around with Reece, just a hair's breadth north of kinky. I've dreamed of Tasso's lovemaking. I'm no longer an innocent, thanks to my dear husband, Buddy, who left to find himself on the sun-drenched

130

beaches of Southern California. "You abused my trust, Buddy. That's bad enough, but you also left us almost destitute . . ."

"I took half our joint account. I left the car!"

". . . almost destitute! But what I really can't forgive is, you reneged on all your promises. And you abandoned Paulie."

"I know, Linda. I know. You think seeing you this way is easy? And finding out on top of everything else that Juanita's sick. I feel so bad. Listen, is she gonna make it?"

"I wouldn't know."

"Is Franklin any help to you?"

"No more than you. Just leave Franklin out of this, okay?"

"I'd really like to talk to him. Franklin and I always got along."

"Talk to my lawyer first."

"And Paulie. I've got a right to see my son . . ."

"You have no rights! You damn well better understand that!"

"Will you listen to me, Linda Jo. I want to help. It's awful news about Juanita. At least, let my dad look in on her. Let him recommend a specialist."

"I've got someone Cal Fowler recommended."

"Is he any good?"

"I don't know if he's any good or not. He's tall."

"Jee-suz," Buddy scowls. "You just don't change."

That tears it. I press down on the horn and let 'er rip; a long shrill shriek pierces the early morning calm. Soon shades angle discreetly; a storm door wobbles open. Stout walkers with golden dogs pause on their strolls through fallen leaves to see what's going on.

Buddy says, "Quit that," and grabs my arm.

The next thing I know we're tussling in the seat, almost like the old days when we wrestled out of passion, not knowing where to light, how to fit our lips, our legs, our arms, how to cope with all that wanting and preserve our precious virtues—both of us, Victorians. Buddy has a grip on both my wrists. I duck and butt my head into his chest. He drops my hands and moans, "Oof," as the breath goes out of him.

I warn him, "Don't touch me again."

I must have got him good. He's rubbing his palm gingerly over his chest. "There's no reasoning with you when you're like this. You always had to fight me, didn't you?"

"Get out!"

"I will. But I'm coming to see you when you're calmer."

"I can hardly wait."

"Are you still in the apartment?"

"None of your business, Buddy."

"Are you staying at your mother's?"

"That's for me to know and for you to wonder."

"I can find out easy enough, Linda Jo."

"Don't go to any trouble on my account." I watch him as he clambers from the car, a good-looking blond guy, sturdier than Reece, but not as handsome, not the sexy stud I thought I loved in high school. That's when I should have given in. We should have coupled on the seat of his Camaro and gotten that part over with and lived our lives, because the solution we contrived was pure disaster. The first day of our marriage I was sure of that.

That morning of our honeymoon, I went out for a swim while Buddy was still sleeping. The sun was not up yet—the sky, a pearly gray with pink streaks brightening the nearby mountains. The water in the lake felt glacial, tickly with silver minnows near the pier and the slippery feel of algae at the shore. I'd headed for the raft, swimming fast to get the warm blood pumping, and thinking as I stroked, "I am Mrs. Burton Paul Merceau III, I am Linda Jo Merceau. Mrs. Linda Merceau. Linda Burke Merceau. Nice to see you . . . nice to see you . . . nice to see you." By the time I reached the raft my fingertips were numb and my legs were tingling like they'd been pricked through with tiny needles. I climbed onto the raft and stretched out on the slippery planks, water roaring in my ears and my body slick and oily-feeling from the lake. The sun rising in the pinkish east was suddenly welcoming and hot. I closed my eyes and slept for maybe an hour or more. When I woke up I felt stiff and burned but somehow riven clean and freed of the depression of the night before. A breeze stirred tiny ripples in the lake. The sun gleamed like pale fire. I struck back to the pier determined to cook Buddy a super breakfast with whatever was on hand and start out fresh and optimistic.

When I got into the house I found he was awake, talking on the phone and giggling. He had a towel around his waist and he looked skinny and young. "Oh, man, it was something. Let me tell you, it was far-out." He blushed red when he saw me standing dripping in my suit, my hair a dark Medusa tangle on my neck. "Hey, man, I gotta split. The little woman's here." He'd hung up, looking embarrassed. When I asked him who that was, he answered, "No one. I just felt like calling up the guys." "You felt like calling? On our honeymoon?" "Yeah." The look I knew: I am Burton Paul Merceau, and I do what I damn well please. "So sue me for that." He'd stalked into the john and left me to mull that over, standing barefoot in the master bedroom of his parents' summer house. There were wide uncurtained windows facing the lake and the sun was streaming in and I was dripping fishy water on the sisal rug, thinking, he's a fool. We're damn fools both of us. Ooh boy, for this; Linda Jo, for this, you've ruined your life.

Nine

A sheaf of gladiola, waxy pink. No floral scent discernible. No softening ferns. Even with the thick stalks trimmed—I've cut them on a slant as Ma has taught me—they're too tall for the vase. I hate the look of these, the blossoms' salmon pallor, the stiff array that makes me think of dull concerts and funerals. The bouquet came to the house this morning. The card from Reece was terse: "You're in my thoughts."

Juanita says, "Nice flowers. Who sent 'em?"

"Reece Cooper. He hopes you get well soon."

"The candy man?" Sliding lower on the tilted mattress, Juanita shuts her eyes. She's wearing a blue satin bed jacket adorned with ivory lace, a present from her sister Viv. Lace frills at the collar and the sleeves and bands of lace over the bosom. Blue satin fastenings. I've never seen anything like it, except in movies. I thought such items were passé, relics of a time women idled on chaises longues and got their mail on silver salvers. Viv who is the same tense, fisheyed type as Ma, doesn't lead that kind of life. "You still seein' Mr. Goodbar?" Mama asks.

"Ma, I'm not seeing anyone right now." I place the flowers on the windowsill where Ma's roommate can enjoy them. An old woman, maybe ninety, with beautiful white hair and frantic, coal-dark eyes, she watches us in fascinated silence, as though we were actors in a play cast for her entertainment. She doesn't talk to me or Ma (I've never heard her speak), but her eyes track our movements, noting and recording. Her daughter, who is older than Juanita, says her mother likes me because I am considerate.

This setup is so out of whack: the woman's daughter, older than my mother; Ma, grumpy as a child; me, fussy and maternal, bearing packets of clean laundry, gifts of talcum and tall flowers. Juanita says her roommate moans at night, and the sound gives her the willies, but Ma doesn't want the curtain drawn between them.

With no protection from the other woman's scrutiny, I flutter at the foot of Ma's raised bed projecting phony cheer. Big, sappy smile. "How're you feeling, Ma?"

"How should I feel? The food tastes like glue. They want me out of bed, up in the chair. Doesn't anybody know I almost died?"

"But you're getting better now."

"Says who?"

"They moved you to this room because you're so much better."

"Horsefeathers! They moved me to this room because they were running out of space in ICU."

"Oh, Ma, they wouldn't do that. Look at you. You're so much stronger. You even sound like your old self."

"A lot you know! A lot you knew the night we came here. They told you I was fine, but I knew better. Like I know now." She beckons me closer so she can talk in a stage whisper that is loud enough to hear out in the hall. "Look at her, Mrs. Foley. She's got great-grandchildren. For her to be here, that's a shame, but at her age maybe you expect it. But me? I'm fifty-five. Why am I here?"

"The doctor says it's just a bad throw of the dice." Greeley calls her trouble myocardial ischemia—blood doesn't travel freely to the heart. He says the problem might be linked to stress. He thinks Ma had other "silent episodes" before that bad one in the pool.

"Bull crap!"

"Ma, don't excite yourself. It isn't good for you."

She mimics me. "It isn't good for you. What am I supposed to do? Lie here like a dud? Not think or speak? Like her?"

"Please, Ma. She hears every word you're saying."

"Believe me, she agrees. I see it in her eyes." Ma bends toward the adjacent bed. "Isn't that right, Mrs. Foley?" She speaks in an exaggerated falsetto, the tone you'd take with a small child. Mrs. Foley stares at her unblinking, seemingly stupefied with awe. Ma says with some degree of satisfaction, "She likes having me here. I give her something to watch. It's not as boring as it was before."

"Who told you that?"

"Nobody has to tell me. When people are as sick as us, we can just tell. There's something . . . a connection. We're on the same wavelength because we're dying."

"Ma, please! You're going to scare her. And you're not dying. *You're not!*"

"At her age you don't get scared." Ma says this with a kind of relish as though she's stumbled onto a wondrous truth. Just hang on long enough to reach great age and then grab your consolation prize—a sweet, rattly-toothed serenity, a benign way to look at death, sharp-eyed, with something like ferocious interest. Ma's words imply some bargaining with fate: Just let me live and I'll get brave, even take a flier into optimism. She asks me suddenly, "Is my son coming to see me once before I die?"

"Oh, Ma. Please don't expect it."

"Just once. I want to talk with him."

"You can talk with him. You can get phone calls now."

"To his face."

"Maybe when you get home . . ."

"Before I die!"

"I told you, didn't I, that Buddy's back? He's staying at his parents' house. Boy, that was some surprise."

"Before I *die!*"

"Oh, Ma!"

She gets a pincer hold upon my arm and squeezes. The strength she shows surprises me. "I know you blame me for the way Franklin is. I know it."

I'm thinking to myself, you bet I do. You kept him where you wanted him, your precious firstborn prince. Free of imagined dangers. No motorcycle wrecks for Franklin. No drug OD's. You kept his laundry starched, his diet fresh, his sex life nonexistent, no fear of prostitutes or forced elopements in our Franklin's life. You kept him clear of life, rooted to one spot, like a hot house plant. And now, when all you crave is seeing him before you die, and all *he* knows is shame and guilt and terminal embarrassment, he cannot budge. What *I* would love to know is why he is so special, and not me? Why don't I rate the same protection?

"Your Pop and I . . . both of us tried. That counselor who came. House visits. Don't you think they cost a bundle? You remember that?"

"Sure I do. Beryl Blackwell. Bouncy Beryl." She had this bone-straight, brownish hair shaped in a soup-bowl cut and a smile so firm she could have been a hopped-up Mona Lisa, spilling with some secret joy. She oozed the phony cheer you find in volunteers who work amid the dying.

"She still with them?" asks Ma. "That rip-off joint?"

"I wouldn't know." Ma found this place called New Behaviors that guaranteed success with phobics through counseling and conditioning. After Ma checked them out, she came home with her eyes agleam, thrilled to know she'd stumbled on a host of kindred, craven spirits—people scared of everything: snakes, crowds, heights, planes, spiders, all of the above.

Beryl arrived three times a week to work with Franklin. She played him tapes of frightening sounds—planes flying, car horns blaring, trains chugging at great speeds—and when he tired of hearing those, they vanished to his room for conversation. He said they talked about her failed romances, or they played backgammon or Chinese checkers. Beryl said that she was building trust. Franklin believed Beryl had the hots for him. She'd given him her home address and her home phone number. If he had problems, he was free to call her day or night. She spoke of having him to dinner at her place, when he was brave enough. She often did that for her clients; they became good chums.

One day Beryl said Franklin was ready to venture out. Just a bus ride down Wisconsin Avenue and back, with Beryl riding shotgun. "Not a long journey at all," Beryl promised. "Baby steps."

Franklin said he'd do it, only if I came along, which flattered me, till he confessed he wanted me as chaperone. He said Beryl had voracious eyes, and she'd make inroads on his virtue given the chance. She had a way of prodding with a knee, or poking with an elbow—nudging, holding, touching, bolstering with a hand firm on his arm. Her lips preached escape, but her eyes dreamed of encirclement, Franklin averred.

We set out on a balmy Saturday, the false warmth of a January thaw. We trooped aboard the bus with Beryl in the lead, Franklin next, and me, guarding the rear, entrusted with Beryl's secret weapon, a paper bag. Beryl had explained, "When Franklin gets tense, he hyperventilates. If he exhales into the bag, and then inhales, he'll find it calms him. His heart beat will slow down, and he'll be fine." I don't think Franklin bought it, but he played along.

It turned out that the bus was pretty crowded. Franklin and I got seats at right angles to the driver. Beryl got stuck clinging to a pole and issuing directives, smiling that steely smile. Seated across from me and Franklin was a motherly black woman and two mean-looking boys in Fila shirts who kept looking at Franklin like he was a freak. He'd turned ashen by then. I could hear him breathing loud and fast. We drove at a good clip, past the Hot Shoppes Cafeteria and The Gap, Woodward & Lothrop, and the stores at Mazza Gallerie. Beryl kept cooing, "Lovely," every time we made it to another corner. Franklin was trembling hard enough to shake the seat.

As the bus took on new passengers, Beryl got shunted to the back. Franklin asked to see Beryl's magic talisman. "The bag?"

I called to Beryl over the crush of standees. "Can he breathe into the bag now?"

"Surely, if he wishes to."

"Not yet." Franklin waved me off and closed his eyes.

We'd tooled past the Cinema Theater and were just passing Discount Drugs when Franklin nudged me with his arm. I asked, "You want it now?"

"Get me off here. I'm gonna vomit."

I shoved the bag into his hand. "Let's go." I was on my feet, elbowing the people looming over us so they'd give us room to bolt. I had Franklin by the hand and was pulling him behind me. I told the driver, "Let us off."

"Can't," the idiot told me. "This is an express."

"My brother's sick."

"This is the T-6; it's an express. It doesn't stop here."

"Do you want him to throw up all over your bus?"

"Let the dude off, man," one of the kids who'd been observing us helped out, and the woman seated near him seconded the motion, "You let that child off now!"

"Look, folks, we got rules," the driver protested; but then, thinking better of it, he stopped the bus with a suddenness that sent the standees falling forward. I heard Beryl call, "Franklin! Do not leave this bus! Franklin, I insist. Franklin, Linda . . . wait for meee."

I pulled Franklin down the steps and out the folding door. We made it to the street before Beryl could struggle to the exit. The bus took off in a puff of black exhaust that left us coughing. I urged Franklin, "Breathe into your bag." He crumpled it and threw it in the gutter. "Just get me out of here, before that driver lets her off," he begged. I told him, "It's okay. It's an express. That guy won't stop until he hits Mass. Avenue." Franklin had doubled over. "Oh God, Linda, go find that bag. I just can't breathe." "You can't use it now," I said. "It's full of germs." "Linda," he groaned. "I'm gonna die." "Not here," I warned, "or *I'll* die of embarrassment." At that moment I pitied him; and yet, I took odd pleasure in his fear, my payback for childhood tortures. There's a mean streak paramount in both of us; it's the fallout that derives from cowardice.

I phoned Pop to pick us up at Discount Drugs. It seemed he took forever to get there. Franklin was fading in the drugstore entry, moaning that his death was imminent. Meanwhile, I pretended to be studying a window full of home health aids: Ace bandages, walkers, commodes, fascinating stuff. Later that afternoon, Ma called New Behaviors to say she had a problem with their methods, and that their Ms. Blackwell was a dud. We didn't hear from Beryl again, though I suspect she added Franklin to her list of failures. He talks of her, sometimes with malice, sometimes with what could be a guilty conscience. I don't know what transpired in his bedroom, but Ma suspected it was hanky-panky.

"We tried, didn't we?" Ma asks.

"You did." I've pulled two nightgowns from her dresser drawer. "I'll take these home to wash and bring 'em back tomorrow. Do you want me to brush your hair?"

She shakes her head, no, closes her eyes. Two perfect tears, shiny as crystal, start a slow trail down her cheeks. I've rarely seen her cry. Even when Pop got hurt and was rushed, dying, to the hospital, her face assumed a masklike hauteur till it was clear there was no hope. And then all she'd permit herself was a single strangled "Oh" of grief, like the soft mew of a cat abandoned.

"I'm hungry," Ma complains. "I'm craving all this stuff I shouldn't have. Rare roast beef, whipped cream cake."

"You never eat that kind of food."

"I know. But I want it now. Couldn't you smuggle something in for me, Linda Jo? A milk shake, maybe?"

"I don't think I should."

"Franklin would do it if I asked. You know he would."

"I doubt it, Ma."

She turns her head from side to side as though buffeted by disappointment. "Oh, why won't you *make* him come to see me?" Agitated by what's she's overhearing, Mrs. Foley looks from Ma to me and back to Ma. Her hands move to her hair; then they flutter helpless to her sides. Ma opens her eyes. "Know what I want? There was this bakery during the war. In Jersey City. They baked cakes with ersatz cream, ersatz chocolate. Victory Cakes, they called 'em. They tasted wonderful. Everything tastes wonderful when you're a kid."

"Did you know Pop then?" I know their histories, of course, but it's better to get her thinking of the past. It seems to calm her.

"I met him at the Jersey Shore, at the dance pavilion on the Belmar Boardwalk. The rat races, we used to call it, 'cause the girls would line up on one side, and the guys would come to look us over. A rat race it was, too. I was only fifteen, your Pop was nineteen and in the army. Way too old for me in every way. But

141

he was sweet. He used to hog the jukebox playing this one song over and over. Carmen Cavallaro at the piano playing the Chopin 'Polonaise.' They made a pop song out of it, 'Till the End of Time.' The end of time . . ." Ma's crying again.

I've stuffed her nightgowns in a shopping bag and set it on the floor beside her bed. I take her hand. "Did you hear what I told you before? Buddy's back. Living with his parents like he's still their baby boy. You could've knocked me over with a feather when I saw him."

"It nearly broke Pop's heart and mine when you dropped out of college. You were smart, just as smart as Franklin. You talked earlier than he did, you know?"

"You never told me that."

Ma, peering at me sharply, could suddenly be Mrs. Foley's twin. "What's with the candy man? He throw you over?"

"Things are on hold, sort of."

Ma nods wisely. "They will be, too. He's a fair-weather lover, wait and see. Buddy's the opposite. He likes a crisis, 'cause it makes him feel important. When things get routine, boring, he falls apart. Watch out, 'cause he'll cut out again."

I force a laugh. "How did you get so worldly wise, Juanita?"

"I wouldn't trust a man named for a piece of candy." With her free hand she beats time upon the bed. She commences humming to the rhythm. *"Dum* de dum. Da Da *dum* de dum de dum. The 'Polonaise' was real dramatic. That's the one Pop liked. Would you believe he was light on his feet? After we moved down here—his army buddy talked him into coming—he was always looking for the big-name bands."

It's inconceivable they danced together. I can't imagine Ma, moving to the rhythms of the Spanish Ballroom (the orchestra replete with fiddles), her hair piled in a pompadour, pinpoints of crystal shining in her ears, a silky blouse, a short flared skirt lifting to show some thigh. But they must have done the steps, must have moved in synch, hips wiggling to the Latin beat, toes tapping on the slick wood floor, bobbing and dipping through arcs of light, columns of smoke and silver dust. "I think I let you talk too much, Juanita. You're tired, yes?"

Her eyelids flutter in assent. She dozes for a moment, stirs, unhappy to be trapped in sleep before making a final point. "Don't let 'em screw you over. Buddy. Reece. Too good for 'em, you are."

"I won't."

"You and Franklin . . . Fast-Track Kids . . ." She is out of it.

In the bed beside the window, Mrs. Foley watches, her eyes bright as black diamonds. Ma's grip tightens on my hand. She pipes up suddenly. "No bypass. Absolutely not!" She is floating in some dreadful limbo, a persistent, frightening dream.

I sit there for a time holding her hand, pondering the little that I know about my mother. Juanita Kirby Burke. Christened Juanita by her parents after the title of a song they sang ("Nee-ta, Juan-eeta") when they were courting. Ma once confessed she would have liked a plainer name, Barbara or Jane, something that didn't sound as though she were "a gun moll for Zapata." She said that without smiling.

Pop told us she was always wound up tight, but turned worse after having children, viewing our bruises and our bumps—cut lips and such—as portents of apocalypse. Although she hovered over both of us, Franklin got the brunt of her attention. When he was small he'd had convulsions from a fever, and Aunt Viv, who was on her annual visit, popped him in a cooling bath that brought his temperature to normal. Ma believed that Viv had saved his life, and though she blessed Viv for acting quickly, Mama resented her for usurping a mother's role. *She* should have been Franklin's savior, not Viv. After that scare, Juanita never let up vigilance. Too much was at stake. If she lost Franklin to illness or accident, she lost her heart.

143

He grew up clever, talented, amusing—the cure for any disappointment she might have in Pop, whose silences or gentle silliness did not bolster her feeling of security. Where Pop was whimsical, Franklin was practical. Where Pop was taciturn, Franklin was glib. Where setbacks in our lives incurred daydreaming in Pop, or meek retreat, Franklin's response to trouble was swift, reasoned, intelligent. Ma dreamed he'd be a lawyer, or a scientist, an architect, perhaps—he had that flair for drawing.

Poor Franklin—bogged down by the weight of Mama's expectations. So many of her hopes were riding on him. Suppose he failed? If he chose the wrong profession, or married the wrong girl, or skidded on a bridge, or drove into a barrier on the Beltway —if he got drafted, wounded, poisoned, conned, seduced, however would he square it with Juanita, his most faithful fan, professing caution as she urged him to accomplishments?

There must have been a choice point in his life, when he felt the first cold thrust of fear rending his gut—terror that clobbered him, choked off his breath, blinded his eyes, left him nauseated, dizzy, more frightened of the feelings fear produced than any of the perils in Ma's lexicon. He grew quiet and couldn't make decisions. He wouldn't see his friends. Professing to be studying, he vanished to his room, for hours, Mama said. Sometimes she'd hear him pacing in the night; the noise kept her awake and wondering.

Around the time of his college graduation, when the world with its requirements was looming close, Franklin stalled, dug in his heels, refused to budge, refused to try; thus, he never courted danger, failure, disappointment. That's *my* interpretation of his illness. The latest wisdom claims the cause is biochemical, which pokes holes in my theories and lets Ma off the hook.

The most she asked of me was that I stay virtuous until I married. She warned of the duplicity in men; she said for all their jolliness and charm, they were programmed by their natures to exploit foolish young girls. She hinted at a darker side in Pop—I can't imagine what, unless it touched on her belief he'd been unfaithful. On their good days they were brisk and kind of pals-y with each other. On their bad days she would glare, unspoken horrors, and he'd retreat to busy work; we'd feel something, a dizzying stir of tension in the air, a heaviness, like storms breeding in the distant atmosphere. She'd mull, tight-lipped and locked into her thoughts, till Franklin broke the silence with a joke or some meandering anecdote. Sometimes I'd come home late from dates to find them yakking at the kitchen table; Franklin would be sitting with his chin cupped in his palm, absorbing Mama's stories like a talk show host, adept at gleaning secrets. Pop would have been long asleep.

She rarely spoke of sex to me except to cite it as a danger. She'd have stayed tight-lipped through torture before admitting she and Pop were "intimate" for any purpose other than conceiving children. She values privacy, restraint, decorum, dislikes the city pool at times because of women in the locker room who "strut around and show it all," down to their appendix scars.

All her lectures on modesty and ladylike comportment left their marks on me, Buddy was quick to say. I want to prove him wrong, but in fairness I concede he has a point. All the secret stuff behind the turquoise curtain, the whispers over supine forms, the clients stifling sobs, hinted there was something shameful in preoccupation with the flesh. One could hardly grow up joyous, free of guilt, with Mama as a mentor. She's an odd model of motherhood—efficient, gloomy, wise, short-tempered, cold, funny without knowing it sometimes. The one consistent feeling I experience in her presence is confusion; she's a priestess of paradox who stirs up warring sentiments in me: anger and compassion, affection and disdain. I love her and dislike her. I want her to love me. I crave her admiration more than anything. I long to separate myself from her, once and for all. If I lose her, I never will get over it.

Ten

Reece may be a fair-weather lover, as Ma says, but I believe he cares for me; I know it for a fact, because presents have been arriving. After the gladiola, a music box, lacquered in red and etched with golden scrolls. The box stands on little legs like the tiny, fancy proppings of a toy piano. When you lift the lid you hear the notes of "Lara's Theme." The card enclosed is printed with the first words of the lyric: "Somewhere, my love . . ."

Gifts come to the office; I think Reece must have guessed Franklin won't open the door if he sees a stranger knocking. The day after the music box, a bunch of foil balloons arrives, shaped like hearts and stars. For a time they waft over my desk like missiles blown offtrack. Then Fowler says they are inappropriate in a business setting, so I haul them down and stash them in my car. It's a rough ride home with balloons drifting at my back, impeding my rearview vision. When I stop or turn a corner sharply, they dance and bob in slow motion, and other drivers drawing up beside me turn and stare as though glimpsing unseemly acts.

The next present is a box of Austrian candies, luscious chocolates, rich as Sacher tortes, wrapped in golden papers printed with the face of Mozart. When I hand a chocolate treat to Fowler he unwraps it with a frown, then asks (blinking at the first tentative bite like one expecting to be poisoned), "Do you have a new boyfriend, Linda Jo?" I tell him, no, just someone who is sympathetic because my mother is so ill.

Gifts come with the morning mail. A string of hand-carved beads, rough spheres of wood clunking on my neck like the dowry of a native princess. A crystal flacon of perfume shaped like a bird. When I dab drops behind my ears the fragrance rises in a cloud of jungle scent, jasmine, I think. Fowler opens windows, fans the air.

He is a tall man with a wrestler's torso, thick graying hair, a handsome face gone jowly. He's assured me he'll be patient with my shifting schedule, as long as I can meet his strict requirements. His out box must be kept empty of paper, files cleared in a wink, quickly scrawled directives acted on ASAP, like military orders. His reference books must stand on a shelf behind his desk, arranged by size, the tallest on the left, the others in descending order, never out of place. His desk lamp must be lit before the stroke of nine, and the desk clock, an antique, must be wound and ticking cheerily when he walks in, or he'll confront me with scowls and a command to set it right. Even if I'm swamped, up to my ears in phone calls and correspondence, he will not wind the clock himself; rote acts, lacking the glamour of a helicopter landing, are not in Fowler's purview.

Times past, I viewed Fowler's eccentricities as harmless quirks. Now, I chafe at his demands, sensing his need to exercise control. Each task, writ clear, like the grim rules of a prison, is a whip over my head. If I bow to Fowler's rules, as I bow to Mama's whims, I won't get dumped.

Sometimes, hooked up to the Dictaphone (like Mama hooked into her life supports) and listening to Fowler's voice spitting out impatient memos, I feel boundless contempt for the coward I've become, fearful of Fowler's anger and hungry for his praise.

Initially, he acts amused at the daily show of goodies, which begin to change from friendly tokens to more pricey stuff. Gloves of lush, expensive leather. A fringed paisley shawl. A pale silk blouse, fastened by tiny buttons and small silk loops. A vest, embroidered with twin birds of paradise, soft spreading feathers on my breast, threads of blue and gold and scarlet like the brush strokes in a painting. A cashmere scarf, dove gray, softer than fur. These arrive with cards marked *R*.

"It would seem that *R* is smitten," Fowler says.

I murmur something noncommittal, my fingers starting hell-for-leather on the keyboard of the new computer (state-of-the-art machine—the software took some time to master, and with all the other business on my mind was not a lead-pipe cinch to learn), to show Fowler I will not be distracted. The other girls take blithe, two-hour lunches and dance aerobics in the conference room, but I, hooked tight to my machines, grab a quick bite at my desk so I can leave promptly at four. Fowler indicates he will be patient so long as the antique clock stays wound, the lamp stays lit, the out box remains empty. He, too, hints at specific gifts. "We thought to add to your responsibilities, give you a title, Office Manager, adjust your salary, of course. But since your situation is so iffy . . ."

"It won't last forever." I offer him my brightest smile, thinking how I'd love the raise.

The girls at work comment that it must be nice—all these guys hovering like planes circling in a holding pattern over National. Monte striving to be indispensable. Buddy, reeling with contrition. Reece, mysterious Reece, who's shelling out a king's ransom in gifts that have piqued my boss's interest. Fowler lingers near my desk to see the most recent arrival, a length of pale green silk, crepe paper–thin, shot through with fine gold threads—something you'd wind around your body like a sari.

Fowler lectures once again about propriety. "Fun's fun, Linda Jo. But there's a time and place."

On my coffee break I phone Reece at the computer store and tell him everything he sent is gorgeous. ("Beautiful! A trip! I should have called you sooner, but there's never time!") Still, he has to stop. "My boss is getting antsy. All those presents coming here, he thinks it's too distracting. Everyone is wondering what's going on." I am too. I add, in a fierce whisper, "I don't know why you're doing this. Maybe we ought to meet and talk about it."

He laughs, ruefully, I think. "It's not that complicated. I know I let you down, and I feel guilty. I've missed our times together," he adds pointedly.

"I've missed them too. Only there's nothing I can do about it now."

"Your circumstances are the same, then?"

It hurts to hear him sound so formal, as though he's taking information from a customer. "Even more complicated than before. Reece, I really need a friendly ear. That lunch we talked about? Could we meet soon? We could find someplace convenient near your store. I don't mind coming into Georgetown, but it would have to be a Saturday."

In the silence that ensues, I imagine he is pondering his calendar, filled with dates with sweet young things who are unfettered by domestic baggage. "Let's do it," he says finally. "That's great." And so we settle time and place and he rings off, sounding relieved, as though the gifts have wrought the magic that he sought. I wonder what he'll say when he hears Buddy is back.

"I suppose I should get lost," he murmurs when I tell him about Buddy. "Give you a chance to work things out."

"No," I say. "Not necessarily." Then, hastening to fill the awkward silence as Reece waits for a fuller explanation, "Gosh, Reece, this food is wonderful. The spring rolls are unbelievable." The restaurant he's picked, in Georgetown, serves Vietnamese cuisine, a mix of French and Oriental he finds intriguing.

The dining room is a converted warehouse, transformed by palest blues and greens and cunningly placed mirrors that give a sense of light and space and cast back images of Reece and me, talking and smiling stiffly as though we'd just met through the Classified. We sit together on a blue banquette. A painting on an adjacent wall shows a tranquil harbor scene, fishing boats and great gray birds skimming the surface of the water. "I like the atmosphere in here. I like that picture." I gesture with my chopsticks toward the painting. "Cormorants, aren't they?"

Reece, mining his store of knowledge, "Yep. They're fabulous fishermen, you know. They dive and then swim underwater till they get their prey and then they bring it back and give it to their keepers. See the bands around their throats; that's to keep 'em from swallowing their catch."

"Interesting. I'll take a little bit more tea, if you don't mind." As Reece refills my cup, I look around, counting the house. There are several modish women sporting smart fall suits and perfect hair. I look okay, I think, in last year's good black skirt and the elegant new blouse Reece bought for me, although one of the buttons at my chest is dangling dangerously. Reece says he should have asked the salesperson to have it sewn. "No, I must have pulled it loose when I was dressing. It's so pretty, I should've been more careful, but I was in a rush."

Reece taps agile fingers on the tabletop, as though beating out a message on his beloved computer. "Linda, what are you gonna do?"

"The usual, I guess. After this, I head out to the hospital."

He sighs as though I've said something profoundly dumb. "What are you gonna do about your husband?" His eyes, metallic green. His hair, the color of cold wine. His skin emits a clean scrubbed minty freshness, scents of soap and after-shave. "Are you going to start divorce proceedings?"

"I saw him for two minutes, and we didn't have what you would call a reasoned conversation. I don't know what to do. That's why I need to talk to you—oh, Reece, look at that baby. Is he adorable?" There's an Oriental family gathered near us at a banquet table—a doll-like wrinkled grandma and her aged spouse, plus assorted younger couples. They are laughing at the antics of a tot who is being passed from lap to lap, accepting adult tribute with a toothless smile. "He's so good-natured, isn't he? If Paulie had ever been that placid in a public place, I'd have fainted. All he ever did in restaurants was whine." As we gaze towards the family, the mother of the baby reclaims her grinning tyke and offers him his bottle. When he takes it in his mouth, the family sits rapt, watching as he swallows, as his eyelids move and flutter like the petals of a flower. "Sweet. So sweet. It must be something in the culture, the way that child responds. The warmth and the security of the extended family."

Reece laughs. "Just hold off on the sociology a second. Are you going to talk things out with Buddy?"

"Yes, I am. But not too soon. I need to calm down first. When I meet with him, I want to be, you know, very composed. Very mature and analytical, very reserved."

"Sounds right up your alley." His smile shows he is teasing.

Still, I feel the blush heating my face. "Oh, don't start that. Just don't. I know you think I'm too uptight. Well, it's the way I was brought up. I led a sheltered life, and I can't do much about it. It's my conditioning. If I'm going to 'be with' someone, I like to think there's something down the road—something more permanent than just fooling around."

Reece selects a spring roll, and dips it into pungent sauce.

Tasting it, he grins with pleasure. Then he leans to me to argue: Can I accept that there are existential pleasures adults can enjoy without probing into motives? We live grounded in the present, don't we, and such factors as anxiety and guilt shouldn't mar the essence of the moment. We are free, he utters softly, in a pointless world, to seize delight, devise our joys from what's at hand. Beyond that, there is nothing. He taps my cheek as though the flesh alone is real, a brief touch, exquisitely tentative and gentle.

"I don't buy that. I can't. Maybe I'm too old-fashioned. Maybe 'old-fashioned' makes sense these days, what with the mess the world is in." Reece shakes his head as though he views me as a hopeless case, then turns back to his lunch.

The baby at the banquet table has given up its bottle and is squirming in its mother's arms. A young man, who must be the father, scoops the baby up and stands, then starts a slow, dancelike circuit of the table, bobbing the infant up and down. The baby coos; the family buzzes with communal joy.

When Paulie was that age I used to stand beside his crib and watch him as he lay upon his back, his skinny arms and legs flailing the air. His face would flush ferocious red, and he would caterwaul discomfort, infant rage. The crying never stopped, whatever ploy I tried. Crazy with the noise and the fatigue of sleepless nights and the awful, lonely dolor of the days, I'd scoop him in my arms, but the sudden movement only startled him. He'd arch his back and holler all the more and Buddy, studying in the other room, or trying to, would yell, "Can't you do anything to quiet him?" I'd holler back, "Can you?" and he'd say he was working, and I was the kid's mother, wasn't I, and ought to know what should be done. I'd sob, "I don't know what to do!" Then Buddy would walk in and grab the baby from my hands and start to jiggle him. And poor Paulie, feeling nothing underneath his feet but shifting air, would scream as though madmen were torturing him. After ten seconds or so, Buddy would hand him back, complaining if he failed organic it would be my fault.

". . . chicken in lemongrass, you gotta try it. Linda, you aren't eating. You look like you're miles away."

"I'm thinking I should be a better mother. I don't do too well with Paulie. Franklin is right. I'm too impatient."

Reece signals the waiter for more water. "You can't always be patient. You have a lot coming down on you."

"That's true enough."

"So, tell me what you want to do?"

"You keep asking that. What is it, a trick question? I don't know." More accurate, I think, to ask: Who do you wanna be? Buddy's wife, or Reece's friend (enjoying existential pleasures—it doesn't sound like he wants more than that), or Fowler's office manager, his martinet and paid informer, purveyor of paper clips and daisy wheels—or none of the above, some luminous free spirit, unencumbered by decisions, playing tag with Paulie in the yard, maybe taking courses back at Maryland, all the tantalizing prospects Franklin wasted. The thought of other possibilities would be intriguing if it didn't scare me silly.

"Everything fine?" A busboy bends to fill our glasses. Reece nods and waves him off. "Look, Linda," he whispers urgently. "You must have got the scoop, by now, I've really missed you."

"A lot of lovely girls in town. Why me?"

"A lot of lovely girls, that's true. Most of 'em expect . . ." he founders, tries again. "Most of 'em think because a guy might look a certain way, he's gonna act a certain way—life of the party, chatty. You know I'm not like that."

"I'd say you were the quiet type. Thoughtful. Introspective. I like that in you, Reece."

"Some of 'em," he shudders. "So aggressive."

"Whereas, *I'm* nicely malleable?"

"You're flakey at times. But kinda sweet. Feisty enough, but you give in." (Super. What a tag line. You could use it as my epitaph: FEISTY ENOUGH, BUT SHE GAVE IN.) "Listen," Reece continues, "You could say *I've* led a sheltered life, all those years

153

tending an invalid. I'm not good on the party scene, but I'm not ready to settle down, either. Maybe there's something permanent down the road for you and me, but to be absolutely honest, I can't deal with that. Not yet. For me to think, long-term entanglements, that's hard. It would take me lots of time, it would take a certain effort on my part."

"What you're saying is, we oughta cool it for a bit?"

As I wait for his reply, the button that was dangling from my blouse drops to the table. Reece scoops it up and studies it very intently before he hands it back to me. "I'm not saying we oughta cool it. I'm saying I can't promise . . ." He hesitates, begins again. "Look, when you've been boxed in for a lotta years, it's hard to let go of your freedom."

"I wouldn't want to box you in. Freedom's great; at least, that's what I hear. These days, I wouldn't know. But Reece, you're the one who's sending gifts. *You* complain you're lonely. So, why do you run scared when I talk about commitment? I'm sorry—I know the word makes people gag—but I don't know how else to put it."

"Your husband's back. You don't know what you want to tell him. So, how can you expect anything more definite from me?"

"You're a factor in what I tell him. Aren't you?"

Reece shoves away his plate and sits in silence for the longest time, as though he's meditating. "Things were going well for us. You might have been a little bit uptight, but we got it on. I know I acted badly when your mom got sick, but I've been trying to apologize. Can't we go back to where we were? We have this special friendship. Do we have to analyze it and define it, till it self-destructs?"

I set my chopsticks down so carefully, as though their weight upon the plate might cause a detonation. "Is there someone you like better, Reece?"

"If there were, would I be here?" There's a tiny purplish orchid on our table. Reece plucks it from its vase and starts fooling with the petals. He won't look at me. In profile, his face is seamless, smooth, like those vacuum-wrapped packets of candy you get from the machines, all the flavor sealed so tightly from the taint of air. "Why are you so quick to down yourself? Why can't you have faith it might work out, if we gave ourselves some time? Can't we just drift awhile? See how it goes?"

"I don't like to leave things open-ended. I like to know where I'll be a year from now."

"Life doesn't work like that."

"I know. That's why life makes me nervous." We sit, reflected in the mirrored wall, stiff as actors in those rented flicks he likes. "When my mother got sick, you said you couldn't deal with illness. Was that the truth? Or just a way to get some distance?"

He lets the orchid fall, a mess of shriveled petals on the starched white of the tablecloth. "It was the truth, and I told you I'm not proud of it. Linda, I want you as my friend. Truly, I want you in my life. But beyond that, I can't make promises."

"Well, I thank you for your candor," I say lamely.

Reece picks up his cup and stares into the dregs of tea as though he's reading gloomy fortunes. I try to sip some water, but it won't go down. I feel like one of those gray fisher birds. There's something like a band around my throat, preventing me from swallowing.

After we leave the restaurant, we stroll in no great rush towards the garage where I have parked my car. When we step down from the curb to cross the street, Reece grasps my arm, and guides me through slow-moving traffic. Once we're on the sidewalk, he walks on the side closest to the curb, the soul of old-fashioned gallantry.

There's a bracing, winey fragrance to the air. Shoppers are everywhere, crowding the cobbled streets, bound for the posh couturiers, the trendy galleries, the sandwich bars and funky stores. People are sauntering, smiling, licking ice-cream cones. For a time we let the crowd bear us along. We even stop at shop windows and gaze at the displays, like two indolent lovers in no hurry to part. Reece points out a display of yuppie toys, computer games and odd-shaped phones and ornaments of twisted neon. "Look," he whispers, "look," like a kid gaping at forbidden treats. I tell him if my brother ever saw this place he'd feel like Rip van Winkle waking to a strange new world. He nods in sympathy at this, and we move on.

There's a flower vendor at one corner, a gypsy-looking guy, sitting amid tubs of roses and giant spider mums. Reece stops to buy a single, tight-furled rose, drops of moisture on the folded petals like an overlay of tiny gems. Cautiously, he strips the stem of thorns, shakes off errant drops of water. "You can tuck this in your blouse. Be decent when you see your mother." He fits the rose into my buttonhole.

"Thanks, Reece. It's beautiful. Listen, you oughta get back to the store. I know Saturdays are busy."

He nods, hesitates. "We were supposed to solve your problems, but we didn't."

"It would take more than a lunch to solve my problems."

"Then we'll have another lunch. We'll keep in touch?"

"We surely will. But no more presents. Promise."

"I like sending you presents. It keeps up a connection. Which is what I want to do." He says this emphatically. When I shake my head, refusing other gifts, he gets persistent. "Suppose I send something to Paulie? To cheer him up."

"No! Please. At this point, it would just confuse him."

"All right. Nothing for Paulie either. You know what's best." His face remains impassive, but I know he's hurt. He'll find somebody soon, willing to drift, I'll bet on that; or love will strike so suddenly and surely, all his existential blather will seem like so much noise to him, as foolish as it seems to me. "Well," Reece is frowning at his watch, "I guess I should get back." He hesitates a moment, "I *will* see you again?"

"Sure, Reece." Why not stay friends?

"Next time, we could try this Indian place I know. They serve these red-hot curries—wonderful if you can stand 'em."

"Sounds like fun." Maybe with the sexual sparring put to rest we could meet again like two old pals and chatter about something other than our thwarted wishes.

"I'll call you soon." Reece bends to kiss me lightly on the cheek. "Ciao, Linda Jo."

"Ciao, Reece."

He lifts his arm gallantly in a farewell wave. As he turns to make his lone way through the crowds, I catch sight of other women casting looks in his direction.

Eleven

Monte says Paulie's falling through the cracks. I feel there's nothing I can do to prevent that. I'm absorbed by my responsibilities—Ma's illness, the bills, the clutter in the house, the tedium at work, the endless visits to the hospital. Franklin is concentrating on his sparrow drawings and his researches in the Britannica. Monte says no one's helping the poor kid who is growing paler, sadder, every day.

When I protest, "He's not that bad—he's doing well in school," Monte counters, "Have you talked to his teacher?"

"There's no need to. Have you?"

Monte draws himself up taller, trying to look more prepossessing. Without his thick-soled sneakers he's a shrimp. His voice

is so drearily pompous, he should be handing down pronounce-
ments in the "People's Court." "That would be a presumption I
couldn't assume, without your permission. But I would do it if
you asked me," Monte adds.

"I'm not asking. Paulie's fine."

"Did you go to 'Back to School' night?"

"How could I, Monte? It was visiting hours at the hospital."

"Then you should have a conference with his teacher."

"Oh, what for? I hate those things. They make me feel as
though I'm five years old again."

"I'd be glad to go with you."

"That would just confuse things."

"I don't see why."

"They would mistake you for Paulie's father. How would I
introduce you?"

"As your good friend, I hope."

"Well, you know what that sounds like. What would they
think?" Monte frowns as though his status as a benefactor to our
family is not a source of gossip. It's hard to fathom, he's so dense.
But he *has* been my good friend. When I complained that house-
cleaning was too much of a hassle, he counseled me, "Don't sweat
it. I'll attend to that." One Friday, very early, before I leave for
work, a cleaning team arrives in an old VW van, Monte's contri-
bution for the week. He says these people do his place and they
are wonderfully efficient.

Indeed, they are. Marching in a single column, like somber,
soldier ants (two guys and a gal in denim overalls and hightop
sneakers), they haul in the big guns—vacuums linked to monster
canisters and floppy mops and spray cans of industrial-strength
cleaner. Presto, it looks as though a hurricane has hit the house—
the furniture moved every which way, the lamps unplugged,
Juanita's dime-store "objets d'art" piled on the mantel and the
tables while this super SWAT team dusts. Franklin, in pajamas,
gets routed from his room, and cowers in the kitchen, begging,

"Tell me when they go away," but it seems to me he's interested, grateful for the bustle and excitement. In record time, the place is shining—the kitchen gleams with piney cleanser, the checked floor of the rumpus room has the dangerous sheen of ice. That night, over tuna salad, Franklin says he would have dressed, in honor of the pleasant, sterile atmosphere, but he has no laundered shirts.

"You can run the clothes through the washer," Monte says. He's popped in unannounced for a quick white-glove inspection. "You can get a coupla loads clean and folded every day, while Linda Jo's at work." Franklin revolves his water glass like it was vintage wine and slowly nods. "And you can do a little of the cooking," Monte adds. " 'Cause when Linda Jo gets home, she's too tired to do everything." Franklin looks aggrieved, as though Monte hasn't grasped the depths of his, Franklin's, disability, especially since Ma got sick. "Simple stuff," Monte advises. "It doesn't have to be the least bit fancy. Tomato soup. Ham 'n Swiss. That's what I fix when I'm busy." Franklin, who is dull-eyed and unshaven, sloppy in food-stained pajamas, sits and blinks as though he's struggling from the confines of a trance. "You won't panic alone in the kitchen, will you?" Monte asks. If it were anyone but Monte Morris, who is nothing if not literal, I'd say he was being sarcastic.

Mostly out of gratitude to Monte, I arrange a conference with Paulie's teacher, who is not as pretty as I'd thought, a plain, plump girl with shoulder-length brown hair rolled under in a too-tight page boy. Hers is a blank moon face that seems bored or maybe sleepy. I've bullied her into an early morning meeting, and clearly she's annoyed. "Usually," she tells me stiffly, not meeting my harried gaze, "we schedule parent conferences much later in the year. Is there something in particular that has you worried?"

"I was worried because I couldn't get to 'Back to School' night. My mother, Paulie's grandmother, is ill."

Iola Patrick is the teacher's name. She permits herself a massive yawn, even rubs her eyes to show me she is still most awfully sleepy. " 'Back to School' night, well . . ." Another yawn, wide enough for me to see her silver fillings. "That's just for general discussion. And for parents to look around the class. You're free to visit any time, of course." Her reproachful brown eyes nail me: We have no secrets here.

"It's a very pleasant room." We're sitting at a child-size table on wobbly child-size chairs, and I, who am of medium height, cannot find a comfortable position. I try bending my knees. Then I thrust my legs out straight into the aisle, reverting to tomboy insolence.

This could have been my first-grade class—the same chalk smell, the same musty residue of glue and paper and spilled milk, the same dust-filled dryness to the air, the same mess of stuff gathered in the name of garnering enrichment: charts depicting liquid measure, and pink and buff and green maps of the world, and posters of cute children in exotic clothes, photos of fuzzy bears and kangaroos and mountain goats, baskets of shells and pots of plants and tanks containing turtles and goldfish, and tall jars topped with lids of perforated paper, holding captive insects. The mandatory guinea pig stands immobile in its cage, staring at a mess of rabbit pellets with a brown, unblinking eye. I think it must be stuffed, till it makes a sudden furtive movement, rustling the shredded paper at its feet, a sound so like despair it makes me shiver. I think the overlay of clutter in the room is calculated to provide distraction, mask the real business at hand, the soothing of bright minds into a dull decorum. I hate it here.

This sleepy girl, Ms. Patrick, is somewhere near my age, dressed in a dowdy skirt and sweater and high socks and stiff, no-nonsense oxfords. Dull-eyed, without makeup, she looks like someone's sullen baby-sitter, cajoled into the job against her will. Yet, on the first day of school, I nearly swooned with glee, clutching Paulie's hand and whispering, "Aren't you lucky? Your teacher is so young and pretty." She doesn't seem attractive now, just a heavy-legged girl who looks as though she'd rather be at home. She's recounted the Social Studies Lesson Plan. Holidays. Customs in Distant Lands. An Overview of Foreign Cultures with Emphasis on Brotherhood and Understanding. It sounds profound. "How is Paulie doing in first grade?" I finally get her down to bedrock.

She sighs, as though she's just been waiting for the proper cue. "He's very quiet and well-behaved. Not a problem at all." She smiles briefly as though she's offered me a priceless gift and expects to be praised for it.

"Well, is that okay? I mean, should he be . . . very quiet? Little boys of six . . . don't they jump around a lot? Make noise?" At that age, Franklin was always in hot water for some kind of prank, always grinning, questioning, upsetting Pop with snobby looks and hints of trekking west.

Ms. Patrick shrugs, willing to tell me what I want to hear. "He doesn't play a whole lot with the other kids at recess. He doesn't like rowdy games like dodgeball, and he's somewhat timid about skills requiring climbing or balancing." She's reciting this as rote. She must have made a point of watching Paulie after I told her I was coming for this chat. "He has his little girlfriend, Hilary. They prefer to play indoors, in the housekeeping corner." She motions to a nook furnished like a cramped apartment kitchen. A pegboard on the wall holds cooking tools and pots and pans.

"Paulie stays inside at recess and plays house? Don't you think that's a mistake? Shouldn't he be encouraged to go outdoors? I mean, a little boy needs to let off steam, doesn't he?"

"I hope you're not basing your objection to your son's play on gender?" There's a cool schoolmarmish tone of threat in plump Ms. Patrick's voice, something they must pick up in teacher training, that very modulated edge of meanness. They all have it, at any age, it seems.

162

"I think Hilary should go outside too, if it comes right down to it, but that's not any of my business." I sound like Monte now.

"Many of the little boys enjoy playing with dolls, and pots and pans. It's not unusual at all, these days."

"Many? How many besides Paulie? There's Paulie and there's Hilary. Who else plays with them?" Maybe my son's a pacesetter; maybe he's started a new trend and all the kids are pleading for their moments in the cramped housekeeping corner and a chance to scour pots. If Paulie's in the vanguard, I need some evidence.

Ms. Patrick shrugs. "I don't keep track of what every youngster does at recess every day." Well yeah, I think, I bet you don't. "Would you like to see your son's work folder?" Ms. Patrick urges us to safer ground. Without waiting for my answer she stands up and lumbers to her desk. She could lose a good twenty pounds, especially around the hips. By now I heartily dislike her, old school prejudices coming to the fore, contempt for goody-goody girls, too cautious and all-knowing, too well-cushioned and smug. The sort of daughter a Juanita would cosset to her bosom and praise as perfection.

Ms. Patrick returns with a folder made of yellow construction paper. On ruled lines on the front, someone has printed in careful lettering, too neat for a six-year-old to manage: BURTON PAUL MERCEAU.

"He doesn't like the name, Burton." My voice trembling at this latest outrage.

"It's that way on his records."

"Is that what the children call him?"

She looks tense, almost fearful. I feel a surge of triumph, thinking, I've got her now, but what have I won? I'm not quite sure. "If he objects, I'm sure he lets them know," Ms. Patrick says.

"Is that what you call him?"

"Mrs. Merceau, I don't know where this line of questioning is leading . . ."

"On the first day—I was here with him on the first day and I distinctly heard you ask the children if they had any favorite nicknames they wanted you to use. You made it clear you wanted them to feel comfortable. I thought that was so neat . . . that he would feel at home here. I heard him tell you, 'Paulie.' I heard it. You even shook his hand. You said, 'How do you do, Paulie. It's so nice to meet you.' " Just like Adele Merceau. The same blank smile, the eyes light-years away, pondering some other galaxy. "Did you forget so soon?"

"Mrs. Merceau, I really resent your tone. You're making me feel as though I'm under interrogation. There are twenty-seven children in this class, and I do my level best to make each one feel warm and welcome, as well as comfortable. Would you like to take on twenty-seven all by yourself for six hours a day, and keep them disciplined, and teach them, and still try to remember each one's nickname?"

"No, I wouldn't, but that's not my job." Her look implies it's not my business either, and my presence here, though it must be tolerated, is totally irrelevant. "May I see what's in his folder, please?"

"Certainly." Her voice is cold. Good going, Linda. I can almost hear Franklin's derisive tone. He was doing well, no problems, no complaints; and now you've fixed it so his teacher resents you and probably will hate him too.

"This is very nice." Trying to mend fences, I wave a paper full of printed letters.

"He's had some difficulty with reversals." Her tone implies that this is serious. "Sometimes, that is a portent of future problems with dyslexia. We'll have to wait and see." She meets me head on now, her eyes alight at this true coup. Gotcha, they say. Gotcha good in your anxiety, which is what I'm trained to do, so don't you mess with me if you want to sleep nights.

I riffle through a pile of crayoned drawings, most of them show chairs and tables, ripples meant to simulate an ocean, mountain peaks. "Does he strike you as creative?"

"Not overly much." We're on the downside now. "This," she points to a stiff cream-colored sheet, folded in half so I can't see the contents, "is a picture I asked them to do of their families. You see he had some problem filling in details." She unfolds the sheet and places it before me, poking it with a stubby finger. Her nails are bitten to the quick, and there's a ragged Band-Aid on her thumb that looks as though she chews on it when under tension. I do that kind of thing myself till the gauze patch gets frayed or separated from the pink adhesive. "You'll agree it's somewhat regressed for a child of six."

The family picture is disturbing. Paulie has drawn the lot of us as disembodied heads, like planets turning in a solar system. Juanita's solemn face is at the center, empty Os for eyes and a downcast mouth. I'm stationed at due north—I assume it's me because he shows me with long straight hair emerging like the rays of a small sun. I look mean or befuddled, I'm not sure which. Franklin is north/northeast, dark bristles for his mangled crew cut and a small, tight smile. There's someone to my west with a nimbus of bright hair. That must be Reece; next to him is a video screen. And there's Monte, for sure, a southern star, with a whistle dangling where his neck would be, if Paulie had bothered to include it. At the top edge of the paper is a tiny head, expressionless, and under that, a rainbow. Is that where he thinks his father is? Over the rainbow? Dead, and gone to heaven, maybe? The heads, devoid of bodies, do seem terribly regressed, except for some of the expressions which are on the mark. There's a black, grouchy face in the bottom right-hand corner, and next to it a yellow flower, wonderfully detailed, a daffodil. That must be Monroe, with a flower from the Merceau garden. It makes me want to weep. "Look at that face and that flower." I tell Ms. Patrick. "I bet he could draw well if he wanted to."

"That's what all our mothers say." The teacher is looking smug.

I stack all the papers carefully as I'm sure this young woman would wish, and hand her back the folder. "Thank you for this conference." Standing painfully, I do not extend my hand.

"I hope you found it helpful." She is standing too, with the folder pressed against her chest. She steals a quick glance at her wristwatch, a tactful hint that I have overstayed my welcome.

"I surely have. I found out all I need to know. I really must get Paulie out of here, out of this class, before you do any further damage to . . . his concept of himself."

"Mrs. Merceau!" She seems truly shaken by the accusation. "I can't imagine what led you to think that!"

"I've found out that my son is shy, withdrawn, and passive and doesn't play outdoors with other kids. He's regressed, possibly dyslexic, and you don't even know his name. His nickname, at least. More to the point, you don't much care. If you were me, would you be upset?"

"I've told you, he's a very pleasant little boy!"

"That picture . . . that picture of our family. Doesn't it make you wonder just a little bit? Do you think he might be troubled? His grandmother is near the center; his father is a dot who's off, somewhere in the ozone. I suppose I ought to tell you, we're separated. He just . . . took off."

"So many of our children come from broken homes. It's not a factor . . ."

"It's not? Maybe not to you, but it is to Paulie. That's what I want you to call him. Paulie. Is that understood? And I want him to play outdoors. Hilary, too. I expect you to see to it."

She is meek suddenly. "I'll do my best." She has grown flushed and earnest, and suddenly I see the prettiness I spotted on the first day after Labor Day when she looked so soft and sweet. Maybe tension does it; that and sex hormones pump up the adrenaline. "Mrs. Merceau, you have to understand, we can't work miracles. The children come to us with so much other baggage. All we can do is hope they learn their numbers and their letters . . ."

That reminds me, I had a whole list of questions Monte told me I must ask: How is Paulie's number comprehension? His study skills? Eye-hand coordination? Emotional stability? Monte knows this jargon from the work he does with kids.

I should have come with Monte, I think grimly. This teacher, who isn't interested in family baggage, wouldn't care about some bachelor's status in our lives. Paulie has drawn a family constellation dotted with clues about who each person is and that person's significance to Paulie. Juanita is the central force, a dying star without much luster, but formidable still, and Franklin and I spin crazily within her orbit, with Reece and Monte looking on. Buddy has broken from the pull of the system's gravity and is off in "La La Land," as good as dead. The more I ponder it, the more I think Paulie has been rather clever; maybe not regressed at all, just lazy.

Like his father . . .

. . . who arrives—unheralded and uninvited on a Saturday near noon, holding two six-packs of Corona like the baggage of a weary salesman, saying he is here to see his son.

"He's a bit young." I gesture to the beer. Memories of the conference are still stinging me. Monte who'd looked wise and pained when I recounted the events of that debacle, had promised, "We'll do more things together. Ball games. Museums." As though Paulie's failings were his responsibility. Monte is encroaching like some household vine that, once rooted, creeps into windows, doors, chimneys. You thought you opted for some ornamental green, and suddenly you are engulfed in boughs and leaves and creepy tendrils. That's not a fair analogy. Monte has been a lifesaver, a good, solemn, stocky presence, offering gifts of time and money, the reassurance of his dull, lumbering generosity. In a better, fairer world, I'd come to love him, but life doesn't work that way. Gratitude's a deterrent to passion. Every time I have to tell him, "Thank you, thank you, thank you," I want to hide out in the comfort of my room, like Franklin. Except for that first gift of cash, I've insisted I will pay him back for everything he's done, every penny.

Buddy swings a six-pack closer so I'll see the classy brand. "These are for Franklin. He used to like a good brew, didn't he?"

"Ask him yourself. He's in the kitchen." Working on a soup stock for Juanita. Chinese chicken broth, the harmful salt replaced by ginger. Franklin wants me to bring it to her with his love. I've told him it'll take more than chicken soup to cure Juanita's blues.

"How's your mother?" Buddy follows me to the kitchen. It's strange to feel his presence after all these months. I sense his eyes boring into me, hear the soft intake of breath, know he's sizing up my hair, my clothes, the breadth of hips and waist, assessing if I've changed. Grown plumper or thinner, stringier or sexier. I feel nervous and defenseless under Buddy's gaze, as though I'm the guilty party, the one who skipped.

"Not too great. She doesn't eat, won't get out of bed, won't agree to any tests. It's like she's given up." I call out, "Franklin, it's Buddy. Don't run away."

Buttressed by the kitchen counter, Franklin holds tight to his cooking spoon as if it is a totem that will shield him from the harm of new encounters. He seems brighter these days, happy with the list of small domestic tasks Monte has set for him. He offers a hand to Buddy, who sets the beer down on the kitchen table and extends both arms. They engage in something like a clumsy bear hug, too good ole boys indulging in some ritual of bonding not comprehensible to a mere female. Franklin, the traitor, astounds me.

"Damn good to see you, sport." Buddy seems moved.

Franklin looks him over. "You got some sun. How was California?"

Buddy acts diffident. "It's the same people telling the same lies to each other, only in better weather."

Franklin nods happily as though that was exactly what he wished to hear. "Thanks for the beer."

Buddy turns to me. "I got something for Paulie in the car."

"He's not here. If you'd called ahead, I could have told you. He's at the Air & Space Museum with Monte Morris."

"What's that jerk doin' around here?"

"Helping with the bills, for openers. Visiting with Juanita since her dear son can't manage it. Looking after Paulie who needs a man around to take him places." I stash the beer inside the fridge making enough noise to let them know I'm royally p.o.'d with both of them.

Buddy turns to Franklin, who is beaming like a stupid chimp, impervious to my sarcasm today, so happy to have an old school chum as company. "Why is he so generous? What does he want?"

Franklin shrugs. "Linda's palpitating body, I suppose."

"Oh, shut up! What is it with you guys? Why does everything come down to that?"

Franklin adjusts the pot lid so that aromatic steam permeates the room. The smell is tantalizing. He suggests, to me, "You tell us why."

"Monte's been an orphan for a good long time. He wants to be part of a family. He wants *troubles.*"

Franklin giggles. "He came to the right place."

Buddy asks, "Can I hang around till they get back?"

"Stay for lunch," Franklin says quickly.

"Now, just a damn minute!" I don't like this at all. Franklin and Buddy aligned. Me, the outsider with the long face, watching these two grin and preen.

"I could go for pizza," Buddy offers.

"Super," Franklin agrees.

I move to burst that bubble. "That's not convenient. I have stuff to do today. Mrs. Lindquist is going to stay with Mama while I do my errands."

"Pepperoni?" Franklin asks.

"Mushroom and anchovy *and* pepperoni." Buddy grins.

"This is no time for a party."

"Hey, sis, we have to eat."

"Some of us don't have time."

"Don't let us detain you." Franklin, bustling to set the table, is all bright smiles, something I haven't seen in months, the Ghost of Franklin Past moving with the old, happy energy. Franklin beaming in the magic cast by one of the old gang. What is the lure that animates these men? What made Buddy, fresh from his marriage bed, toddle to the phone to call the guys? Look how these two grunt and shuffle, beam bright-eyed like they were lovers. Neanderthals, more likely, circling home fires. Warriors in the cave pledging loyalty to one another. Compañeros. They cherish friendship like it was some mystical religion only the high priests can attend. We softer types with hips and bosoms are forever barred. Thinking this makes me feel old and tired, superior and jealous, too.

"Hey, Linda, lighten up." Buddy nudges me, and the sudden unexpected pressure of his elbow on my arm makes my stomach flutter, like the old days when our bodies were all mystery to one another, and I was crazy for his kisses, and he poked his tongue with gentle insolence inside my mouth and, groaning, told me afterwards I was a virus in his blood. "Don't go, yet," Buddy pleads. "God knows, we gotta talk things over."

"Yeah, make her stay. She needs a little recreation. Too much serious, serious thinking gives our pretty little girl here frown lines."

"Franklin, you louse!" But I stay, straightening stuff around the house and primping just a bit while Buddy goes out for the pizza. We end up in the basement, me and Buddy lounging on the floor in front of the TV, as we used to in our dating days, and Franklin on the couch, clicking the remote so that it fans through all the channels. Nothing on but football games and cowboy movies. There's a mess of pizza boxes spread around us as well as empty beer bottles. The house smells of oregano and chicken soup and brew. The beer, not cold enough, has turned me woozy, just pleasantly relaxed. Blinking at the TV screen I watch a quarterback run a zigzag course to glory in a contest between Oklahoma and Nebraska, exciting stuff. "You never ran that good," I say to Buddy.

He pats my hair, the old gentle touch of those mornings in high school when he marveled that anything could be so soft. "I did. You're saying that because you're bitter."

"Bitter? Who, me?"

"Oh yes, she's bitter." Franklin hiccups softly.

"Franklin, shut up!"

"No," Buddy insists. "You let him talk. All of us need to talk. What we need here," Buddy stops to belch, then grins angelically, beseeching our forgiveness for this gross act, "is an absolutely frank encounter. The sort of thing I'm trained to lead."

I bellow, "That's a hoot!"

"Be fair, Linda," says Franklin. "The man is trained."

"Oh yeah," I say. "I ought to know. I worked to pay for it, and then he never finished. Just picked up and ran away."

"Good," Buddy says. "We're cutting through. We're getting to the nitty-gritty."

"What might that be?" Franklin sounds supremely interested.

"Resentment, rage, and pain," Buddy intones. He shuffles through the paper in a pizza box, hunting a last wedge of mushroom and anchovy. There's only a single pepperoni left. Buddy regards it sadly. "Do you resent me too?" he asks Franklin.

Franklin clicks off the game. The silence startles us into sobriety. I turn to peer at Franklin whose sleepy grin has faded. "Sure I do. You did something contemptible."

"Interesting," says Buddy, staring at the soggy pizza.

"What's interesting?" I want to know.

"Interesting to hear Franklin accusing me . . ."

Franklin says, "I fail to see . . ."

171

"You took off too," says Buddy. "Didn't you? Four years ago. Didn't you just bug out?"

"That's none of your damn business, Buddy." I flare in my brother's defense, though heaven knows why.

"Apples and oranges," says Franklin. "Don't cloud the issue. If I'm a head case, that screws up *my* life. You cut out on your family. Wiped out your bank account. Left Linda with a slew of bills. What do you expect to get for that? A medal?"

"I got scared too, Franklin. I had to split."

"Excuse me," I say softly. "I didn't know I terrified people. Me and Paulie, monsters both of us."

"Oh God." Buddy sets the slice of pizza back inside the box and looks at it, like staring, hoping, wishing, will get him the mushroom topping that he wants. "I hated school so much, Linda. I hated that damn social work, all those sob stories, those miserable people with their awful, stunted lives. I should have been a doctor, shouldn't I?"

"Plentya sob stories there, Buddy. Go visit Mama at the hospital." I'd heard the same complaint from him every day he was in grad school. His misery would get so bad I'd sit and shake, listening to him rant. I became convinced that he was planning something desperate: OD'ing on bad dope, taking a flier off a bridge. One night, when we were arguing, I turned my fear into a joke. I pretended I was Brando in that scene from *On the Waterfront.* Buddy started the drill, "I could've been a doctor, Linda Jo. I could've done something important." So I piped in, mocking but scared to death: "Gee, Cholly, I could've been uh contenduh." I had the Brando slur down pat, the earnest look, the slouch. Buddy got so mad he picked up one of his textbooks and let it fly, just winging me over the ear. We had one of our doozies after that, with those creeps next door threatening to call the cops—Paulie sleeping through it like our voices raised in screams were oft-repeated lullabies.

"Let's get something straight, Buddy," I've started picking up the remnants of our lunch because I need something to do to calm me down. "If you didn't go to med school, it was not my fault. It was because you couldn't pass the damn organic chemistry! So stop blaming me and Paulie. Stop making us pick up the tab for your so-called wasted life."

"You bet I blame you, Linda."

"Truth time, truth time. Time for old Franklin to get lost." Franklin is on his feet, not walking a steady course. He wavers for a moment, smiling foolishly, and then sits down again, looking confused. "What does it mean, Doc, when the room spins around you? Brain tumor?"

"That sounds so much like your mother, it's incredible," Buddy marvels.

I will not let him off. "What do you blame me for, you rat? How dare you walk into this house and start accusing?"

"Hey, Linda, do you remember . . ." Franklin is grinning foolishly again. "Once, when we were kids, Ma took us to the Medical Museum at Walter Reed. How many mamas take their children to that den of horrors?"

If I remember correctly, quite a few; trailing their nervous kids through rows of shelves that show the secrets of the lab, remnants of grim pathology—lumps of diseased tissue bobbing in jars, black-petaled excrescences floating like flowers *(Les Fleurs du Mal,* Franklin had called them) in clouded fluids. Ma meant to educate us in the sciences.

That day, Franklin and I had gotten giddy, as we were assailed by all the poor ivory-tinged fetuses set upside down in bottles, the gross gnarled limbs swollen by the blight of elephantiasis, the cross sections of failed brown lungs. We'd wandered down the line of escalating horrors, giggling, shuddering, staggering (almost faint), the laughter risible as bubbles in our throats, bursting to choke off tears. Juanita, realizing she'd goofed, had steered us to the section marked HISTORICAL. Another kind of gloom. The empty shells gleaned after acts of carnage. Mr. Lincoln's undershirt tinged rusty red with blood. "Ma didn't know it was that gruesome. Besides, Franklin, we were not that young."

Buddy intervenes. "I bet she did so know. That's her idea of protection. Scare you to death. Make fear the great deterrent. Don't screw. Don't get preggers. Don't smoke. Did you know, the day Paulie was born, she called me up to remind me of the Lindbergh story. The kidnapping, you know? I was not to let strangers come near the baby. Or let you hire baby-sitters."

"She didn't, Buddy."

"Linda, she did. You were in the hospital. You didn't have an inkling."

Franklin pipes up, "You ever watch the Super Bowl with Ma? The Goodyear blimp comes on? You know what happens then."

"Oh, do we know!" yells Buddy.

Franklin, catching Ma's tone to perfection, "You don't recall the *Hindenburg* disaster, do you?"

Buddy chimes in, pretending to be broadcasting. "It's May 1937. Night over Lakehurst Naval Station. The great airship is drifting towards its landing, when suddenly . . ."

"A burst of flame," says Franklin. "A monstrous orange explosion like the ending of the world."

"Over in minutes," counters Buddy.

"Thirty-six lives lost," says Franklin. "The poor man on the radio, describing it and crying."

"Some say," Buddy is doubled over, laughing. "Some say, a charge of electricity in the atmosphere met with a leak of hydrogen . . ."

"I don't know why you think that's funny. You guys can be so dumb."

"Speaking of leak, I gotta take one," Franklin says. "The beer . . ."

Buddy drones on, "But others suspected *sabotage.*"

"And that," Franklin, standing again, wavering toward the

174

stairs, "could happen here. Over the Super Bowl. Inside the Goodyear blimp."

"Disaster televised," says Buddy. "What ratings that would bring."

"Gotta get upstairs," says Franklin. "To the john before disaster strikes."

"Ah, stay," laughs Buddy. "We're just warming up. We haven't gotten to the *Andrea Doria.*"

"No shipwrecks, please. No water pouring through the hold. Not yet." And Franklin, howling, lurches to the stairway.

When he is gone, I sit hunched on the floor, face buried in my palms, crying. In a minute Buddy is beside me. "Ah, babe. Ah, don't. What is it? Tell me."

"How dare you say I ruined your life! Where do you get that kind of nerve after what you pulled?"

"Ah, babe." He puts his arm around my shoulder and pulls me to him till my head is resting on his chest. We're on the area rug beside the couch, sprawled amid greasy pizza boxes and empty beer bottles. "I only meant, you should have had the smarts to say no when I suggested we get married. You were brighter than I was. You should have nixed it. That way, I could've gone to Dartmouth, and you could've finished Maryland."

"That isn't what you mean. What you mean is I should've let you do it, and then you never would have mentioned marriage. I would not have seen you for the dust."

"Oh yes you would. It was you for me, babe. Always. It still is."

"Don't make me laugh."

"I can understand why you don't believe it, but it's so. No one like you in California. No one." He is planting little fluttery kisses on my face, my ear—the old, gentle necking he's so good at, that I like so much. Just the tender foolishness. Little snuffles, nuzzles, long wet kisses, sighs. "Come with me to California," Buddy whispers. "That's why I came back. To get you and Paulie. I've been working with my uncle Bob Merceau in real estate. The commissions are fantastic. You wouldn't need a job. You could stretch out on the beach, perfect your tan."

"Till you get panicky again? No way."

"You could forgive me, babe. To love is to forgive, isn't that so?"

That sounds like something in Ma's household magazines, wisdom you'd cross-stitch on a dish towel. I used to gobble up that stuff, looking for advice and comfort. Juanita should have warned me I was devouring fantasy. Nothing in the Household Hints ("How to Save a Marriage"; "How to Bake a Pie") jibes with my knowledge of reality. "Maybe I never loved you, Buddy. 'Cause I don't feel forgiving."

"You love me, babe." His hand fools with the topmost button of my jeans.

I warn him, "Cut that out."

"Your mother ruined you for enjoying sex, you know."

"I know that's what you think."

"So jumpy. Everywhere I touch, it's like you're wired."

"Electric charges in the atmosphere. Me and the *Hindenburg.*" I can't help it; I begin to giggle.

"Umm. And then the hydrogen explosion."

"You guys are gross. Laughing at that awful tragedy."

"It's fifty years ago. Frankly, Scarlett, I don't give a damn." He presses me down till I'm stretched out on the rug and he is over me, kissing me hard. He has his hands under my sweater and he's fiddling with my bra, working on the hooks. He gets them undone pretty handily. Practice makes perfect, he used to say. "Missed you, baby, so," he's murmuring between kisses, and his lips are everywhere.

"If you missed me, you have a strange way of showing it."

"Linda Jo, you need to break free of your crazy family. Don't get mad, you know they're nuts. But they keep this iron hold on you. Anything they tell you, you believe. The doom and gloom. Shot your nerves to hell."

"My mother's sick. You expect me to ignore that? Quit pawing me, Buddy, I mean it, stop!"

"Couldn't quit it if I wanted to." His wet lips nuzzling. "You taste so good. Umm." He chants, "Pretty little Linda Jo. Fragrant with o-reg-an-o. Baby," croons Buddy, "we need to be away from them. Go for good times again. We had some fun there for a while. Didn' we?"

California? Orange blossoms. Gold, Pacific sands. I know there's no way I would go. No way, not unless Juanita got well pretty quick and Franklin catapulted into health and took on some responsibility. No way. But wouldn't it be rich, if all our childhood playing, all of Franklin's chanting in the swing, turned out to be prophecy for me? I'm pondering that so hard and Buddy is so engrossed, we don't hear footsteps on the stairs, don't hear Paulie's treble piping that he saw pictures of the astronauts and climbed inside the space lab. I must have heard. If I know what Paulie said, I must have heard him on the stairs; but I'm not paying attention, so intent am I on kissing Buddy and at the same time fending off his hands, which are lighter, softer, more insistent, more tickly and gentle than they ever were before. They seem to have acquired newer, subtler life, dabbling in real estate, than they ever had coping with the problems of humanity.

"Linda! What are you doing?" It's Monte's anguished voice that rouses me. "Linda!" Monte's mild eyes wide with accusation, maybe a prior claim, won't leave my face, stare as I sit up swiftly and begin to rearrange my clothes. Paulie, holding a bakery box, pipes, "We stopped at Dunkin' Donuts."

"Hey, son." Buddy has risen to his feet and now holds out his arms. Paulie stares, not comprehending.

Monte gazes straight at me, the old question unspoken, but hanging in the air as though the Goodyear blimp is trailing a bold banner: LINDA, DON'T YOU KNOW, THE BODY IS A TEMPLE?

Suddenly, Paulie is screaming, the awful keening of a child trapped in a recurring nightmare. Buddy pleads, "What is it? What's the matter, son?"

Paulie has dropped the bakery box. Doughnuts spill over the area rug and roll across the checkerboard linoleum. Instinctively, I rush to pick them up before they attract ants. Paulie presses against Monte, his face buried in Monte's trouser leg, his narrow shoulders heaving awful sobs. Buddy confronts Monte, "What's the matter with him?"

I say, "He thinks you're dead, a ghost." A disembodied head, no bigger than a pea floating in space beyond a rainbow.

Buddy wheels on me. "Bitch! What did you tell him?"

"Nothing. He never asked."

Monte advancing with Paulie clinging to his leg. "Don't you dare call her that? How dare you say that to a woman!"

Buddy raises his fist. "You wanna tell me what to call my wife, Monte? You wanna just c'mere and tell me? You just c'mere, okay. But first, let go of my kid."

Monte warns, "I teach karate twice a week."

Buddy sneers, "Big deal. You let go of my kid and you c'mere. I'm gonna deck you, Monte."

Monte bends to Paulie. "Go upstairs to your Uncle Franklin, sport." When Paulie hesitates, Monte says, "Mush," and Paulie runs, wailing, to the stairs. I start after him, but Monte holds a palm up, like a traffic cop, or a guru, beseeching peace and pursuit of sweetest reason. "Let him alone. Let him calm down a second. It's a lot for him to grasp."

Contrite, I move to Monte, knowing I must make amends. "Listen, I'm sorry you guys walked in on us."

"Get away from him, Linda," warns Buddy.

"Don't tell me what to do."

"Just get away."

"I won't. Monte's the best, the kindest, the most generous person I have ever known. I practically owe him my life." Beset by a misguided impulse, I place my hands on Monte's shoulders, thinking to embrace him out of simple friendship. He blanches at my touch, gasps as though a bullet hit him, rebounds, shakes me off, commanding, "Don't."

"Sorry." New tears are starting. "Excuse me for living, Monte."

"You're still married, Linda Jo." And still the fallen woman whom he can forgive, but cannot hug. I never thought that Monte, engrossed in being noble, would think of me as tainted, hardly pure enough to touch. Monte's lips move as though he's practicing a further explanation. As usual, his confusion is such, he can't articulate. He stares from me to Buddy for a wretched moment; then he bolts, lurching up the stairs in Paulie's wake.

"A fine mess we got here," Buddy says, as though the crumpled boxes and the messed-up lives are one and the same.

Twelve

Later that afternoon I seek out Franklin. Having heard the controversy rising from the cellar, he has opted for the safety of his room where he sits tight, out of range. Noise and commotion rattle him, send him scurrying to solitude. The Chinese broth can boil away for all he cares.

I find him reading, stretched out on his bed, the blinds drawn, the lights lit as though it's midnight. The air in here is stuffy, musty as the tomb. Even the efforts of the cleaning team can't dispel the heaviness. "This room is like the land that time forgot. You could open a window sometime, Franklin. Just to stir things up a bit."

Reluctantly, he looks up from his book, then glances down,

affecting interest in the chapter. Conrad again. More chronicles of sea disasters. This one must be engrossing. For once, the TV set is silent. The shade over the bedside lamp is tilted to cast brighter light upon the page. I see my shadow on the wall, looming over Franklin like a woeful harbinger. I'm carrying a plate of doughnuts, the ones I salvaged from the cellar floor. "I don't feel psyched for fixing dinner. You want one of these?"

He shakes his head. "Paulie not here?"

"Gone out for barbecue with Monte. I said he could stay overnight at Monte's place."

"You think that's such a good idea?"

"He feels safe there, more so than here. I don't know if it's good or not. I don't know what to do about Paulie, Monte, anything." I sink onto the floor, the plate of doughnuts balanced on my lap, my back to Franklin. He rests a palm upon my shoulder, implying brief, tacit sympathy, then withdraws his hand. I've noticed lately that he's wary of touching. He'll reach out like a blind man to assure himself of where he is, and then backs off, as though protracted contact is too threatening. I hear him turning pages in his book. Clearly, my presence here is not desired.

Franklin asks me, "Ma okay?"

"I called. The nurse on duty said she was asleep."

"No progress there."

"No progress anywhere."

Franklin sighs heavily. "I feel a lecture coming."

"Not from me. Believe it or not, I have been boning up on agoraphobia. Trying to find out what you're up against. I was too bushed to run my errands, so I've been reading." Monte, who doesn't miss a trick when it comes to getting us on track, has left some books, selected from the library in Chevy Chase. This afternoon, I sorted through them with a firm purpose in mind. Most of the volumes, out-of-date, call Franklin's ailment "housebound housewife's syndrome." He'd raise holy hell if he heard that. One book I like, documenting what is known of panic syndrome, defines the problem as *Platzschwindel,* German for dizziness in public places. That too is out-of-date, for dizziness is now regarded as a minor symptom, one of a vast complex involving fear of crowded places, public transportation, tunnels, bridges, supermarkets, dentists' chairs. That last, at least, sounds logical, innately sane. "Here's something I learned today. I'm supposed to tell you, be afraid. Go with the flow. Drift into fear. Drown with it. Embrace it as you would a lover."

"Those doughnuts smell good. You got any with chocolate frosting?"

"Yep." I select the one he wants and hand it up to him.

He inches backwards till he's sitting, propped against the headboard of his bed. After he bites into the snack, I hear him brushing off his shirt. "Crumbs in bed, I hate 'em."

I choose a glazed doughnut for myself and turn to face him. "The cause of the fear is relatively unimportant." Ignoring years of our Mom's warnings, I lecture with my mouth full, certain to choke. "It could be clinical depression, coffee nerves, hypoglycemia, a form of epilepsy, though that's thought to be unlikely, even sexual inhibition."

Franklin laughs, seemingly enjoying this. "Ah, Freud. I knew he'd show. Something awful in my past?"

"Perhaps. *Platzschwindel.* I like that best."

"And the cure? I'm assuming that you found a cure?"

"Depends on the book you're reading. And the year of publication. Anything from diet to long walks to prayer to therapy to drugs."

"To Beryl Blackwell?"

"Franklin, she wasn't completely off the beam. Probably, she was too patient."

"No baby steps?"

"Uh-uh." I shake my head. "Total immersion. Jump in over your head. You swim or drown. When you struggle for a little bit and find out suddenly you're floating, you know you can get better."

"This is a lecture, after all."

"Franklin, you need to spring me."

"Meaning?"

"Buddy wants us to go back with him to California. I know it's crazy, but I am considering it."

"Crazy all right! You must be nuts!"

"I thought you liked Buddy. Today you acted like he was your long-lost brother."

"He's decent company. Everybody else I know acts like what I have is catching, or seeing me upsets them. Linda, Buddy's okay for a day's diversion, but the long haul? Never. I thought you found that out the hard way."

"Buddy has qualities . . ."

"Yeah. Don't we all. Grow up, Linda. Buddy's a good ole boy. He'll bed you down, and get you pregnant, and then he'll go off somewhere with the fellas. That's what Buddy loves. The team, the crew, the crowd at homecoming. Everybody singing, reminiscing, watching sports. It's not sex he wants so much. It's . . . compañeros. Isn't that the word you like?"

"Maybe I want that, too. Just a household with stability. Paulie knowing his own father. Someone to pay the bills. Besides Monte, who threw me for a loop today. He acts like I'm not good enough to breathe his air."

"Poor Monte. He's more scared of you than I'm scared of going out. Trust me, you're always safe with Monte. He wants to worship from afar. Maybe he'd like a date, so he can show you off, make the other turkeys jealous, but that's about the size of it. He wouldn't have you as a lover or a wife."

"Oh yeah? Why not?"

"I told you, you intimidate him. Men don't marry women who scare them. They might desire them, but they marry gals who make 'em comfortable. Like well-worn shoes." Franklin chuckles. "Kinda tarnishes the old image of romance, don't it, but it's true. Men marry gals who make 'em think that they can be themselves, and women marry men they think they can improve, which explains why eventually most marriages go down the tubes."

"That's just your point of view. Cynical and warped, what I'd expect."

"So, put it to the test," Franklin says, chewing on the doughnut. "Come on real strong with Monte. See how he reacts."

"And if you're wrong and he responds?"

"Enjoy the oddness of the experience. Go with the flow."

"Easy for you to say."

He sighs. "Always easy to give advice to others."

"Also, easy to be smug when you're holed up in your room."

Franklin, forever mocking, holds a cupped palm to one ear. "Hark! What is it that I hear. An old refrain. Repeating. Forever repeating. It's the 'Rondo à la Linda.' A haunting and persistent theme which is, by now, extremely boring. Go away and let me read my book, would you?"

"Shipwrecks again. That's all you know. What a waste of time for someone clever."

He flips the cover toward me. "It's *Heart of Darkness,* better every time. I lent this to Juanita once. I figured she, if anyone, would know what 'the horror' was. She told me it was much too boring, and gave it back."

"Ma deals with specifics. Conrad is too abstract; his symbols are so general. They could encompass the whole world. His horror could be evil incarnate or anything you ever dreaded. Ma deals with stuff that she can measure, smell, taste, see."

"You think so?" Franklin pats the bed, inviting me to sit. He loves this kind of conversation, the way we talked when we were teens, when he, a college freshman, and I, in AP English, would match our knowledge of books.

I settle on the space he's made, facing him. "I always thought that it was lazy of Conrad not to spell it out, tell us what Kurtz saw before he died."

"Lazy, no. Clever, making the reader wonder."

"I think his ending is a cop-out. He got painted into a corner. Invention failed him."

"No, Linda, he needed to be vague, for the ending's irony. For Marlowe telling that final lie about Kurtz's death to his fiancée."

"Marlowe could lie, and we could still know what Kurtz saw."

"It's Marlowe's voice, Marlowe's limitation. Not the author talking. Marlowe can't know what Kurtz saw; he can only surmise. Therein, a deeper horror."

"Oh, Franklin, I don't care. The whole thing bores me, like it bored Juanita." I stand up again, ready to leave.

"Wait a sec." Franklin, from the pit of loneliness, implores me. "What about the 'character in motley'? What do you make of him?"

"Who's that? I don't remember."

"Yes, you do. The enigmatic Russian, dressed like Harlequin. Depicting youth and glamour? Or the wise fool laughing in the face of danger? Or crass colonialism?"

"You answered it."

"No, I didn't," Franklin says. "Which one?"

"All of 'em? I don't know. Maybe, the wise fool laughing in the face of danger."

"Maybe." Franklin slaps a palm upon his knee, relishing the thought. "When I read that part tonight, I thought of Pop."

"Pop! Franklin, you're really nuts."

"Sometimes, when Ma was off and running with her stories, Pop would catch my eye and wink, like it was all one big joke."

"I know. And thank God for it."

"Only I listened to Ma. I thought he was a fool."

185

"Well, he wasn't. At least Pop kept his sense of humor. Till the *Star* folded, anyway."

"I never understood him, Linda Jo. Pop was a walking non sequitur to me."

I know Franklin so well. I know we're no longer discussing Conrad, or even Pop and his idiosyncrasies. Franklin has always been the explicator for me, the one who gave coherence to my world. I remember when I was a kid, no more than nine or ten, and I discovered sex. I was visiting a friend from school (a sly girl, darkly pretty who went on to study math at MIT) and she produced a volume from her parents' shelves, *The ABC's of Sex,* which was an alphabet of terms arranged from *A* to *Z.* I remember the confusion and despair I felt poring through the letters—*ejaculation* and *epididymis* in the *E*s, *penis* and *penetration* in the *P*s, *masturbation, menstruation,* all the way to *zygote!* I came home reeling in astounded shock, and swiftly went to talk things out with Franklin, who marched me to the high grass of the yard for a conference. He sat me in the old swing, still intact and rusted, and listened to my fears. "It's all right, Linda," he told me finally. "It sounds strange, but it's . . . workable." At that point, Franklin's assurance was all the comfort I required. Now, although I have no reason to explain it, I suspect he's leading up to something heavy. "Too bad you didn't like Pop better."

Franklin says, "I liked Pop; I didn't like the way he died. Stupidity or calculation, I never could be sure. Maybe he had the answer."

"What are you telling me?"

"Don't go to California, Linda. Buddy will make a slave of you the way he did at Maryland, and then go off and do his thing. You heard him today. He has this crazy feeling of entitlement; he thinks he has the right to do just what he feels like, and there's no need for explanations."

"That's probably right on the mark, Franklin, but you tell me what I'm supposed to do. I feel . . . completely drained. It's like

I'm on a treadmill, trying to keep up the pace, and every time I think I've got the rhythm, someone speeds things up and I can't even run in place. I try to work and look after you and Paulie and pay the bills and keep Ma's spirits up, and I just can't do it. I can't go on living off Monte. If what you say is right, I can't even pay him back with an offer of my 'palpitating body,' as you so crudely put it today, 'cause he doesn't want me, either."

"Would you if he did? Would you?"

"Oh, why not? It's the only thing I've got that strikes me as negotiable."

"That's sick, Linda. That's how you got yourself in trouble in the first place, trading sex for what you figured was security. When are you gonna wise up?"

"When are you gonna help me?"

"I don't know how I can. If you go, it's curtains for me."

"You'll be okay. I'll ask Aunt Viv to come and stay. Or Buddy will help me hire someone. If he's telling the truth about his big ⋅commissions . . ."

"I won't live through it, Linda Jo. I'll do what Pop did. Step right up to the horror and let it crush me."

"That isn't what he did!"

"It doesn't matter. I will. What's the point of living like this anyhow?"

"Oh, Franklin." I'm heading for the door now, wanting nothing more than distance between myself and my brother. "Franklin, you little rat. Don't you dare pull this on me. Don't try to blackmail me, pretending if I go, you won't have anything to live for. Don't think for one damn minute that that's gonna sway me. If I decide to go with Buddy, I will go, and you can live or die as you damn please!"

"You're all heart, little sis."

"The last thing you need is my pity. I told you that before. When there's something you want enough, or someone you love enough, you'll overcome your lousy panic and get up off your ass.

Juanita knows it! That's what's killing her, that you don't love her enough to come and see her, in spite of how you feel."

Franklin flashes back, "Don't you pin that rap on me. If Ma's not getting better, I am not the one responsible."

"You're responsible that she's depressed. It's a matter of appearances right now. She's got her roommate, Mrs. Foley, who must be ninety-five if she's a day. She's got all these kids and grandkids marching through the room, and who sees Ma? Me, when I'm able, and stupid Monte sitting there with his long face, and some of the clients from electrolysis who come to say she had a light hand with the needle. Where's her pride and joy, her darling, brilliant boy, light of her life? Hiding in his room, 'cause somebody might look at him cross-eyed, and he can't take the discomfort."

"You don't make my life sound as if it's worth a damn."

"So kill yourself! Blackmail me with that. See if I care. No matter what you decide, there's one thing you had better get damned used to."

"And what is that?"

I turn to face him from the doorway, ready to milk the moment of all the drama I can find. "If I decide it's best for me and Paulie, whether you like it or not, whether Ma is well or not, we're going to Cal-i-*forn*-ya."

Franklin wets his index finger with his tongue and draws a straight line in the air, like someone writing on a blackboard: Chalk one up for Linda. "Whatever happens, kiddo, I forgive you."

Thirteen

"**P**icture a pirate." An actor, in old-fashioned sailor getup, is standing center stage, rumbling out a prologue in Shakespearean tones. A spotlight bobbing in his wake, not quite on target, wavers and goes black, then flares, surprising him. There's a novice in the light booth, I suppose. Spitballs fly. The crowd of hyped-up kids and weary parents shifts and coughs and snuffles as though cued. Paulie, sitting like a buffer between me and Buddy, wheezes softly. Buddy taps his neck in hope of calming him.

"Picture a pirate," the actor starts again, bending as though confiding in the audience. Suspended well behind him is a tall white screen, no other scenery in view.

"He said that," Paulie observes.

Buddy agrees, "He did indeed."

"Just listen to him, honey." I have my palm firm on Paulie's shoulder, an inch from Buddy's hand, which is tap-tapping a secret message like Morse code.

Today, ungodly early for a Sunday, Buddy was on the phone, proposing he and Paulie spend the day together. "There's a kids' play at the theater in Glen Echo Park. *Blackbeard the Pirate.* Sunday matinee, 1:30," Buddy read from the *Post.* "If you will give permission," Buddy requested with exaggerated courtesy, as though he was begging favors from a head of state.

I asked him what made him think Paulie would go with him, after the way he scared the poor kid yesterday.

"We have some fence-mending to do. We have to get to know each other all over again."

That's surely true. The present Buddy brought Paulie from California was a football uniform, the colors of the L.A. Raiders, black and gray. Paulie, who's scared of contact sports, surveyed the gift in silent horror and turned away, not deigning to touch the colors of the enemy. I told Buddy he'd made a foolish choice. "Why the Raiders? If he liked football, which he doesn't, he'd want a Redskins uniform. If he wore that thing to school, he'd be attacked."

"Paulie's not home anyway. He slept over at Monte's, and I don't know when he's coming back. They'll probably sleep late, it's such a gloomy morning." The day had started with a brief, fierce shower. I'd found the Sunday paper soaked, only the sports pages salvageable. Franklin, who sometimes professes interest in the football scores, was still in bed, still marveling over Conrad, I supposed, or pondering how he might be soon abandoned, or snoring. I didn't know and didn't care, my head pounding from yesterday's surfeit of beer, my stomach grumbling for solid food. I'd put the kettle on for instant coffee and was munching Paulie's chocolate cereal dry, like popcorn. "The only way I'd let him go," I said after some thought, "is if I came along."

Buddy took his good old time responding. "You aren't going to the hospital?"

"I'll go tonight. Ma has this roommate with a million relatives. Sunday, they're all over the place."

"It was supposed to be us guys, Paulie and me."

"Well, would it freak you out if I horned in? 'Cause it's the only way it's gonna happen, you going anywhere with Paulie."

"Happy to have you," Buddy laughed, as though he'd planned all this from the beginning and I'd jumped to the bait.

"This evil hombre is a giant, seven feet tall," the actor stretches his arms high over his head.

Paulie wriggles taller, dislodging my hand. I set it back upon his neck, my fingers brushing Buddy's, who glances at me, in response. "I bet he wishes he were playing Hamlet," I tell Buddy. He signals with a finger to his lips, be quiet.

Imagine me with Buddy at Glen Echo. They've transformed the old place into an arts center of sorts, spruced it up a bit, though most of it is still a ruin. I don't like the improvements. The Clara Barton house is painted lemon yellow, and the old ballroom is yellow too, with green and crimson pennants on the battlements. I've heard there's been a problem with the roof; raccoons are damaging the tiles. Still, folks convene for square dancing on Friday nights, phony cornstalks on the walls and propped up scarecrows on the fine, wrought-iron balconies. Not the palace I remember, but I guess people are having fun, and Pop would grin at that and say, "Right on."

The park leaves Buddy cold. He thinks the whole place should be leveled and used as an athletic field. He looked blank when I told him why I like it so—how we'd come here that first time, Franklin and I, with Pop; and Pop had acted carefree as a kid. How he'd laughed and danced and crooned his silly song and

I'd felt so safe, like God was in His heaven and the world was right. I'd been so happy to find that even grown-ups could be silly. You could be old, with all these terrible responsibilities, and still have fun. That's no big deal to Buddy, whose family is into pleasure in a major way, but for me it was an awesome revelation, like learning that my folks experienced sex, at least twice in their lives.

"The pirate's beard falls to his waist." With exaggerated motions, the actor demonstrates a flowing beard. Children giggle, sneeze, pop gum. Someone hurls a jelly bean on stage. The actor eyes it sadly as though it were a deadly missile. From deep in the front row there is a flurry of applause. Buddy bends to whisper into Paulie's ear, so close, I can sense how it must tickle. Paulie has calmed down in the presence of his dad. I guess his memory of our time together is still sharp, because he gazes back and forth from me to Buddy, like he's wondering who will start the screaming. All at once he's jiggling in his seat like the tension is too much to bear. I suspect he needs the little boys' room.

". . . and the beard is twisted into tiny braids and every braid is knotted with a scarlet cord, the color of *red blood,*" the actor menaces.

"Sit still, honey, please." My hand is back on Paulie's neck. Buddy toys with Paulie's hair, just to assure him all is well. In the dark, we're like a loving family, Mama and Papa Bear tending their frightened cub. Buddy is like a bear, solid and strong.

"This pirate, Edward Teach, is better known along the bounding main and in the secret coves where treasure chests lie buried, as," the actor pauses as the soft beat of a snare drum in the pit picks up in intensity, *"Blackbeard!"*

Laughter from the kids, the nervous kind. Paulie is cuddled in the curve of Buddy's arm, having shaken free of me again. Buddy's hand brushes my shoulder as he clutches Paulie's arm; he pulls Paulie closer so there's distance between them and me. Annoyed by this, I inch closer to Paulie.

"Picture this pirate, preparing for a battle to the death." A round of sneezes in the crowd, and I'm thinking of the viruses Paulie could catch. The hall is warm with wet, packed bodies. There's a noise like gravel pummeling the roof. Rain again. It seems as though the showers haven't stopped, since the night Ma had her heart attack.

The actor, crouching on one knee, is whispering now. "Blackbeard lights the tip end of a long, slow-burning punk," the actor pantomimes striking a match.

"What's a punk?" asks Paulie.

"It's a kind of stick that burns. Now, Paulie, shush," I warn him, "or we'll have to leave."

Ignoring me, Paulie asks Buddy, "What's a punk?"

"It's a fresh kid who doesn't listen to his mom." Seeing Paulie tense, Buddy amends "Actually, it's what your mom said. Now, settle down, old man."

"Did they have matches then?"

"I think so. Ask the expert." Buddy flashes me a grin.

"Did they, Mom?"

"I tell you what—we'll get Uncle Franklin to look that up in the Britannica."

The actor gesturing: "Blackbeard coils the blazing punk around his ears and up under his hat brim like a snake." The actor, standing tall now, moves downstage.

Paulie is leaning forward in his seat; if I glance sideways I have an unobstructed view of Buddy. He is staring at the stage with a half smile on his lips, absorbed like a young kid. In profile he looks innocent and sweet.

"When Blackbeard moves, the punk hisses and sizzles like a thing alive. Thinking of the fun to come, the pirate grins. His teeth are long and sharp, like tiger's teeth. His eyes gleam in the dark, alight with evil thoughts. In his right hand he holds a sword, and in the left, he's carrying a pistol. . . ."

"But if he's right-handed," asks Paulie, "how will he shoot?"

"Not very well," says Buddy.

"At last the evil pirate king . . ."

"And if he's left-handed," says Paulie.

". . . is ready *to attack!*"

The stage goes black. The drum deep in the pit is rumbling. A rustling through the audience as the beats hit fever pitch, the theater dark. Suddenly a picture flashes on the background screen. A pirate magnified to giant size. Red coils in his beard, and a blazing, snakelike punk burning from beneath his hat, his long teeth bared, his eyes glowing with wild, bloodthirsty lights. The children in the theater scream. Instinctively I grab for Paulie who has bolted to his feet, ready to run. Buddy has a grip on Paulie; so do I. We get him sitting down; somehow Buddy and I are clasping hands against Paulie's tensed back, laughing a bit because we got scared too. Buddy squeezes my hand. I tell Paulie, "It's just a picture, honey. Like a slide projector, only magnified."

He whines, jiggling up and down, "I gotta go."

Buddy says regretfully, "I'll take him." And slowly drops my hand, but not before another fervent squeeze. They clamber past me to the aisle, as music starts and the footlights brighten to reveal the setting listed in our programs as: SCENE I, ABOARD THE PIRATE SHIP. I whisper, "Hurry back," and settle in my seat, not sure, exactly, what is going on.

We're careful not to touch again, although the play is really scary and all of us are jumpy and Paulie can't sit still and wants to go and wants to stay and wants to change places with me because he can't see the stage clearly and wants to go back to his seat and wants to sit with Buddy. Buddy, who is unusually patient, takes Paulie in his lap and strokes his neck and whispers in his ear—all of it very sweet, that mix of tenderness and kindness that's so attractive in a guy; I can't help feeling lonely, solitary in the dark, thinking that must feel nice, fingers at the nape, lips against the ear and secrets told.

As events on stage start building to a frightful climax, Paulie cowers low in Buddy's arms, and Buddy booms out loud enough for me and everybody in the first ten rows to hear, "It's okay, sport. It's all pretend." Which sort of kills the eery mood. A woman turns around and mutters "Shush," and Buddy tells her earnestly, "Fuck you, ma'am." Paulie, who's been warned about the consequences of repeating certain words, is rapt; he is gazing at his father with a mix of horror and enchantment, waiting for the lightning to descend on Buddy. "You didn't hear that, kiddo, did you?" Buddy asks. " 'Cause if you did, I'm in big trouble." Paulie shakes his head and snuggles against Buddy's chest.

Walking to our cars, Buddy apologizes, "I didn't know the thing would be so bloody."

"Well, he seemed to enjoy it." The rain has stopped; the sun beams with a yellow glare that hurts my eyes after the darkness of the theater.

The dirt path we are following winds past a row of artists' studios, conical wood huts fashioned to resemble ancient yurts. Each hut is topped with sod, and planted in the sod are yellow marigolds that bob and beam like tiny suns. From a distance, the wood huts look like hats, peaked toppers bright with flowers, clown chapeaux. Seeing them, you have to smile, meld with the shabby, loopy ambience of the place, suspend disdain. The Crystal Pool is still a ruin—so is the shed that once housed bumper cars and the Laff House and the Cuddle Up—but the carousel is said to be in working order.

Paulie, skipping on the muddy path, detours to slop through puddles. "I liked the part best when the British captain cut off Blackbeard's head, and the sailors dumped his body overboard, and then when they looked down, they saw him swimming around the boat, looking for his head, and they got *so scared.*"

"Keep it down, honey, okay? When you yell like that, it makes my head hurt."

"And how the captain thought he was so smart, killing Blackbeard, and then he looked out across the water and he saw these lights, and they were moving faster than the wind, and they were Blackbeard's eyes shining in his head, and the head was following him."

"Will he have nightmares?" Buddy asks.

"You better believe it."

"And the head is going to haunt him, ever and forevermore, because the sneaky British captain tricked Blackbeard into coming on board his ship, because Blackbeard didn't know it was a trap . . ."

"Paulie dear, just simmer down."

"So really Blackbeard won, didn't he?"

"Well, I wouldn't say he won exactly."

"Didn't he, Dad? Because he's still haunting that guy who is just so scared."

"You got it, sport. Blackbeard got the best of 'em." Buddy suggests, "What say we go for ice cream?"

"Ice cream. Yay!"

"No, Buddy, we can't. We have to have an early dinner, so I can make it to the hospital."

"You're always going to the hospital," says Paulie.

"That's right. You want to come with me?"

Paulie concentrates on kicking water from a puddle. His feet are soaking, muddy; his eyes look glazed as though he has a fever.

"He's just a tad worked up," notes Buddy sorrowfully.

"I hope he settles down; otherwise, he just won't eat."

"What's for dinner anyway?" asks Paulie.

"I don't know yet. Maybe Uncle Franklin will surprise us."

"Uncle Franklin?" Paulie slaps a flat palm to his head with fine dramatic flare. "Om-o-lets! Oh, yuck!"

"Paulie, please calm down!"

"He needs to let off steam."

"I know. The play was kind of long." We are walking past the Spanish Ballroom whose yellow walls and rain-bedraggled pennants make me sad today.

"It's just a shame the carousel is closed," Buddy says, " 'cause he could have a ride and work off some excitement."

Paulie is looking wary.

"No, Buddy, it gives him motion sickness."

Buddy flashes me a frown. I can bet what he's thinking—my nay-saying is crippling the child. Well, I'm sorry, but that slow up-and-down gallop, coupled with the turning, does make Paulie sick. Push comes to shove, I don't like carousels that much, or any rides (forget about the whip, and I would die if you dragged me on the roller coaster), so I can understand where Paulie's coming from. There are kids for whom childhood is just a pain. They are born careful—old men—just marking time before the kid stuff fades and they can get on with their quiet, cautious living.

"Bet you'd give the carousel a try if it was with your old man, wouldn't you?" Paulie sneaks a hasty look at me and nods he would. Buddy grabs him in a sudden hug and growls tigerlike in Paulie's ear and starts to tickle him. It's like he's got this pent-up passion he has got to spend somewhere, and Paulie is the likely object.

He's hoisted Paulie on his shoulders and they're trotting down the path ahead of me, past the artists' studios with their roofs of flowers. Paulie is bucking like a cowboy, slamming his sneakers into Buddy's chest and yelling, "Giddyap!" and Buddy is jogging at a healthy clip. By the time I catch up with them, Buddy has eased Paulie back to the ground and both of them are whispering like they're cooking up a secret.

"We men have got this good idea."

"If it has to do with ice cream, I don't want to hear it."

"Suppose Paulie and I head out to Roy's and grab a bite, while you visit your mom, and then you stop by my place afterwards and pick him up."

"Buddy, I can't."

"Because my folks are at a medical convention in New Orleans and it's lonely in the house. There's this Ping-Pong table that needs using, and a soccer ball going to waste."

Paulie yells, "Yeah!"

"Quit it, Buddy. That's not fair."

Buddy, softly, "If I have to be unfair to get you someplace where you'll talk to me, without your brother and that Monte fool putting their two cents in, I will."

"Let's go there, Mom! I want to go."

"You can't, honey. Because there's school tomorrow, and you need to be home early. And we've already been gone most of the day. Uncle Franklin will get lonely if we don't get home."

"Best thing in the world for him," says Buddy. "Let him get lonely. Let him get an inkling how it's gonna be when we head for the coast. Maybe it'll shake him up enough to make some changes."

"You're jumping to conclusions, Buddy."

"I'm trying to make repairs out of this mess I made. I'm guilty and a fool, but there's my side of the story. You could allow me a brief half-hour to plead my case. Is that too much to ask?"

"You had your brief half-hour yesterday. I heard it then."

"Ah, Mom? Let's go with him. We can, can't we?"

"Oh, Paulie, I don't know."

"We can," says Buddy. "And we will."

"You had this all planned, didn't you? Before you called this morning?"

"I had nothing planned at all. I'm a desperate, sorry guy, seeking desperate measures."

"Oh, Buddy, please."

"And I want us back together like we were meant to be."

"I wouldn't count on that. Too much has happened."

"Baby," murmurs Buddy, "I know you pretty well. And therefore, I don't count on anything."

Fourteen

"The thing that got me angriest is when you made me give back Adele's sweater. You remember that?"

"Angriest? That didn't make you the angriest. That made you pretty mad, but angriest? Not quite." Buddy's smile, in the pale glow of a single candle is sad and sweet. "You'd get so mad sometimes. Furious. What did I do?" Sighing, he runs a finger down my arm, tracing a line from the shoulder to the elbow; a pause, then a slow trek to the wrist and back again. He's the med student tonight, studying the long bones of the skeleton. The softer flesh, the deeper crevices, and dark declivities come next, after the elementary stuff is mastered.

"The business with the sweater really hurt, 'cause you implied that I was nothing but a gold digger. You said I was taking advantage of a poor woman's confusion."

"That was the graduation party, right? Baby, I was wasted."

I guess he was. I remember him, teetering on the deep edge of his parents' pool, like he meant to try a swan dive fully dressed. He held a beer can, cupped in his palms, as though it were fine brandy. He kept shaking his head, grinning this dopey grin and muttering, "You got to give it back. You got to. This isn't worthy of you, Linda Jo. It isn't right."

Buddy asks, "You like the wine?"

"I guess I do. I'm not sure it's a good idea."

Buddy surveys the ridges of my collarbone. "It's a wonderful idea."

"If Paulie wakes . . ."

"The kid's out cold. We played soccer till it got too dark. Then, Ping-Pong for a half an hour. He fell asleep in front of Disney. When I carried him to bed, he didn't budge."

"How will I get him home?"

Prodding my ribs, like he's testing for hidden fractures. "You can stay here. Both of you."

"I can't. I'm due at the office bright and early. Paulie has school."

"Skip it. Both of you could skip a day. Like we used to do sometimes. Such brats we were, remember? We used to fill those soda cans with my Dad's bourbon and toddle into class completely buzzed. And the teachers were so clueless. Remember what's his name in algebra: 'When we mull-tiply, the bi-no-mial . . . Will you work it on the board, Mr. Merceau?' And I'd be staggering, almost, and hiccuping, and couldn't manage x from y, and you'd be back there in your seat, laughing hard, really losing it. Goodness, you're soft." Stroking one breast and then the other; then his hands move downward, tentative.

"Oh, watch it, Buddy. No."

"Why? Because you like it. Am I getting near some magic place?"

"Lotsa magic places."

"Zattafact? God knows, I make an effort finding them. God knows I try."

"This is very California, isn't it? Candlelight? The wine?"

"I don't know if it's California. It's like old times."

"No. Old times would be Paulie waking up and screaming, and me saying, for God's sakes, do it if you're gonna do it, so I can go to him."

"Bite your tongue."

"Someplace better I can bite?"

"Hey now, I don't think so."

"I don't mean bite exactly. Something like this?"

"Well, yeah, that's very pleasant."

"I bet it is."

"Say, Linda Jo."

"What, Buddy?"

"Don't do that, please."

"Why not?"

"Because you never wanted to."

"That's true, I never did. But now I do. Must be the wine. Maybe the company."

"I never asked you to. I never expected that. It just doesn't seem right."

"You said that it was pleasant."

"It is. But you're my wife. And you shouldn't want to do that."

"But you do what you please? So why can't I?"

" 'Cause it's the way things are. I take the active part. I give, and you receive. It's the way we're built. It's programmed in our anatomy."

"I thought you would be glad if I got into this a little more. I mean, more than I usually do."

"Yeah, baby, I know. And it makes me crazy to say stop, but it just doesn't seem natural for you and me. It isn't right."

"Well, pardon me for living. I didn't know there was a right or wrong to it."

"Hey, babe, don't be that way. Don't get all huffy. 'Cause we're both feeling so happy and so close, and up to now it's all been perfect, and I'm learning all about your lovely body, all over again . . ."

"Look, do it if you're gonna do it, Buddy. 'Cause, it's getting late, and I have to be at work tomorrow by eight sharp."

Solemnly, he raises himself on one elbow and peers at me, trying to read my face in the faint glow of the candle. "Linda Jo, have you been with anyone since I've been gone?"

"You have no right to ask me that. I could ask you the same, only I bet I know the answer, and I don't want to hear."

"It's different for a man."

"You think so, Buddy, but it isn't."

"If you've been with someone, I forgive you. Then maybe you'll forgive me too."

"I haven't asked for your forgiveness."

"Well, I'm asking you. Can you do that, Linda? Can you forgive me, because I want you to so much?" He lifts himself on top of me, his weight so heavy on my chest and his face pressed hard on mine till I can hardly breathe, and something warm and wet, his tears, flowing hot upon my neck, and his body moving now to its appointed place, programmed by anatomy, pumping desperately and fast, like he means to wipe out his mistakes and mine in one grand rush of passion. I know what he expects of me —participate, but don't get too unbuttoned. Soft sighs are fine; maybe a little mew of pleasure, but moans and grunts and raking of the nails across the back (how Reece would go for that!) are tacky and unladylike. "Love you, babe," says Buddy suddenly and rolls away.

I lay still for a time, eyes closed, arms crossed over my chest—

Elaine, the Lily Maid of Astolat floating down the river on a bier. The bedsprings creak as Buddy moves from bed. I hear him, fooling with the wine, snuffing out the candle. When the room is truly dark, I look around again. Buddy swings open the bedroom door. A wave of gold light from the hall brightens the place. Buddy stands still, framed by light, observing me. "Back in a flash. Don't go away now." He hesitates. "Tonight was far-out, wasn't it?"

He wants a testimonial, I guess. "Real good. You know, Buddy, it *is* late. If you could promise to have Paulie home by breakfast time, I'd let him stay the night." He nods okay and stands, hoping for more—a cute guy with an athlete's build, broad shoulders, solid pecs, hips lean enough to die for, bright, blond hair. A lover, waiting for my verdict on the evening's sport. In the hazy light, it could be Buddy, Reece, some compañero, anyone.

Later, he wants to know, "Does tonight mean we're back on track?"

"You'll wake him. Shush." We have come to check on Paulie who is sleeping in the big four-poster in the Merceau guest room, curled upon his side, his mouth agape, his fists bunched to his chin like he is deep in thought. He has good color for a change, darling freckles on his nose (a last residue of summer and those swim lessons he hated so). His lashes, which are wonderfully long and curly, wasted on a boy, cast faint, quivery shadows on his cheek. I notice that his hair is darkening, losing its blond sheen to something brownish and mundane, like mine. I'd hoped it would stay fair. When he was born, he had this goldish fuzz over his head, that looked like pollen dust, and dark blue eyes that gazed at me so warily I feared he knew right off we weren't a good match. His breath is coming noisily, "Ka poo, ka poo," something between a snuffle and snore. Poor baby, has a permanent stuffed nose because of allergies.

"Linda, you haven't answered! Does tonight mean we're back on track?"

"Hush, Buddy, please. I don't know what it means. It means we went to bed, and it was nice."

"Nice? That's all it was?"

"If we're going to let him stay the night, let's let him sleep. Just leave the door open a bit, okay. So if he wakes, it won't be dark."

Buddy follows me into the hall. It's almost daylight bright, a plush chamber of memories, soft carpet underfoot, faint floral scents, Adele's perfume held captive in the draperies. Buddy's voice is shaky with emotion. "I'll tell you what it means to me. It means we're married and we ought to be together. It means the past is past and we should get on with our lives."

"That's what we were doing when you split."

"Is it possible you'll ever let go of that? I acted like a jerk, we both agree on that, but let me tell you why I left. For openers, my folks kept harping that I was messing up my life."

"Oh, sure. I wasn't good enough."

"You didn't help. Every time I did something clumsy or stupid, and, God knows, I did my share, you'd throw this look at me: Who is this oaf? Every time I'd reach for you in bed, you'd get this terrible long-suffering frown, same as you did before: please God, let's get it over with."

"That's not exactly what I did before, and *that* got you bent outta shape."

"Maybe I'm not the greatest lover, or the best provider, but I do better in California. I like the work. I like the climate. You can get out in the sun and run. You're only minutes from the beach."

"Hot diggety."

"That kind of crack just proves my point."

"What do you want from me? A medal, 'cause you got a suntan and you kept in shape?"

"Out there, I feel more manly. I want you with me when I feel that way. Maybe you'd respect me more."

"Buddy, I have these other things to think about. My mother, Franklin. Last but not least, Paulie."

"What's Paulie got to do with this?"

It's typical he'd need to ask. For a time tonight, while he was dressing, I'd lain in Buddy's bed and thought about a whirl of things, mostly our son. I'd gone back to that picture he had drawn in school. Something has bothered me about it; something beyond the obvious. All at once the answer hit me and I sat upright in bed: in the drawing, we were all set down so carefully—Buddy, Franklin, me, Juanita, Monte, Reece, even Monroe scowling in the garden; but there was no child in the scene, no Paulie claiming his position in the constellation. Like he didn't know where he would fit, or, in the turmoil of the scene, his presence didn't matter. That has to be our fault, Buddy's and mine.

"Buddy, we fight so much. We aren't together two minutes before it starts. We never notice Paulie's there, and all the time we're arguing, we're scaring him to death."

"We never used to fight that much till you quit school. And then you got so sour, people didn't want to be around you. All our friends stopped coming by."

"They were your friends, and once I stopped going to classes, they never had a thing to say to me. They were all reading books I hadn't read, discussing stuff I didn't know. I hated it. I felt inferior."

"You could have told me that."

"If I had, would it have mattered?"

"Yeah, it would have mattered! You could've told me how you felt. See, that's the way it is; you always assume the worst of me!"

"Maybe you give me reason."

"Okay, I do." Frustrated, Buddy runs both hands through his hair. "Baby, it's silly standing here like lumps, trying to thrash this out. Let's go downstairs and talk."

"No, Buddy, I'm going home. I hate it in this house. I hate everything that ever happened here." The day we told his parents we'd eloped, their gazes floated past me like I wasn't there. The doctor cased the room, then stared down at his hands as though the talent they possessed astonished him. Adele had seemed perplexed. I looked familiar but she didn't know me; I was someone she had seen in a receiving line. She'd drifted past me toward the stairs, mewling that she had a headache and couldn't cope. Like an idiot, I'd followed, as though I still felt designated as the one to rescue her. As I watched her mount the stairs, I heard the doctor's voice, resonant with fury, carry to the hall. "I guess you've kissed off Dartmouth. I guess you better figure out how you're going to support yourself, because you'll get no help from me." And I heard Buddy's response: "I don't need your goddam help. I'll cash in my bonds, and Linda Jo and I will go to Maryland." I thought I loved him then. I thought we'd stick it out, no matter what, and teach his stuck-up family a thing or two.

"Are you telling me we're quits, Linda?"

I used to write down Buddy's name and mine, circled by hearts and flowers, wedding bells. I used to write out combinations of my married name—Mrs. Linda Jo Merceau, Mrs. Burton Paul Merceau III, and thrill, seeing the letters on the page. "I need to think about what's best for me."

"And the little guy? What's best for him?"

"Don't push me, Buddy. You got what you wanted today. Paulie's intrigued with you all over again. And you had your thrill tonight. Be glad."

"I had my thrill? That's what that means to you, when we're in bed?"

"Bed never solved a thing for us."

"If you don't enjoy sleeping with me, don't do me any favors. Buddy Merceau doesn't have to beg anyone."

"Please have Paulie home by breakfast. So he'll get to school on time."

"It won't kill him to skip a day."

"I know that you like sleeping in, but I want him home for breakfast, so he can go to school. If you can't do that, I'll wake him now."

"I'll have him home for breakfast."

"Thanks."

"You're going now?"

"I'm going, yes." He stares at me with stricken eyes. I think we know it's been decided but we can't say it out loud. All that I can think of are lines we used to read in AP English, gloomy words I never liked because they sounded like Juanita spewing out her dreary prophecies: This is the way the world ends, this is the way the world ends, this is the way the world ends . . .

"Well, then, drive carefully."

"I will, Buddy." In a whimper, in a whimper, in a whimper.

Franklin, who's left the safety of his own turf for the living room, is waiting up for me, his eyes alight with pleasure at the prospect of fresh gossip. He has been lolling on the sofa, studying the Britannica. He holds the volume up for me to see he's made it to the *B*s. I nod to him. "Impressive."

"You got a phone call from guess who."

"If it's Reece, I can't talk to him tonight. Maybe not ever. If he starts sending presents to the house: flowers, candy, anything, do not accept."

Franklin is stifling a smile, "From Juanita. Tomorrow, you're to bring her warm bathrobe and her ski socks. It's too cold in that place, even for her. She says they keep the air conditioning on Igloo."

"All right."

Franklin is eyeing me like I'm one of those sorry freaks we gaped at in the Medical Museum. "Does this mean you're on again with Buddy?"

"It means nothing at all." It means I'm tired of sex and its deceits, tired of seeking safety in the company of men. I want to live somewhere with Paulie, our own home, bright and calm, where I will be affectionate and wise, and he will have his place within the galaxy, a shining Paulie face to call his own.

Franklin looks perplexed. "Where's little toot?"

"With his father for the night."

"That's sweet. Nicely domestic. I bet you two are on again."

"Oh, Franklin, think what you damn please." I hurry past him, headed for my room.

His voice trails after me, profoundly sad. "No presents from the candy man? Too bad." Louder, so I'll be sure to hear and get annoyed. "I liked that damson plum he sent."

Fifteen

Saturday, the first cool day of autumn, is the anniversary of Pop's death. Franklin stays in his room most of the morning. I hear the drone of the TV and the slow thud of his pacing back and forth. As I listen, I hear noises from his closet as though he's rearranging his possessions.

Juanita phones at eleven to remind me of the date. She sounds weepy and glum, but not that frail. She wants a photograph of Pop so she can see his face before she too expires, of loneliness. This afternoon, they're moving Mrs. Foley to a nursing home. "She won't last there ten minutes," Ma predicts. "In here, at least, she's got distraction. With me around, she finds life more interesting."

"We all do, Ma."

"You could bring Franklin today. Today of all days, he should come."

"You know he won't."

"Franklin should come today. Explain to him why it's important. One year today."

"He knows what day it is."

"If you can't manage to bring him here, don't bother to come."

"Oh, Ma, be reasonable," I start to beg, but she hangs up.

Buddy stops by at noon to pick up Paulie. They're heading to the zoo and for Big Macs afterwards and more Ping-Pong and soccer after that, because Paulie can't stop talking about the fun he had last Sunday.

When we meet, Buddy and I are courteous, but cool. Buddy maintains a glum, wounded demeanor, like he's the victim in the piece. He seems to think I'll change my mind if he acts somber enough, or solicitous enough of Paulie. I know I want a severance, quick and clean, but I still can't say the words. Some meanness in my soul keeps me from telling Franklin that Buddy and I are close to quits. The talks on child support and visitation rights are just on hold till I can wangle time to see a lawyer.

Posted at a window, I watch Buddy and Paulie leave the house. Buddy saunters in the lead, wearing a Members Only jacket and pale, tight jeans he must have bought in California. A few paces behind, Paulie, in khaki windbreaker and rolled-up Wranglers and running shoes with Velcro closings, apes his father's gait, that lazy, loose, uncautious walk that scuffles on the pavement, toes turned in. Paulie is getting tall, losing his baby clumsiness. Watching him swagger to the car, a cocky replica of Buddy, I feel a rending in my chest that has to be a breaking heart.

Franklin surfaces for lunch, wearing Pop's brown robe over ancient, grimy jeans (that he must have kept hidden from Ma's compulsive launderings) and a blue work shirt. One of Pop's wide painted ties is hanging from his collar like a tinted noose. He has an Indian bonnet on his head, eagle feathers, everything. "You think your son would go for this?" Grinning, he pulls the bonnet off and sets it on a kitchen chair as though it were a priceless artifact. A wispy trail of feathers flutters to the floor.

"It's molting! Where'd you find that thing?"

"In a box inside my closet. Do you remember Indian Braves?"

"Sure. I remember crying 'cause girls couldn't join. And you went off on a weekend to Prince William Forest and got caught in the tail end of a hurricane and never made it there."

"Right. Worst outing of my life, bar none. Ask me why Pop could be a pain."

"Please, Franklin, not today."

"Today is most appropriate." Franklin sits down at the kitchen table, waiting to be served. "This headpiece was Pop's. There was a smaller one I wore. I ripped it up. So much for pleasant memories."

"Nice kid you were." I set out peanut butter and grape jelly, bread and milk. If he wants me to serve him, that's the best he can expect. "What was so terrible about the trip?"

"We got lost, for openers. There was Pop and me in Pop's old Chevy, and Petey Lindquist and his dad, and a kid named Barry Greer, whose father was a hotshot lobbyist, the four of them together in the Greer's big van. Pop, who was supposed to be our fearless leader, lost his bearings in the rain. We kept passing the same landmarks, a motel and a convenience store, but no one would get out to ask directions. We were learning self-reliance." Franklin grins.

He says that when it started to get dark they made camp in a field. The Greers and Lindquists shared a four-man tent. Pop and Franklin had this tiny job that kept collapsing on them. Once you crawled inside, you had to stay crouched on your hands and knees or lie flat on your back and stare up at the canvas. Pop's long legs protruded in the rain; he had endured that with good humor. Pop was a city boy, not adept at camping skills. For Franklin's sake, he was determined to enjoy the outdoor life.

Franklin recalls, "It rained all night. Of course, the tent, when it was up at all, leaked like a sieve. We were lying on these plastic ground cloths, and they were wet and muddy. It was like drowning in a swamp. Our sleeping bags were soaked. I have never been so cold, so wet, so miserable in my whole life. Finally, we crawled into the car to get some sleep.

"In the morning, it's still raining. Greer drives to the motel to get directions to Prince William Forest. He comes back with jelly doughnuts; that's the good news. The bad news is, the motel guy says the streams are flooding, and the roads north and south of us have been closed off. We have a powwow in the mud. Pop wants to build a bonfire and cook a good hot breakfast and settle in until the weather clears. Lindquist points out we're in a field, no woods around, and even if we gather up some sticks they'll be too wet to burn. Greer proposes we check in at the motel and relax with the TV. Everyone agrees except for Pop. We have driven to Virginia to experience nature, and nature in its wildness is what we are experiencing. It's all part of a bigger lesson, and when the rain stops, we will enjoy ourselves just that much more."

"Well, that was Pop."

"That was an idiot talking. Lindquist tries to ram some sense in him, but Pop won't budge. Greer loses patience pretty quick and tells Pop to do what he damn pleases, he's pulling out. That just makes Pop more stubborn. I'm yanking on his arm; he's wearing those green fatigues of his and an army jacket, and they're soaked. There's water streaming down his face like he's in tears. I'm begging, please Pop, oh, please let's go with them. Please! He says, 'You'll thank me for this, one day, Franklin.' And I know I'm dead. I'm six years old, freezing, hungry, thirsty, constipated, wet to the skin, and he's telling me, 'You'll thank me for this.' I tell him he can stay alone, and I'll go with the other guys, and he says, 'I want you to learn from this experience.' If I'd had a gun, I would've gladly shot him."

"You would not."

"For a warm bed and indoor plumbing, I'da wasted him. The other guys take off. When they pull away, I start to howl, like I've never howled in my entire life, but Pop hangs tough. We spend the weekend in the mud. Pop tries to fix the tent, but he never gets it right, so we live outta the car most of the time. Pop can't get a fire going, 'cause everything is wet, so we eat this dry granola shit and cheese sandwiches and warm apple juice, which tastes exactly how piss must taste. When the rain stops, which it finally does, the bugs come out. Pop's got a first-aid kit of course, leave that to Ma—everything you'd ever need for major surgery— but she forgot insect repellent. We go on nature walks and the bugs eat us alive. Pop's scared of snakes, but I'm not supposed to know it."

"Did anything good happen?"

"Not that I recall. At one point, the sun got really hot, and Pop said he'd pitch a few to me. I had my baseball bat, but the balls and mitts and stuff were in the van. Pop said we'd just go through the motions and he'd analyze my swing. He spots this grassy kinda hummock and he stands on that. It's really hot, and he's taken off his shirt, and he's in those flood pants that he wore, and they're shrunk up to his calves. He makes me move in close, 'cause he's gonna critique me, right, while I aim at a phantom ball? Crazy! He starts pitching to me, and as he bends, there's a rustle at his feet, and a hundred, maybe, of these small white butterflies float up from the grass and fly away. There's this quick, bright flutter for a minute and they're gone. For a second, when he heard this stirring in the grass, Pop looked like he'd keel over. I knew that he was thinking, *snake*. I enjoyed that part."

"Well you survived."

"With a sore throat and a million chigger bites and the worst cough of my life. And Pop got poison ivy. Ma read him the riot act, when we got home, and he, in his defense, which cut no ice with her, said that he was teaching me the virtue of persistence. Finish what you start. Hang in, no matter what. The other guys had a stupendous time. Nonstop TV, and all the junk food they could eat."

Franklin fingers the war bonnet again. "Maybe I'll trash this too."

"But Pop was right, wasn't he? He wanted you to tough things out. What's wrong with that?"

"Look where the lesson landed me. The other guys are doing fine. Petey Lindquist's playing pro ball in the minors. Barry's in business school. I'm a basket case. And the wise guru who preached the doctrine of self-sufficiency is dead by suicide."

"That is not so. It was a stupid, tragic accident."

"You know that for a fact, do you?"

"A man who spends the weekend in the mud to prove a point wouldn't give up his life 'cause something in it disappointed him. Pop would hang in, no matter what. He might consider bailing out, he might lose heart, but he'd hang in."

Franklin is working on his lunch, swirling peanut butter over bread, spooning out jelly, with the swift no-nonsense motions of a master chef. "It doesn't matter now. It's done."

I grab his hand before he lifts the sandwich to his mouth. "She wants you to visit her today. It's one year since he died and she is in a state." He shakes my hand away and reaches for the milk. "Franklin, please. She told me not to come without you. If I do, she probably won't talk to me. I can deal with that, believe me, but if she shuts me out, *she* won't have anyone."

"She might as well get used to it."

"What does that mean?"

"Push comes to shove, she'll be alone anyway. You're going west with Buddy, aren't you? You're gonna 'tough things out, no matter what'?"

"Suppose I do?"

"Suppose I do?" he mimics me. "Suppose you do, you'll end up sending him to med school, so the next time he walks out, he can say he did it 'cause he got too good for you."

"If I did go, it would end this argument. You could do what you damn please. Stay here and die."

"That could be worth something, you know? Go," says Franklin suddenly. "I'm urging you."

"Don't push me, Franklin, because you might be sorry."

"I'm as sorry as I'll ever be, whether you go or stay. Go, Linda. Have a life. I'll make out fine. Aunt Viv will come. Monte'll cope with Ma."

"You make it sound so easy."

"Go."

"Damn it, maybe I will!"

"What 'maybe,' Linda? Do it. Get off my case. You want to drag me to Juanita like a farewell gift, Franklin on a platter. Then you'll cut out anyhow. So go. Because I'm not leaving this house. Once and forever, understand that. I'm comfortable the way I am. I'll be the family grotesque forever, the nut who never leaves his room. Say my name in whispers. Trot the children here to see me every Christmas, creepy old Uncle Franklin, drooling in his soup and quoting useless facts. I will not change for you or Ma or anyone, because I'm happy with the way I live. I'm happy. You got that straight?"

"Great, Franklin. That's just great. You're happy wasting in your room, and Ma's happy sitting in the hospital and I'm happy facing life with Buddy. We're that rarest of commodities, a happy family!"

Stacked behind the turquoise curtain where Ma received her weepy ladies, my suitcases and Paulie's duffel bag have gathered dust, and the faintly soapy smell of Ma's pink creams. The lingering scent sparks memories. Ma, standing at the curtain like a prima donna, nailing me and Franklin with the serpent's look and muttered threats, "Quit that carrying on, you two, or you'll be sorry. No TV for a week." Ma, calming her ladies, clucking over female woes and rumored infidelities. With clients she would turn maternal, her voice a soothing buzz over the zap of the electric needle. She sounded wise and calm, the essence of authority, a shadow moving swiftly behind turquoise panels, trim in her spiffy uniform and slick white shoes. Recalling fragments of the past, I'm caught in this creepy nostalgia, as though Ma died and I was sorting her effects. Sneezing from the dust and streaming tears, I lug the suitcases upstairs, satisfied the thudding on the steps will give Franklin good cause to panic.

I start packing Paulie's stuff. The Raider uniform goes in the duffel first, followed by his pint-sized underwear, his scruffy corduroys, his little-boy pajamas bright with drums and bears. His books and toys, the Jiminy Cricket lamp, are things I'll send for later. I say this to myself, pretending I am being rational. Franklin has pushed me into a corner; pride decrees I won't retreat, but I'm giddy with panic, praying that one of us will call the other's bluff. Franklin and I are the same blood and bones, stubborn as Pop, unyielding as Juanita.

I'm starting on my dresses when I hear him pounding on the door. "Open it, Linda Jo."

"It isn't locked."

Franklin, deathly pale, flings open the door and stands posed in the entry. In the long dark robe, he looks like the Commendatore in *Don Giovanni,* risen from the tomb and bent on vengeance. He takes in the clutter on the beds. I've heaped my clothes in piles with no practical scheme. I don't know where we'll live, can't gauge the weather on the coast (summery, with earthquakes, I suppose), can't predict a future beyond fuzzy thoughts of me and Buddy quarreling, with Paulie looking on. Franklin says, "Listen."

"I am."

"Sometimes, I act like a damn fool."

217

"Agreed."

"Will you forget those things I said?"

"What things, specifically?"

"Linda, don't cave in to Buddy. Give it time. Once Ma's on her feet, you can make it on your own, you know you can. Get your head straight first. Figure out what you want. Then cut out if you have to, and I'll be back here cheering." His eyes are closed and he is talking quickly, as though he's got to spit the words out fast, before the bitterness of what he's tasting poisons him.

"Stay here for my own good? You're such an altruist!"

"If you promise not to leave with Buddy, I'll go with you to the hospital."

"When?"

He looks at me, his eyes wide now with fright. "Tonight? After dinner?"

I shake my head. "Now. Before you lose your nerve."

He nods. "Now. I'd better change."

"Exactly as you are. This minute. I'll leave a note for Buddy. In case he gets back here before we do. He can get a house key from the Lindquists."

Franklin, fighting for time, his breath already sounding shallow, sighs, "Yeah. Leave a note." He manages a smile. "A long one, yes? While I regroup."

I'm fumbling for my pocketbook, my keys, pondering what the actual sight of Franklin looming like a ghost beside her bed will do to Ma. "Let's go." I grab his hand. Pulling him toward the hall, I get a quick glimpse of our faces in the dresser mirror, both of us pale with fear, so zombielike and stiff, I'd laugh at the absurdity, if I weren't shaking with unseemly terror.

Sixteen

In the car, we drive in silence for a time, with Franklin clutching Pop's gnarled stick as though he means to beat off terrors. When a vivid splash of sun shines in his face, he looks alarmed, then shakes his head from side to side and groans, like someone fighting his way back to consciousness after a trance. He doesn't move into the shade or shield his eyes.

"The sun visor, Franklin. You can pull it down."

He murmurs "Yeah," and sits immobile.

"Is there too much air for you?"

" 'S okay."

"It turned cool kinda early, don't you think. I know it won't last—we'll slide back into summer—but it feels good, doesn't it?

Almost like New England in the fall? If it keeps up, the leaves will soon be turning." I hear my voice, soothing and low, this phony calm I take on when I comfort Paulie, as he struggles out of dreams. The studied, tranquil tone, the carefully contrived, "professional" serenity sounds eerily like Ma, jollying some nervous lady in the basement cubicle: "Relax, now, hon. Just hold on for another second and we're done."

"Franklin? You hangin' in?" He's breathing like a diver with the bends. "Should I have brought a paper bag? In case you hyperventilate?"

"Don't know. Can't breathe good, Linda Jo."

"Not too far to the hospital. Hang on."

"There's a crowded lobby, right? Elevators?"

"We'll take the stairs if you want to. Don't quit on me, Franklin."

"Can't catch my breath."

"You only think so. You're doing fine."

"Ears ringing. Scared to death."

"Go with it, Franklin. Be scared. Nothing will happen."

"Says you."

"Listen to me, Franklin. We're all in the same boat. Everybody's panicked half the time. Paulie's scared of swimming, and that bitch teacher he has. I'm scared Fowler will can me, if I take too much time off. Juanita's got her catalog of historic disasters and impending calamities. You know 'em better 'n I do. But they don't throw her. That's the point we sometimes miss about that lady. She talks a blue streak about her worries, but she toughs 'em out."

"Yeah. Juanita's feisty. I'm the family weak link."

"No way. You're here, aren't you? It's a big adventure for you, going to see Ma."

"Park somewhere, would you? Till I get my breath."

"It's bumper to bumper, Franklin. I can't go anywhere."

"I think . . . feeling faint."

"Bend over. Let the blood go to your head."

"Seat belt's too tight." He tugs hard at the strap crossing his chest.

"Then, loosen it. No, don't!" I think better of that as we stop short, in gridlock on Wisconsin Avenue, missing the car ahead of us by inches. That's all I need, a fender bender, and Franklin clobbered by the windshield, knocked out cold. "It's safer if you stay buckled. Try this, breathe deep. Relax and breathe. Relax and breathe. And think of something, anything. An interesting topic of conversation."

"Don't be a jerk. Can't breathe . . . can't talk."

Then I will talk him through this till he's safe, my brother whom I love and can't abide, whose pop-eyed craziness makes me ashamed and breaks my heart, who pulled me skyward in the backyard swing with silly songs, and giggled with me in the turquoise cellar, and shored me up in battles with the common enemy, Mama and Pop. Franklin, who told me sex was "workable."

"Linda, please get me home!"

"We can't go anywhere till traffic eases up. Franklin, would you believe the changes in Bethesda?" Cheerful and falsely calm, I start spieling this travelogue about the escalator at Bethesda Metro, which is the longest in the world ("When you descend, your ears pop; it's like Dante going down into the netherworld."), and the busy central plaza with its new ice-skating rink and modernistic sculpture (which looks like hubcaps strung upon an abacus, to me) and French cafes with festive awnings and fancy shops. "It's getting like New York, losing its small-town flavor, don't you think?"

He's not listening to me. "Linda, I had the best intentions . . . but I can't."

" 'Can't' ain't in the dictionary, Pop used to say, the Gospel according to Ann Landers." We lurch forward a foot or so, brake sharply and proceed and brake again—slow torture for a quarter mile, and the gas gauge is hovering near Empty. "I'll have to stop for gas when there's a chance. You mind?" No sound as we progress another block except the din of traffic and Franklin's labored breaths. "Hello, there, Franklin? Space to Earth. This is your pilot calling. Is anybody listening?"

"I don't . . . want to stop for gas. I don't want to see Ma . . . in the hospital. Even if I could hack it . . . getting to her room . . . I don't want to see her dying. Please, Linda Jo. That's worse for me than anything."

"The worst of it is in your mind, not in reality. Ma's holding her own. If she had let them do their tests, I bet she could've come home weeks ago. Greeley wants to quit the case. He'll hang in as a favor to Cal Fowler, but Ma is driving him straight up the wall. Maybe you can talk some sense to her."

"Don't wanna talk to her. The whole idea . . . was crazy. You conned me, didn't you?"

"You conned yourself." My tough-guy act is purely bluff, and I am feeling the contagion of his panic in my throat, which I've talked raspy and dry, and in my legs, which have the same numb feel they had when I was having Paulie and someone zapped me with a shot, an "epidural" that turned my limbs to stone. Franklin has a death grip on Pop's stick, and he's gasping "huffa huffa," like a frightened child. It strikes me it was arrogant and dumb to wrest him from the house, cold turkey, and drag him through these crowded streets, without Beryl on hand to pump him up, without a simple paper bag to offer as a talisman. If he dies of shock or has a seizure, it is on my head.

There's an Amoco station on the corner, the first good omen I have seen all day. We swing into the entrance on a bone-dry tank (with me offering silent thanks to any powers kindly overseeing us) and coast the last few feet to the self-service aisle. Grateful for the chance to walk and stretch a bit, I flick my seat belt off and push hard on the door handle, which doesn't always give on the first try. This time it opens handily. "Hang in, Franklin, okay? I won't be long."

He grabs my sleeve. "I'd rather slit my throat than see her in the hospital."

"It's not that bad."

"Please, let's turn back. Figure I blew it this time. For a change."

"Just sit and take deep breaths, because we aren't going home or anywhere till I get gas. Then, if you still feel bad, we'll park somewhere till you calm down."

"Always the little mother, aren't you?"

"Until you grow up, I had better be!" Shaking him off, I climb out of the car and let the door slam hard behind me. When I turn around to look at him, he's staring at me through the windshield, bug-eyed, like a hostage in the mean grip of a terrorist. So pitiful a sight, I soften just a bit and signal him, thumbs up. He shuts his eyes.

Something is out of kilter with the pump. I can't get the gas flowing freely, and the fumes are starting tears and a dull constriction in my chest. Tension does that, or maybe it's the fuel's toxicity. After a few moments' struggle with the hose, I give it up and go back to the car and tap on Franklin's window. He takes forever opening his eyes, and when he does, it's like I've roused him from a trance. I motion that he should roll down the window, but he only sits there like he's paralyzed. Finally, I pull open his door. He shrinks against the seat as though he fears a beating from the likes of me. "Could you help me pump the gas?" He shakes his head. "Wait for me, then? I'll get someone." I leave the door open, figuring that a whiff of air might perk him up—he looks that pale and shaky—and head inside the gas station to beg for help.

The kid behind the desk takes in my runny eyes and asks, "Somebody die?"

Explaining, it's the fumes from the self-service pump, and I'm probably allergic, and I think the line is jammed, I ask him, will he help? He clears his throat, "Um-hum" and starts this scribbling on a piece of paper, taking his sweet old time. Finally, trying clumsily to flirt, he says, "All righty, little lady." He's wearing dark gray coveralls with his name stitched on the breast pocket in red: Eric. "So, how about it, Eric?" He grins, hearing his name. He has a chipped front tooth that makes him look goofy and diabolic when he smiles. "All righty," he says again, in no hurry to move.

The car is as I've left it in the self-service aisle. The door on Franklin's side is open, but I don't see him huddled on the seat. My first thought is, I must've dropped my charge plate or my keys, and Franklin's on the floor retrieving them. Only, I've got my car keys in my hand, and the charge plate, as near as I recall, is in my purse, which is visible on the front seat, with no Franklin beside it. So then I think, my God, he fainted, and it's all my fault for not bringing a paper bag to help him breathe. He could've moved into the back, where he might've wanted to stretch out if he felt woozy, but the backseat is empty, and he's not slumped on the floor, and he's not sprawled on the greasy concrete of the service aisle. I even check inside the trunk, knowing he wouldn't hide in there—he wouldn't be that crazy—still there's no gauging how scared he is. There's nothing in the trunk but the funny-looking spare that resembles a toy tire, and tangled jumper cables. I have to face the truth. Franklin is gone.

Even then, I don't exactly panic. I watch while the kid fiddles with the hose. The gas flows for a time, then peters out. The kid says something's the matter with the line, just what I said to him, and I'll have to move to the full-service pump, but he won't charge me extra. So I do, turning the key in the ignition with steady hands, backing up and then pulling forward with a nice easy motion, the way Pop taught me. Breathing slow, deep breaths, the way Beryl counseled Franklin to inhale when he felt panicked. I figure Franklin's gone into the rest room, and will soon come out chortling that even phobias can't resist a call of nature. After I've paid my bill and he's still not there, I ask the kid, who's still trying to come on with me, to check the lavatory. "Please look into the men's room and see if my brother's there."

He grins warily, intrigued by what may be a household drama. "Boyfriend skipped, huh? He must be crazy."

"Please. He's a very nervous person. Just look and see if he's okay."

I can tell he's wondering, "Nervous, how?" But he goes to take a look, and comes back after what seems eons, sauntering, wiping his hands over and over on an oily rag, and says there's no one in the head. "Pahdon, me." He winks. "The men's room." I ask if I can wait; I'm sure my brother will be back in just another moment. He frowns. "Hey, miss, this ain't Union Station. If you're gonna wait, you'll have to move outta the way."

"I need to make a call. Do you have a pay phone?"

He shakes his head. "Ma'am, please move your car. People are waiting for the pump."

I know this is crazy, wasting time. Franklin can't be far. He's certain to attract attention from people on the street, a gangly fellow with a funny haircut, wearing a long brown robe and toting a walking stick. It's possible a cop detained him.

Four blocks north of the Amoco, at the point Wisconsin Avenue becomes the Rockville Pike, the office complexes give way, and the tower of the Naval Hospital looms tall and cold over the landscape like the mast of an ungainly ship. Across the roadway from the hospital, the campus of the National Institutes of Health spreads lush and green, like a well-tended park, plenty of trees and leafy hedges, plenty of brambly nooks and shadowed groves, where a scared rabbit like Franklin could lie low.

There's an odd-looking domed tent pitched at the entry drive to NIH where pet lovers assemble every day to protest animal experiments conducted in the labs. People are sitting at tables in the shelter of the tent; a few march along the sidewalk, brandishing posters of doleful sheep and baby monkeys. The signs plead: STOP THE KILLING and HONK IF YOU LOVE ANIMALS. Some days I honk timid support, and other days I drive by silently, thinking how the tests are necessary—maybe they saved Ma's life. Today I have the notion that, if I honk, Franklin will appear, posing at the entrance to the tent with a faint, embarrassed smile (his brown robe flapping in the breeze like the caftan of an Arab sheik, who's paused to count the passing caravans) and yell at me to stop and take him home. There's no logic to this, but there's surely comfort in the fantasy, so I try, honking as I pass, two brief, shrill blasts that rouse hard looks from passersby who don't support the cause. I honk a third time, louder than before. A woman carrying a sign waves and hollers, "Thank you and God bless you," which is comforting to hear, but only brands me as a charlatan and doesn't help my case because there's no Franklin in sight.

At the Metro stop near NIH, I manage an illegal U-turn and backtrack into town, where I encounter gridlock again. I have the sour taste of panic on my tongue, like one of Reece's recipes gone bad.

What would I do if I were Franklin, without money or friends, terrified? Nothing computes.

The car inches past tailor shops, the dark arcades of rug merchants, a pasta store, a health spa, a motel with emerald-and-white awnings and a billboard touting Happy Hour. There's no Franklin, huddled and pale beside a wall, confused and scared in some dark arch, or arrogant and mean outside a bar, extracting vengeance for the way I've badgered him. "Okay, Franklin, you've made your point," I whisper as I drive. "Cut out this shit, and I will take you home." It makes no sense that Franklin, scared to death of strangers and anything that smacks of new experience, would venture to the streets, the urban heart of darkness, worse than anything in books. No point to it. Unless he means to act upon his threat and end things. How would he do that? "Oh, babe," I hear his voice, as clear as if he still were here beside me, holding the old, gnarled stick and frowning at the clamor in the street, "let me count the ways."

Seventeen

Familiar, musty clutter in his room. Stuffier when he's not there. It's like he moves in his own sweep of light; his foolish, quirky smile brightens the place. Nothing startling in his dresser. Pop's jumbled ties. T-shirts and shorts and mismatched socks stuffed in scrunched-up piles. With Ma sick, no one tends to him.

Nothing of interest in his desk. Recipes scrawled on index cards. Red beans and rice. Sausage and apple casserole. Polenta dumplings. Onion pie. Forget it, please! The bird pictures are whimsical, lovingly detailed, so much effort devoted to a furl of wing or curve of beak, it's clear he has a talent. One sketch of a fat mockingbird, perched singing on a wire (I can almost hear the loud, sweet notes piercing the summer dusk like a diva's aria), could win him kudos from the Audubon Society. Some clippings from a magazine describing home computers. Franklin, you devil, you. I bet you figured since I was putting out for Reece, he'd get you a PC at discount. For every new position or perversion garnered from some dirty flick, he might throw in a floppy disc, a printer or a modem, even, and your life would gain a new dimension.

A second drawer. The usual mess of pencils and old stamps, dried glue, and cherry LifeSavers from the year one. It's a miracle you don't have bugs. Stale crumbs and sticky lozenges. Oh, Franklin, my poor Franklin, no proper bug would live with you! A postcard, never sent, depicts a circus elephant, a renegade, trapped by its captors on a country road. The animal lies on its side, held down by ropes and chains, as cautious troopers move to it with guns in hand. It wears a pointed hat; its fancy, tasseled saddle lies askew on its broad back. The postcard is called, "Runaway." It seems too appropriate. Sad. Do you feel like that trussed beast, ludicrous and trapped in its peaked hat? It hurts my heart to look at it.

I don't wish to invade his privacy, but I am searching for a key that might explain him. I want a folder full of Proustian reminiscence or sexy poetry, a cryptic observation from the underground. Something to tell me where he's gone or what is going on inside his head beyond the whir of panic.

When Pop died, we found silly stuff tucked in the welter of his papers. Fillers he'd clipped out of the *Star:* MAN FOUND EMBEZZLING CORPSES. CHILD SAVED FROM DROWNING BY COURAGEOUS PIG. Cartoons he'd cut from magazines of Thurber dogs and Addams witches. Booth's surly terriers. Larson's high-minded ducks and sober anteaters. Funny stuff, gently absurd, that fed his taste for whimsy. One mildly dirty business card, the gag, old as the hills. "Older than vaudeville," said Ma. A man stands at a urinal and smiles, WE AIM TO PLEASE. YOU AIM, TOO, PLEASE.

In Franklin's desk, there's nothing serious or silly. No outlines for a novel or letters to the editor. No diaries or treasure maps or secret codes. Another index card. Cornbread dressing with jalapeño peppers. Oh, yuck, as Paulie says. If I find you, smiling and alive, I'll murder you, Franklin!

Shamelessly, I prowl his room. At last, something turns up in the book that's on his bedside table. A folded sheet of paper in *Heart of Darkness* is scribbled with his thoughts:

"A Rationale for the Examined Life: Suppose the ancient anchorites who lived during the Middle Ages embraced seclusion more from fear than piety? Suppose their world filled them with terror—that whole medieval bustle, stench of wars and plagues—and all their mythic wrestling with devils was literally a struggle with their fright? Fear of life became more powerful than fear of death, and so they cowered in the woods and pondered the After-life as something more desirable. Suppose their solitude led them to wondrous insights—a mystic sense of oneness with the origin of life and goodness—CRAP!"

He adds a terse rebuttal: "No rewards for cowardice in history. Someone said (Churchill? Ask LJ check the quote): The best virtue is courage because it makes all other virtues possible."

"Pondered the Afterlife?" I don't like the sound of that. Poor lonely Franklin, seeking consolations in the intellect, only finds more reason to heap coals upon himself. Choking back the press of tears, I promise him I'll look up the quotation about courage in the library if it interests him so much. "Anything you want, Franklin. "Anything! If you will just come home!"

In the top drawer of his night table he keeps a flashlight and assorted keys and his wallet, which still holds a few dollar bills, his expired driver's license, and his student ID from Maryland—and photographs. There's one of Ma and Pop, dressed to the nines, headed for a New Year's party at the Lindquists. There's one of me with baby Paulie in his stroller. Paulie, who's bundled in a bulky snowsuit and a knitted hat, stares into the camera with a wise, unblinking gaze, a model of toddler dignity. I'm kneeling at his side—a good shot of me—smiling in a glory of maternal pride. There's a photograph of me and Franklin on the steps of the Lincoln Memorial, taken the summer of the Bicentennial by one of Franklin's high school pals. We're wearing jeans and matching T-shirts, printed with a slogan we adored: I'M NOT A TOURIST. I LIVE HERE. I look as though I'm choking back a burst of laughter. Franklin, with an arm around my shoulders, appears protective and superior. His chin is raised in a parody of homeboy arrogance—my brother assuming an attitude, scowling at the tourists crowding "his" domain. That day we'd traipsed to all the monuments (because Franklin deemed that pilgrimage was appropriate on the Fourth) before claiming our turf amid the picnickers and celebrants gathered on the Mall. Franklin kept us chuckling with his version of "historic" facts: "Dolley Madison invented ice cream and used the profits to finance the War of 1812. Lincoln kept a diary of scandals in his administration known as the Lincoln Log." When dusk fell we clapped our hands and stamped to the beat of Sousa marches booming from an outdoor concert by the National Symphony. When it was dark we stretched out on the grass and watched the starbursts of fireworks, green and gold and rose: flowers and waterfalls and wildly waving plumes, floating in the sky like the gorgeous tails of birds. Showers of light sparkled near the white dome of the Capitol. "Oo-wee," Franklin had shouted after each display. "Oo-wee," a schoolboy's explosion of exuberance. "Excellent!" had been his verdict of that day. "Completely excellent!"

Marveling that he's kept the photo of us all this time (why not some sexy number from his college years?), I pull the picture from his wallet for a closer look. On the back he's written in the date, July 1976, and under that our names, as though he needed a reminder, and under that a label, copied from the old Batman and Robin series on TV: DYNAMIC DUO.

The picture blurs as I sink upon his bed and let the tears flow freely now. "Oh, Franklin, please come home! Please! Just get here, and I promise I won't pick on you. You're silly and a Grade A pain, but you're my brother and I love you and I want you back. That's all I want. I want you back!"

Intermittently, I try calling up Monte. There's no answer at his apartment. When I phone his store, a cautious female voice finally tells me he's headed to the Fitness Show at the Convention Center. Her wariness enrages me, as well as Monte's taking off without a murmured by-your-leave. Imagine, plodding unimaginative Monte, daring to have a goal that doesn't fix on me, daring to leave his store without telling me his whereabouts. He's been a gadfly in this house. Now, when I need him most, he takes it in his head to vanish, as though instinct warned him I would ask something too difficult. After that last encounter in our cellar, he seems content (relieved) to hover on the border of my life, assessing me with gloomy eyes, a voyeur, nothing more. We have a tacit understanding since that day. I do not flirt or tease or even touch his hand in any way that he might misconstrue. He doesn't criticize.

Somewhere near six o'clock it dawns on me I'm starving, so I tiptoe round the kitchen, scared of noise, as though the clattering of pots and pans, such a normal sound, will brand me as heartless, craving food when Franklin's missing, perhaps dead. Scrambled eggs and toasted muffins. Earl Grey tea. I find a jar of English marmalade Franklin has been hoarding and heap spoonfuls of bitter orange and butter on the bread, savoring how the flavors meld and seep into the muffin's crevices. Even with the saltiness of tears, nothing in memory has ever tasted more delicious.

Gobbling, ravenous, halfway done—rumblings in the stomach are a perfect counterpoint to grief—the phone rings with an urgency that portends news. For a moment I pretend I don't hear and go on eating, stoking up driblets of egg and crispy muffin, so good—*so good.* Bad news will always find you, Juanita promises.

A hasty gulp of tea; a last morsel of bread. I've propped up the picture of me and Franklin on the kitchen table. Before I dare to get the phone, I offer a last plea to the haughty fellow in the photograph. "Don't let this be bad, Franklin. You hear me? Don't!"

It's a woman's voice, breathless and rushed, too lively for Adele's. No one I know from the office. Possibly a nurse with news of Ma. "Is this Linda Jo Burke?"

"This is Linda Jo Merceau."

"Oh right. Sorry about that. I forgot your married name. Linda Jo *Merceau.* I bet you don't remember me." A chuckly, chortly huskiness like a frog got in her throat and she's stuck between a giggle and a cough.

I really hate this, guessing games. "Who is it, please?"

"Linda, it's Beryl Blackwell."

"Beryl!"

"You do remember me?"

"Oh yes."

"How are you, Linda Jo?"

"I'm well enough. How are you, Beryl?"

"I'm pretty well. I guess you're wondering why I called."

"I guess I am."

"Well, the reason, as you might suppose, is Franklin."

"Is he with you?"

"Yes, Linda, he is, and feeling calmer after a dreadful afternoon."

"Is he all right?"

"He's had a sandwich and a nap. I believe he will be fine."

"A sandwich and a nap. After a dreadful afternoon? And he'll be fine. Well, good for him!"

"He said you'd be upset."

"He said that, did he, Beryl? He is astute. When did he mention it? Between the sandwich or the nap?"

"Linda, please. He feels sufficiently ashamed for what he must have put you through."

"Well, I don't know about *sufficiently*. Can I assume, since he's rested and had a snack, he's ready to come home?"

"He'd like to go home, yes. I offered to take him there, but we didn't know if we should chance it, not knowing where you'd be."

"Well, right. I could be tearing out my hair. Roaming the streets. Not to mention crying, hysterical. There's a lot I might be doing so it's good you called. *Finally.*" I emphasize that last.

"Linda Jo, there are things we should talk over. Calmly." No flies on Beryl. Calmly indeed, she takes control.

I try a couple of seconds of deep breathing. Count to ten. "May I have your address, or is there something else that Franklin wants to do before I come for him?"

"Do you have a pencil handy?"

"No, I don't. Just tell me where you are, okay? I promise, I'll remember it."

She hesitates as though I've failed a most important test. Linda Jo Burke Merceau. The sister in the act. Not decorous enough or kind. A mean, sarcastic brat, not sensitive to brother Franklin's whims. Slowly, as though she's talking to a child, Beryl tells me her address on Battery Lane, a stone's throw from the gas station. I must have passed her place a couple of times, during my search for Franklin. "I'll be there in fifteen minutes."

"Franklin will be glad to see you." She hesitates, "Linda, I cannot emphasize enough that anger will not help Franklin. If you could cool it for a bit until you hear him out . . ."

Ah, well. You see, Beryl, here's the thing. Anger will help *my* case. 'Cause if I don't scream and holler good and loud, I'm quite likely to kill him first, no questions asked. "Tell Franklin to be ready, please."

Ready or not, I'm on my way. Tears stream and dull my vision. Hands tremble as I lock the door, the note for Buddy still in place. Wait for me, Buddy, please, and we will hightail it to California. Franklin has made the leaving easier. He went to Beryl's. He went to *Beryl's!*

After he left the car, he waited at the crosswalk till the sign said WALK. He crossed the street, not sure of which direction he was headed. He ducked into the nearest building and waited in the dark lobby to catch his breath. He saw me move the car. He saw me talking to the boy in coveralls. He saw me drive away. When the car pulled out of sight, he stood a long time, paralyzed. He was aware of people moving, some eyeing him with curiosity. He saw the wall of pay phones in the lobby and thought of calling Monte. He fished through his jeans to find a coin, one of the quarters he always has on hand for practicing his magic tricks. In the mess of crumpled tissues, gum wrappers and such he pulled out of his pockets, he found a wadded scrap of paper, legible, thank God, bearing Beryl's address and phone number, a remnant of the days when she'd counseled him to call her, day or night.

"I was planning to work all afternoon at New Behaviors; then I decided I could do my paperwork at home. Can you imagine if I hadn't?" Up to this point, Beryl has droned without embellishment. Now her voice takes on a richer, deeper timbre, as though she's thrilling to the tale. "It was hard to pin him down to where he was—he was so agitated, he couldn't get his bearings—but then he talked about the Amoco station and the new building across the street with all the fancy marble in the lobby—people are calling it the Roman Baths—so I knew just where he was and thank God it's not far from my apartment. I told him just stay put; just do not budge. I could've walked, it was that close, but I thought he'd have it easier if I drove." Beryl laughs. "I *flew*. I almost ran down two pedestrians. People must have thought I was a lunatic."

She hasn't aged. That adamant fixed smile, that fierce, determined perkiness must keep the flesh firm as cement, although she's taken on some weight, grown broader in the beam, and the girlish pleated skirt she wears, along with thick black tights, is hardly flattering. She's kept her hair cut in its soup-bowl do, an homage to A. A. Milne. I note bold henna glints and a sweep of bluish shadow on her eyes, as though she's lately, clumsily discovered glamour and hasn't got it right. There's a fat, angry pimple on her chin. She must have had a fit when Franklin turned up after all these years and she had to greet him with a shiny zit on her face.

"He'll be out soon," she promises. "He's in the john, just freshening up."

She has a pretty nice apartment. Chairs. Pictures. A couch. We wait together on the sofa, in a welter of small pillows, wooly throws. "He's hiding from me, right?"

"Frightened of your anger, certainly." She looks prepared to give a sermon, friendly in her cheerful way, but infinitely earnest. She's wearing a tight black sweater, not demure, one of these cotton ramie jobs that don't conceal a lot. "In any case," says Beryl, "I'm glad we have this chance to talk."

I nod, sinking into pillows like a swimmer pulled down by the tide. It's stuffy in the room, as though the heat has been turned on too early. A clock bongs noisily behind us—a sound like springs uncoiling.

"I suspect Franklin has got you very hurt and angry, but I want you to know this. The fact he took off on his own—the fact he left the house at all—I take to be a most positive sign."

"I view his disappearance as sadistic."

Beryl's smile transmits rueful rebuke. "Linda, I know you're mad at him, but give him this, it's something of a triumph." Grinning, Beryl shows fantastic teeth, so uniformly white and even, I figure that they're capped. She has a delicate small nose and dark, bright eyes that crinkle almost shut each time she laughs. It strikes me with a shock she must have been a pretty kid, someone who hit her peak while she was young and hung on to her girlish airs with the view that what worked early on would work through life. If we'd been peers in high school, we might have been good chums, two adolescent charmers, lively and cute.

"He took his damned sweet time informing me that he was here."

"Well, Linda, he was in bad shape. Couldn't catch his breath, and sweating so, I thought he was dehydrated. I made him drink a ginger ale, plenty of ice, and later on, he had a chicken sandwich."

"Bully for him."

"And I insisted that he try to nap, but he'd do it only if I promised I wouldn't call you right away. He was ashamed, and needed to . . . regain composure."

"He was so ashamed, he fell asleep? You know, that's just so like him."

"When he woke up, we had a good long talk. I assured him that he can be helped. Now more than ever. We know so much more than we did four years ago. The latest research points to medical disorders, far more than emotional . . ."

"He knows that, Beryl. He keeps up with the literature."

Beryl folds her hands like a good girl launching into a recitation. "We have drugs that nip these episodes of panic in the bud. Linda Jo," she leans to me, her dark eyes shining, "I have seen miracles. People who were crippled by their fears, just as Franklin is, going back into the world and functioning. People who lay trembling in the night, frightened by the sounds of their own hearts. These people, getting jobs. Succeeding. Making contributions to society." She speaks this in an earnest whisper. Her eyes have taken on this saintly glow, like she's Mother Teresa telling the story of the poor and lame. She's getting just a tad carried away, but that's our Beryl. I think about her clients coming here for parties. Do they huddle on this sofa, grasping platters on their laps, scared they'll spill their food, or spatter wine over the rug? Are there certain dishes Beryl prepares to comfort them, like macaroni casseroles or meat loaves? Do onions make them queasy, or do they tote fat bulbs of garlic to ward off evil spirits?

"I'm not sure drugs would work for Franklin. There's our family to consider. You know my mother's an alarmist. Both of us grew up hearing nothing but worst-case scenarios. That has to leave its mark, doesn't it?"

Beryl waves this off with an impatient waggle of her head. "I don't think Franklin blames her; and even if she were the cause, you cannot change your mother's personality. You can accept it, and forgive it, and," she pauses as though ready to impart a magic formula, "push past. For God's sake, Linda Jo, don't dwell on it. You have a husband and a child. You're old enough to know you have to take responsibility for your own life." The fine edge of contempt chilling Beryl's voice is payback, I presume, for our caper on the bus. "I could tell you stories about families." Beryl's look hints at dreadful histories. Franklin's and my problems hardly qualify.

But love can be a burden, I know that much. Ma's vigilance warrants our loyalty. Her fierce, unswerving interest in our lives deserves response, and so we tremble on command, and walk the safer path and shrink from disappointing her until we founder and sit paralyzed, or act like simps. Sometimes, sitting in the waiting room with Tasso, I dreamed that she would die and I'd be free. Then I prayed for her to live, so I could beat her at her gloomy game. Where is the medicine for that?

"You're quiet, Linda Jo. Are you upset?" Beryl wears a dense, musky perfume. I picture her dabbing her wrists and ears as Franklin slumbers in her bed. I picture her coming to him naked, bearing ginger ale with ice, and a hefty chicken sandwich, garnished with picnic gherkins and frilly toothpicks. She'd bend to him, her soft breasts swinging in a cloud of scent . . .

"Look," Beryl's voice is cordial now and businesslike, "let's not confront past shadows. Let's deal with problems we can solve. Franklin needs a full medical work-up and probably a course of drugs as well as psychotherapy. If he's ready to start treatment, if he wants to help himself, and Linda Jo, he has to want it, I can give him several good referrals. I've told him that." She smiles sadly now. "I don't think he should work with me."

"What did he say when you suggested therapy?"

"Oh, he got quiet. He thanked me for my concern. He assured me he would think it over. He did not look overjoyed." She giggles now. "Leaping to health, that's scary isn't it? He needs some time."

"Speaking of time, Beryl, he's been locked away a good long while. What's keeping him?"

Gracefully, for someone bottom-heavy, Beryl rises from the couch. Her hair gleams in the lamplight. "I'll go and see." Without exactly knowing why, I move to follow her, like we're kids involved in some brisk game of tag. She leads me through an alcove to a hall. The floor is polished wood and slippery. There's a small, bright rug, an Oriental. Green and garnet flowers. Bands of fringe. I take a stand upon the rug, dead center, as though it represents some bright island of safety. Beryl points to a closed door. We can hear tap water running. Beryl calls in a wheedling voice. "Franklin, Linda is waiting for you."

"Franklin, let's get going."

"Please, Linda Jo, let me. Franklin? Are you all right? Please answer, dear."

I tell her, "Try the door."

Beryl tests the knob, then knocks again, ever so gently, as though she's summoning him to tea. "Franklin, open the door please."

"Franklin, you jerk, come out of there!"

"Franklin, it's Beryl. I need something in there. Please open up."

"Don't do this to me, Franklin! Don't!"

"Please dear, come out."

"Franklin, you lunatic, open the door!"

Beryl, in a loud whisper, "Perhaps I should find the super. He has a master key."

"Yes. Get him here."

"Oh, look, I know he's fine."

Her perfume in the tiny hall is stifling. "Just get the man here, will you!"

"I'll phone him, if I can just remember where I put his number. Somewhere, in the kitchen." Suddenly the water in the bathroom stops and Franklin swings open the door, tall in the long brown robe, his face composed but chalky white, his hair dampened and slick. "Franklin!" cries Beryl. "Why didn't you answer?"

"Water was running. Didn't hear."

"That isn't so, you lying bastard!"

"Linda Jo!"

"Running away wasn't enough? You had to find another way to torture me!"

"Don't yell. My head hurts."

Beryl asks, "What took you so long, Franklin?"

"Washing up. Looking for this." He holds up a jar of aspirin. "You got any with buffering, Beryl?"

"You lunatic! You think I don't know what you're up to. You think I'm not on to your game? You worry me to death, so when you finally turn up healthy I'm supposed to be so grateful I ignore everything else. Not this time, bub. No way!"

"Let's not make a case of this, okay?" Something steely in his eyes, something anguished and yet cold, like he's looked into the heart of fear and stared it down. "Let's go if we are going, please." His voice crackles with urgency, as though it's life or death for us to leave, without further argument. He turns to Beryl. "Listen, thanks." He's as churlish as he ever was to her. She seems untroubled by that. Grinning, she seeks my eyes as though she's just pulled off a major coup, delivering him to me intact.

Tonight the sky looks phony like the scenery in those old-time movie palaces downtown, where tiny stars stay fixed against a dome of blue, and fat clouds dangle near a bogus moon. It's cool, a blast of northern air turning Bethesda into Canada. The car engine is chugging jumpily on idle. When the air turns snappish, as it is tonight, you have to let the motor run a good long time, or you'll stall out. I've rolled my window down a bit so we don't die of the fumes. Franklin is shivering.

"How many did you take?"

"Don't know what you're talkin' about."

"How many? You took your sweet time in the bathroom. Don't tell me you were in there primping."

Franklin lets his head loll on the head rest. "Six, maybe. Seven, tops. I started getting nauseous. Know something? It's hard to keep 'em down. And I didn't want to, anyhow."

"Jesus, Franklin! Should I get you to a doctor?"

"Nah, I'm fine." Surprising me, he chuckles. "You ever peek inside Beryl's john? It's furnished with the damndest stuff. She's got this knitted poodle cover that fits over the toilet brush and the same doggie cover on the toilet lid. She's got this fluffy, pinkish carpet on the floor. She's got this soap dish that's a swan, and a bird cage with this little stuffed canary that sits there on a perch and stares at you with dead, glass eyes. At least, I think the thing was stuffed; it didn't move, even when I started barfing. If it's alive, it's catatonic. Living with Beryl could do that to a bird. She's got this Kleenex box covered with shells, and shell picture frames and wallpaper that looks like silver ripples with fishes swimming. You can see your face in it. She's got these framed things of embroidery on the wall and each one has a different motto. ONE DAY AT A TIME. LOVE, FAITH, COURAGE. Crap like that. I started on the pills, and I was getting sick, and they were coming right back up, and I was feeling so disgusted, thinking, even this you can't do right. And then I realized that, if it worked, if I was gonna die, the last place in the world I'd see would be this little shiny room, with shells and fish and that mean-looking, stuffed bird. It looked like Juanita, you know, puffed up and mad."

"So Beryl's lousy taste kept you alive?"

"Hardly," Franklin says. "It had nothing to do with Beryl. I'm sitting on the floor, hugging her toilet bowl, thinking I have finally hit rock bottom, dying in a sea of kitsch, and then I get to wondering about Kurtz, and I think I know what was the horror. Not the evil in his life. Not even a preview of hell. I think it was this sudden sense of nullity. He would die and there'd be nothing. No grief or guilt or wickedness or good, or opportunity for penance, anything. A cold, dark void. I heard you knocking, and I knew how angry you must be. I realized our deal was probably off and you'd cut out with Buddy, and I'd be left alone to sit and ponder what a dud I am. No one to talk to about anything. And even that seemed more desirable than . . . nothing. Is that amazing? Those stupid mottoes on the wall started to sound heavy. Pop would've loved 'em, philosophy from fortune cookies, right?"

"And then? What happened, then?" I expect he'll say that love for Ma and Paulie, regard for me, helped change his mind.

"Nothing happened then." In the darkness of the car I can just make out his sheepish, exhausted face. "Nothing happened," Franklin whispers. "I decided . . . to hang in."

Eighteen

Above us, pinpoint stars. A fuzzy drift of clouds covers the moon. His breathing, noisy and precarious. A groan escapes him as he leaves the car.

"How do you feel? Tell me what's going on, Franklin."

"The usual shit."

"But you can do it, right?"

"Don't know."

"You can. You're motivated. Beryl says so."

"Beryl—doesn't live inside me."

"Then, count your blessings." The car door closes with a thunk, cheap metal on cheap metal, no satisfying heaviness. For a terrible split second, I fear I've locked the doors and left the keys in the ignition. I find them safe within my fist. "Dummy! I am a dummy, Franklin. Bordering on senile. I always go into a panic, always think I lost my keys when they're right there in my hand. You set to go?"

"Yeah, set." He lurches for my arm. In his free hand he is holding Pop's dog-headed stick, tapping it on the pavement with a sound like Old Blind Pew tapping in the darkness toward the Benbow Inn. Or was that Long John Silver dragging his wooden leg? Franklin is shuffling at my side and struggling to breathe. He gasps, "Is there a plan?"

"No plan. We walk across the parking lot. We go into the lobby. We go upstairs."

"No elevator," Franklin warns.

"We'll take the stairs. Four flights, but that's no biggie, right? Piece of cake." My voice rings with souped-up glee; it's the tone I use with Paulie when I take him for his shots.

Franklin says he's too damn tired to climb that far.

"Too bad! I can't bring her to you! Though, if she knew that you were here, she'd drag herself downstairs."

He mumbles this is nuts, and I am putting both of us through needless agony.

"Shut up, Franklin, and save your energy."

The bushes bordering the parking lot bend under gusts of wind. Franklin and I are shivering. This afternoon (flipping TV channels to see if Franklin had been found somewhere, a suicide), I watched a weatherman explain we were in for an unseasonal chill.

Franklin's strange attire is attracting double takes. A blonde woman in pink velour, pink sneakers, and white tennis socks with pom-poms at the heels, has turned to stare. "Nice night," I tell her, and she moves off hurriedly, the white poms bobbing into blackness. "Franklin, you are an oddity."

"I'm sick, Linda. Really sick."

"Should I take you to Emergency?"

"Hell, no! They'll kill me there."

"You'll feel better indoors. It'll be warmer."

"That aspirin that stayed down. Feels like a hole burning in my stomach."

"We'll get you something. An antacid. I'll ask one of the residents."

The barrier to the doctors' parking lot is down, a slim pole marked with zebra stripes, like the gate to a frontier. Ages have passed since Shantar labored on his car, stroking a square of chamois lovingly over the garish paint. If he'd persisted, I'd have gone with him, joyriding.

"I'm cold, Linda."

"Me too. Look, Franklin. Monte's here." His car, sporting a bumper sticker that says JOGGERS DO IT ON THE RUN, is jutting at a funny angle, as though he parked it in a tearing hurry. "He must've come straight from the Fitness Show."

"Isn't there—a limit—on her visitors?"

"Nobody notices. Visiting hours end at eight, but you can stay till nine, or even later. Nobody cares."

"I couldn't stay that long."

"We'll trot you in to see her; then we'll go."

"You promise?"

"Scout's honor."

"You never were a Girl Scout, Linda Jo."

"Well, you have to trust me, Franklin."

"I have, haven't I?"

At the main entrance he balks, frightened by the sliding doors, which are triggered electronically to snap open and shut as people come and go. As we draw close, the glass panels hurdle open like the twin blades of a trap. I have to drag him forcibly over the threshold. Then the noise assails him and the stuffy air and the poison mix of gloom and terrible anxiety that hangs over the lobby like a toxic cloud. People are bunched in droves outside the elevators. A grim-faced volunteer commands the information desk. In the window of the gift shop, Paddington remains unclaimed, sitting atop a pyramid of boxes. Franklin stops to get his bearings; then he darts straight for the fire door as though he's read a blueprint of the premises. He must have played this entrance over in his mind a thousand times.

The stairs are certainly the better choice, but if he faints, it will be a horrendous fall. He could break a leg or get internal injuries. I pray we make it to a landing first. Then, if he passes out, I'll get him loaded on a gurney and whisk him up to Ma and tell her I've brought her a get-well present, and she'll know right off what I'm alluding to and look from me to Monte and declare, "Is she some pistol, or what?"

Those books that Monte made me read argue that phobics rarely faint, although the likelihood of losing consciousness dismays them. Anticipation does them in. Anticipation and the recollection of their past attacks haunt phobics the most, but they don't lose consciousness, they cope, even while they're laboring for breath. If I tell Franklin that, he won't believe it. He has a death grip on my hand, like Paulie did the first morning of school.

Someone is tottering behind us, holding a cardboard poster of a man-size bunny, with loppy ears and stiff white whiskers and a big-toothed smirk. The bunny stands erect on trousered legs. "We miss you in the cabbage patch," is the greeting drawn in script across its belly. That apparition bobbing in a sickroom door could give a groggy invalid a relapse.

"Imagine? Giant greeting cards," I say to Franklin, whose breath is sounding ragged. He grips my hand so hard I groan with pain. The bunny card, which looks too cumbersome to fit inside an elevator, is bobbing in our wake like a misguided pet. Franklin turns to stare at it. "Franklin, don't dawdle." I'm terrified that looking down will get him dizzy.

"Why is he following us?"

"He's not. He's going to see some lucky patient."

"Lucky?" Franklin exclaims, and I see hope in that burst of spirit.

"Don't drag so, will ya, Franklin." I'm tired enough to drop. If Buddy gets into the house, he'll find the dirty dishes I was too hurried to soak—the greasy frying pan, the egg-stained silverware. Maybe he'll have the grace to clean things up. More likely, he'll set down a glass of milk and Paulie's favorite Mallomars amid the tea stains and the muffin crumbs and say, "Your ma's okay, kid, but she's no kind of housekeeper." If Buddy peeks into my room, he'll see the clothes in disarray and affix some hopeful meaning to the mess. Paulie will see his duffel packed and get upset. Maybe the Lindquists won't be home and Buddy won't get the key. Maybe he'll go with Paulie to his parents' place and leave me time to think. "Franklin, will you make some effort."

"God, Linda, my ears are ringing. I can hardly hear you."

"You'll be okay." Near the third-floor landing, two teenaged volunteers in pink-striped pinafores are sitting on the stairs, whispering and puffing furtively on cigarettes. Batting at the smoke, they move to let us pass. Well, we're a caravan. Me, almost sobbing with fatigue, tugging Franklin by the hand, and the faceless messenger bearing the doughty bunny, its ears at half-mast and its smile sappy and intransigent.

"We miss you in the cabbage patch," one girl repeats in wonderment, then bursts into a giggle.

The bunny bobbles past us and disappears behind the fire door, and after him the smiling girls in a haze of bluish smoke. Under their pink-striped skirts, their hips are soft with baby fat.

Franklin's pallor worries me. When I tell him we should stop and take a breather, he quickly drops my hand and settles tailor-fashion on the landing, with the stick across his lap. I ease down to the topmost stair, grateful for a chance to rest my legs. Franklin has closed his eyes. "Are you okay? Are you faint, or what?"

"I don't know what I am."

"I know it isn't easy, Franklin."

"Damned straight."

"You're doing good."

"If I die, Linda, you oughta know, I want to be an organ donor."

Laughing, without much mirth, "Let's not get too dramatic. You're not about to die. The worst that happens, you'll pass out."

His eyes are open now and darkly earnest. "I mean it. If I die, I want my heart, lungs, kidneys, everything, to go to someone who's a real daredevil. A ski jumper or a test pilot. Maybe an astronaut. That way, Franklin the coward gets buried; but the part of me that stays alive goes on and has adventures. I think that's kinda neat, don't you?"

My brother, bona fide rare bird and looney character. I used to wish that we were twins. I used to envy the sure grace with which he'd push off on his bicycle, or park the car in a tight space, or barrel off the diving board, or pee so casually into the grass without having to squat. "Sure, Franklin. If you die, I'll beat the bushes for a daredevil who might be shy a kidney. No sweat."

Franklin persists. "Maybe a deep-sea diver. A marine biologist. That would be interesting."

During the time his fears were coming on, I was too absorbed in my own woes to pay attention. Ma would phone to say Franklin was acting strange, and she was worrying. That cut no ice. Ma's worrying is as natural as her breathing—the sudden lump, the freckle changing color, the clouds of poison drifting from Chernobyl. I laugh at her. What else is new?

Grinning at Franklin now, "Better to stay alive and have your own adventures."

His color's better, and he's sounding calmer. "Don't forget the corneas. The corneas to a scientist."

"You're weird, Franklin, you know?"

He nods, "Yeah, weird. There's weirdness in the family. Bad luck for both of us."

A many-windowed passageway leads to Juanita's wing. The windows in the hall outside her door overlook the outside entrance to Emergency. There's a yellow clover painted on the blacktop where helicopters land with trauma victims. The first time I saw the rescue helicopter landing on the pad, I thought about Cal Fowler and his glamorous arrivals from the Phillie office. The hospital landing looked more disorganized, as though the team on call were novices. The voice that called the code on the PA was trembly with apprehension, and the people who assembled on the blacktop looked anxious and stiff, like raw recruits. When they lifted out the victim, it seemed like they were carrying a stretcher full of dirty laundry. They broke into a run—odd to see them racing to Emergency with what looked like a mess of bloody sheets. I looked that day for Shantar, but he wasn't there.

It's quiet on Juanita's floor, save for a sudden clash of dishes in the nurses' kitchen and the groans of somebody in pain, soft calls like a child venting some secret grief.

"Be careful, Franklin. The floors are waxed and slippery." Gingerly we tread, still clasping hands. I hear the sound of quick, short breaths and realize it's me, panting like someone terrified. When we passed the waiting room for ICU, I peered in for a glimpse of old friends passing food around or knitting, even weeping, but there was no one I knew—only two, dazed older women sitting stiffly on the couch, eyeing the forest scene like they were waiting for a show to start. Like our silent, sweet, hospital "family" never had existed. The sharpness of that loss has got me trembling worse than Franklin.

He worries, "You okay?"

"Just nervous over what she'll do when you walk in. You better let me prepare her." He nods and shuffles miserably beside me, the gnarled stick dragging.

"You think the shock will be too much for her?" He's set to cut and run.

"Not if I tell her first. Just wait in the hall a second, please."

"Okay."

"No funny stuff? You won't run off?"

"God, Linda, I'm too tired."

"Wait for me, then."

She's propped up in her bed, watching Monte toy with the TV. Mrs. Foley's bed is empty, the mattress stripped down to the ticking.

Seeing me, Ma gestures toward the windowsill, which once held rows of greeting cards and pictures of the Foley grandkids in athletic poses. The flowers are gone, but one red helium balloon is stuck against the ceiling. "She'll miss me, Linda Jo."

"I know she will." I sit down in the bedside chair.

Monte, trying to get a movie into focus, tells me, "Hi, Linda, you're looking good."

"He lies," Juanita says. "You look like hell."

"Today was just a little tiring." I slap on my all-purpose smile. "How are you feeling?"

"Crummy as usual."

"It's a William Holden film," Monte announces.

"Good-o," says Juanita and begins to cry, one lone tear inching down the crease beside her nose, so slow, it seems it has nowhere to go. "She'll die," she tells us simply. "Without someone to divert her. To take her mind off herself. She's not outgoing," Ma adds unnecessarily.

"Ma, there'll be people at the nursing home. Visitors. Her family."

"Without someone to discuss the soaps. To keep things lively."

"She'll have TV to watch."

"Without me, she'll be done for in a week." Ma plucks a

tissue from the box on her bedside table and blows her nose, noisily. "I'm everything to her." Wadding the tissue, she dabs her eyes.

Her dinner is still sitting on the bedside tray. I peek under the dish covers to check this evening's menu. Chicken and baked potato without margarine. Two rusty clumps of broccoli. Red Jell-O turned to soup.

"Ma! You didn't touch a thing!"

"So, sue me, Linda Jo. I have no appetite." A flare of evil temper. The serpent's look, chilling my blood. "They don't know how to cook, anyhow. The broccoli's like mush. The Jell-O tastes like Kool-Aid, reminds me of the Jonestown Massacre."

"I could ask the nurse for sherbet."

"I want something to chew! I want a lamb chop, medium rare. I want a steak, smothered in onions."

"Mama, you're a vegetarian."

"That's right! Look where it got me. Did you bring me any clean nightgowns?"

"I didn't have a chance to run a load, but I brought you something better."

"Not presents from the candy man?"

"No way."

"Franklin," Ma says firmly.

"He's right outside."

"Just bring him in here, please."

Wearily, I rise to get him, resenting how her face has come alive, the sallow tone receding, and a sudden glow of joy flushing her cheeks. "Just a sec, Ma." My back is going stiff and there's a hard knot in my chest from the strain of lugging Franklin up four flights. You'd think she'd thank me for the effort.

"Don't bother with that now," Ma says to Monte, and her voice sounds faint and brittle as a little girl's.

Franklin is slouched against the wall, his chin sunk to his chest, his eyes squeezed shut as though he's catching Zs or deep in prayer. "She wants you to come in." When he opens up his eyes to look at me, I do my darndest to be kind. "She's fine, and there's only Monte in there."

Dragging his feet, he follows close behind me till we reach the door; then he pauses at the threshold, as though he means to vest his entrance with a certain drama. Ma's sitting very straight, tiny and tense, bony and frantically alert, a captive bird. Her eyes are hollows, big and dark, scouting the corners of the room as though she's looking for a way out of this place. Her hair is wild, a mix of gray and ginger frizz and flattened curls. Sounding his most seductive, Franklin says, "Hi, babe," and saunters to her bed as though he came here every day—this visit, no biggie, the usual routine. He bends to kiss her cheek, then sits down in the bedside chair and takes her hand.

"It took you long enough," Juanita says. "How come you look so pale?"

"He's been shut up for four years, Mama, remember?"

"And no jacket on either one of you. Monte says it's turned real cool."

Franklin says solemnly, "A polar ice cap is descending. Dinosaurs are dying in the swamps."

"Don't get smart with me," warns Ma. To Monte and me, "I'd like to see my son alone if you don't mind. Something confidential that I need to tell him."

"Hey, Juanita, no problem." Monte is staring, bug-eyed, like he can't believe what he is seeing, Franklin, big as life. The TV is still flickering out of focus. "I'll get that later." Monte gestures to the floating picture on the screen. Bill Holden and Grace Kelly in *Bridges at Toko-Ri.* "Linda and I will wait outside."

"I'll ask the nurse to take your tray." I look from Ma to Franklin. He's got her hand against his lips like he's d'Artagnan paying homage to the queen of France. Swift kisses on the fingertips, better than Greeley's medicines. If his kisses perk her up, who am I to criticize? "If you need something, we'll be close by."

Docile as orphans, Monte and I troop to the hall, and walk a ways down to the nurses' station, where I tell them Ma declined to eat, and the nurses go "tsk, tsk," the sound of dire prophecy, and shake their heads. Monte and I admire the flowers sitting on the nurses' desk, and comment on the oddness of the weather, and greet the practicals we know, who are wearing bulky sweaters buttoned tight over their uniforms. (Ma's right; the air-conditioning is set on Igloo despite the coolness of the night.) We wander back, and stand beside the glass wall that overlooks the helicopter landing pad. The yellow clover on the blacktop glows like an heraldic crest.

Monte asks me finally, "How did you get him here?"

"It's complicated. I got upset. We had a fight. He ran away and ended up at Beryl Blackwell's, that's the lady from the phobia place. Then we came here."

Monte nods as though I've said something coherent.

"Bill Holden's fading. She wants Monte to fix the set." Franklin, appearing in the hallway, looks bemused and tired, not overly tense, but somberly preoccupied as though Ma slapped him with a doozy of a lecture, and he's still absorbing it.

Monte moves so quickly to the task at hand, I figure he is grateful to be rid of me. I linger in the hall with Franklin. "How does she seem to you?"

"She's pretty feisty, but the roommate's leaving has her bummed."

"Well, she's got you here to compensate. What was the hush-hush thing she had to tell you, or should I not ask?"

"She bent my ear. A lecture on the current danger, sex and AIDS. Assuming I get active anytime, I'm to take all the precautions. Condoms, a must, but only certain kinds, and she rattled off a list—do you believe this?—brand names she deems acceptable. Real mother-son talk, right? God, what a family! You know a

Japanese outfit called Tokyo Knights? Her research says they're best."

"What research? In this place!"

"How the hell do I know? Maybe her roommate clued her in. Maybe the residents. Anyhow, Ma's covering all the bases, in case I'm AC/DC or just your standard psycho pervert." Franklin looks amazed. "Even if I was, where does she think I'd get the opportunity?"

"Maybe she thinks you haunt the streets at night like a vampire. Stalking cats and an occasional German shepherd."

Franklin grins, "My secret's out."

"That was it, then, a lecture about AIDS?" A worldwide plague would naturally grab Ma's attention, and Franklin's safety would loom uppermost. Never mind that he stays home, and I'm out in the danger zone.

"I'm to keep my eye on you, so you don't do something dumb."

"Thank you, Juanita! She doesn't trust my judgment, right? Only yours, and Monte's, that's what counts."

"You count. Don't be a dope. It irks her that she can't bully you."

"Who says?"

Franklin, patiently, "You count. She surely knows who got me here."

"Why can't she say so? Just once, couldn't she manage a 'nice goin', Linda Jo, and thank you for the effort'? Or, 'you're a good daughter, and I love you.' Is that so much to ask? I think if she would only say it once, it would be such a huge relief, just to know she really cares for me."

"She cares for you, you dope! Every gloomy warning that she ever gave you—every old wives' tale and grisly story was because she loves you and she wants you safe. You must know that!"

"I'm not sure what I know. I don't think she respects me. Don't stare at me like that—I don't! Suppose she died thinking I never accomplished anything? I'd feel so worthless. She zaps me with her look and I feel worthless now. She does that to me, Franklin."

His sigh reveals the depths of his exhaustion. "You give her too much power. She's your convenient alibi for everything that goes awry. It isn't fair. Beryl told me this today; wait, let me get it right." Briefly he shuts his eyes as though he's quoting from a tract he's had to memorize. "Beryl says the choices that we make in life are our responsibility. If things go wrong, we have to give up laying blame on other people and find our own solutions. That's what it means to be adult, and we have to grow up sometime, like it or not." Franklin looks sorrowful. "I'm not saying I like it. I'd rather blame the past four years on anything—the planets out of whack or some foul-up in the genes—but I know I could've changed things if I wanted to. Beryl says what happens next is up to me."

"Beryl says! Beryl says! She gave me the same lecture. She has the expert scoop on everything, so I assume she's right, only," I try to smile as though the truth of Beryl's perceptions hasn't stung me, "it's easier laying blame."

"Or hiding," Franklin murmurs.

"Well, you're not hiding tonight, and I'm proud of you!" Franklin has the guarded look of one who's witnessed a potential miracle and fears to speak of it, lest it dissolve in air. Gravely, he smooths my hair; the gentleness, the hesitancy of his touch, prompt me to a fresh assault of tears. "Oh, Franklin, I'm a jerk! I'm trying to take all the credit for your being here, when you're the one who did it. You managed, in spite of everything!"

"We did it, kid. We are a team. Hey, Linda Jo, I don't feel all that bad, you know? Tired as hell, but no dizziness. No trouble breathing, anything. I feel hopeful; is that allowed?"

"Should we put the heart transplant on hold?"

Franklin beams. "You're such a little witch. When we were growing up, I must've set a good example."

We cross the hallway toward Juanita's room with Franklin in the lead, striding with unexpected vigor, as though upheavals in the air—a clash of ions, stir of winds—have turned the whole world topsy-turvy, and he's become the sturdy one.

Monte has the TV in sharp focus, Bill looking gorgeous in a navy pilot's uniform and Grace too beautiful to be believed, both of them so loving and so noble you know right off you're watching fantasy. Monte is worrying. "A war flick? I doubt you want to see it to the end, Juanita. 'Cause, you know, he gets shot down. And it's depressing."

"Yeah," says Ma. "But first he zaps 'em."

Franklin, in an aside, "Someone's starting to sound chipper." He bends to Ma. "Here's the deal. You start listening to your doctor, or I don't come back."

Ma flashes him the look. "When Dr. Sorry Eyes says anything I deem intelligent, I certainly will listen." She sits bright-eyed and tense, breathing rapidly, but evenly; her hands, flat on the bed, tremble a bit. "You will be back? You're gonna lick it this time, Franklin, aren't you?"

"Hey, Ma, I'm up for it this time. Counseling, medication, paper bags, barfin' on the T-6 bus, if that'll work, anything but elevators. I draw the line at elevators."

He's flushed and way too hyper, the new Franklin touting optimism like it's something he invented. Boldness is like a drug that's pumped him up. Fearing that his welcome spurt of bravery will dissipate before too long, I tell him we should think of heading home. For a moment he looks shifty-eyed, as though he's pondering the trek back to the car and doesn't relish it. "Let's do it, Franklin. I think Ma's getting tired."

"Are you tired now, Juanita?" Monte pipes.

"Hell, yes. Tired of being here."

Franklin nods. "Tired of being here is a good sign." He is standing in the area between the beds, passing Pop's dog-headed stick from palm to palm as though he's working on a magic trick. "She'll be on her feet and out of here in no time."

Ma's eyes search Franklin's face as though she's storing every curve of bone and skin to memory. "Have you talked some sense into your sister, yet?"

"Please, Ma, I don't need any lectures. I've told you every chance I could, Reece and I are ancient history. You may as well know this: Buddy and I are splitting up. It's definite, except for meeting with the lawyers. Once we work out child support and you're on your feet, Paulie and I will move to our own place." That last is pure ad-lib. Monte eyes me with his customary puzzled stare, as though the idea of my being on my own is an affront to common sense.

Franklin's face, so haughty and austere (the supercilious jaw, the tight, patrician smile) has creased into a goofy grin. Slyly, he nods at me, as though I have affirmed some prior knowledge. He rests Pop's stick against the wall and moves to where I'm standing in the harsh glare of the bedside light. "It's a good call, Linda Jo. A good, gutsy call. You and the little toot will make out fine."

"You think so, Franklin?" I wish I were that sure. There is a time in life when things you thought were certainties get proven false. The perfect love, the perfect compañero, turns out selfish and uncaring; the perfect life you planned turns out a dud, and you can't trust your sensibilities, your instincts, anything. I don't know how people make reasoned choices. I don't know how they grow to be adults, or find courage to live their days. Beryl's grinning, whispered sympathy isn't sufficiently encompassing. It's all of us, scared in the night. All of us, counting heartbeats.

"Oh yeah, babe, you did right." Franklin folds me in an awkward hug. The old, warm smells of Pop cling to his robe, as though they've seeped into the seams and will not be displaced. Tobacco, printer's ink, and cherry LifeSavers. Stale chocolate and glue. "Pop would have said it too. A gutsy call." Franklin bends to my ear, suddenly conspiratorial. "Hey, Linda Jo. Didn't we just have crazy times? Didn't we just raise holy hell practicin' our dancin'?"

He has captured Pop's inflection to a tee, the meditative, gentle voice, giddy with tenderness and cherished recollections. But Pop, who kept the ghosts of loneliness and gloom at bay for us, is gone; Franklin and I must help each other muster courage for a leap of faith: hurtle (kicking, screaming) into adult life, and even learn to savor the experience.

"Yeah, Franklin, we had fun."

"Didn't they just play the nicest music?" He's really into it, the sweetness of that day. "Not bands, you know, but orchestras? You know the difference, don't you?"

"Yeah, I know. Bands have horns. And orchestras have—"

"Fiddles!" Abruptly, he spins me in a turn, then as if we've both reacted to the same brisk cue, we're laughing, floundering through the motions of the box step. Forward, to the side, and back and forward, faster now, and bend the knees and let the hips move free and hearken to the rhythm. "Hips!" cries Franklin. "Hips." Contemplate the probability of ice cream sundaes.

"You guys," Monte complains. "You guys! This is a hospital."

"Oh, what a rumba they teach," sings Franklin, and we whirl, the Fast-Track Kids—spinning through gold light and velvet dust —dancing to the tune of distant fiddles in the Spanish Ballroom.

"It's a joy when they don't fight." Ma's voice booms in the sudden silence when we stop for breath. "I'm glad she finally found her senses, 'cause it's crazy for anyone to live in California. The place is gonna fall into the ocean one day soon. You'll see. One minute, everyone is sitting in the sun and happy. The next, the ground gives way; and it's all gone." She snaps her fingers in the air. *"Poof.* Like that."